W9-BDT-056

ALSO BY CHRISTINE WENGER

Do or Diner
A Second Helping of Murder
Diners, Drive-Ins, and Death
Macaroni and Freeze

IT'S A WONDERFUL KNIFE

A Comfort Food Mystery

CHRISTINE WENGER

AN OBSIDIAN BOOK

OBSIDIAN

Published by New American Library,
an imprint of Penguin Random House LLC
375 Hudson Street, New York, New York 10014

This book is an original publication of New American Library.

First Printing, February 2016

For more information about Penguin Random House, visit penguin.com.

ISBN 978-0-451-47409-4

Printed in the United States of America
10 9 8 7 6 5 4 3 2 1

Penguin
Random
House

For Santa's helpers,
Andrea and Wladziu (Walt) Kaczor,
whose beautiful Thistle Dew Inn
has inspired many writers.

For all those who keep Christmas
in their hearts 365 days a year.

For all those who preserve their family traditions,
stories, pictures, and rituals and pass them on
to future generations.

For all others, repeat after me:
"I do believe. I do believe. I do believe!"

Chapter 1

I just love Christmas.

At times, the holiday season might be stressful. It always seems like there's never enough time to decorate, bake, shop, write out thoughtful messages on cards, entertain, and enjoy the numerous events. But even though it's busy and crazy, it's a wonderful time of year.

I am a big list maker, and intentionally I write, "Stop, sit down, relax, and smell the cocoa." And I make my cocoa with real chocolate, milk instead of water, whipped cream, a sprinkle of cinnamon on top, and a candy cane for a stirrer. . . .

After a long day of cooking, I was looking forward to making cocoa in my special red Santa Claus mug that Grandma Bugnacki bought me decades before when we visited Santa's North Pole Village. I was going to sit down with a big plate of my mom's snowball cookies with a fresh dusting of powdered sugar and wash them down with the cocoa, and maybe heat up more, if needed. . . .

I looked around at all the boxes and bins that I'd just brought up from the basement or lugged down from the attic of my Big House. Now, where was my Santa mug?

But no matter how much I loved Christmas and all that went with it, I would *not* decorate until the dishes were in the dishwasher after Thanksgiving dinner and all my guests were either gone or in recliners, sleeping off the tryptophan from consuming mass quantities of turkey.

Right then, on Thanksgiving night, all my guests were indeed gone. The only one sleeping in a recliner was my pal Antoinette Chloe Brown (who recently shed her married name of Brownelli).

So I could begin to decorate my diner, the Silver Bullet, which was only a few hundred yards off the main road, Route 3, the road that split Sandy Harbor, New York, in half, sort of diagonally.

I decided to take my sweet golden retriever, Blondie, for a walk in the thirteen-degree temperature and three feet of snow on the ground. Mother Nature and Lake Ontario had gone easy on us so far, with only one blizzard, but this balmy weather wouldn't last.

"Blondie, come!" I said, and she grudgingly lifted her head from her cozy spot under my thick oak kitchen table. "Let's go for a walk!"

She didn't hurry to get up. "Come on. You love the snow."

Ty Brisco, a Houston transplant who worked as a deputy with the Sandy Harbor Sheriff's Department, and I had rescued Blondie when she'd appeared half-frozen next to the Dumpster at the back of the Silver Bullet. Poor thing.

We shared her, but I had primary custody. It got lonely

at the Big House, my huge white farmhouse with green shutters and a wraparound porch.

I got winterized—puffy parka, hat, boots, and gloves—and picked up a couple of plastic bins and a couple of boxes. I called for Blondie one more time, and she appeared at my side. Juggling everything, I opened the door, let her go out in front of me, and then closed it. Carefully, I felt my way with my boots across my back porch and down the five steps that would lead me to ground level.

Or was it *eight* steps?

I dropped to the ground like a cut Christmas tree. My packages soared through the air and a box of lights landed on my head. I did a split that any gymnast would envy, but I bet they'd never heard anything crack as loudly as a couple of my bones.

My teeth hit the snowy and icy sidewalk, and I spit out a tooth. Oh, sure. I'd just paid off Dr. Covey after a root canal. Shoot!

Blondie was barking, and I couldn't calm her down. I couldn't even calm myself down.

"Blondie, go get Ty. Go get Antoinette Chloe!"

She just stood there, barking. Then more barking.

"Get Ty, Blondie. Go get him!"

She stopped barking for a while, then tilted her head as if to say, *Trixie, I'm not Lassie, for heaven's sake!*

"Yeah, I know. Just keep barking. Maybe someone will hear you."

I tried to get up, but I felt like a manatee swimming through quicksand. Everything hurt, but mostly it was my right leg and ankle.

As I lay there trying to catch my breath, I noticed my big Santa Claus mug that I had been thinking of. It had fallen out of the box and was broken.

It was then that I began to cry.

I don't like to cry, although I am a pro at it. I cry at sappy movies. When the channels start putting on their holiday movies, I am one big blubbering mountain of tissues.

But I was crying for myself then, because I saw my Christmas season melting away before my watery eyes.

Who was going to decorate?

Who was going to finish my shopping?

Who was going to cater the three dozen holiday parties (and counting) that I'd booked? Or the rehearsal dinners each evening for the holiday pageant at the Sandy Harbor Community Church? Most everyone was coming right from school or work during the four weeks before Christmas Eve, and they needed sustenance, so Pastor Fritz had hired me to provide food and drink.

And on top of all that, I was supposed to cater the community's annual Christmas buffet after the play in the church's community room.

I wasn't going to be able to drive to make deliveries. I wasn't going to be able to stand to cut, chop, and cook if all my bones were broken that I thought were broken.

I was getting pretty cold there, sprawled out in the snow and ice. My parka was usually jacket length, but right then it was midriff length, and I couldn't pull it down no matter how hard I tried.

"That's it. Keep barking, Blondie."

Silence.

"Blondie, can you spell *SPCA*?"

She ran off to jump like a gazelle in the snow.

Finally Antoinette Chloe appeared at the back door.

"Trixie? What are you doing down there?"

"Counting snowflakes."

"Interesting." She yawned. "Why was Blondie barking? She woke me up. Want any coffee? I think I'll have a cup before I drive home."

"Antoinette!"

She knew something was wrong because no one, and I mean no one, ever left off the *Chloe* in her name if they valued their life.

And no one called me Beatrix for the same reason!

"What's wrong?" she asked.

"I need help. I fell. And I heard bones snap, crackle, and pop."

"Oh! I thought you were putting lights up around the sidewalk or stairs."

"By lying on the ground?"

"I thought you were being . . . creative."

"Not that creative." My leg and ankle were throbbing. "Antoinette Chloe, call an ambulance for me. I'm hurt pretty bad." I sniffed.

"I will! I will! I have to get my cell phone. I'll be right back. Don't go anywhere."

"Don't go anywhere?" I mumbled grumpily. "I thought I'd go Christmas caroling with the church choir, but I don't have my sheet music with me."

I waited, and waited, and finally ACB returned. "You're in luck. The ambulance drivers are at the Silver Bullet on a dinner break. Ty is on his way, too."

"Good. Thanks."

Under normal circumstances, I would've had to have been half-dead to want to travel in an ambulance, but these weren't normal circumstances, and I felt half-dead.

I took deep breaths of the cold air and listened to ACB ramble on. She did help pull down my jacket, and I felt a little warmer.

Finally I heard Blondie barking and Ty's deep voice in the distance. Then I saw red lights flashing. I didn't know which made me feel better, but it wasn't ACB's talking about the upcoming auditions for the Christmas pageant at the Sandy Harbor Community Church.

"Trixie, why on earth do they have auditions? Everyone who wants to be in the pageant gets to be in it, for heaven's sake. I think that being pageant director has gone to Liz Fellows's head."

"It's her first time heading up a pageant," I said, panting out each word. Where was my ride to the hospital? "She's finding her way."

"Margie Grace's pageants were certainly entertaining. People are still talking about the shepherds tending a flock of salmon along with their sheep."

I shivered. "But people didn't get it when the shepherds did the tango with the sheep. It was a little over-the-top, even for Sandy Harbor."

"Margie is hopping mad. She wanted to be asked again."

"Trixie? What happened?" Ty finally arrived with Blondie, and I relaxed a little. "The ambulance guys are here."

"I—I . . . f-fell . . . down the s-stairs." My teeth chattered, and I tried to get them to stop. "My right leg and ankle hurt."

"Don't move."

"I c-can't anyway."

"Here come Ronnie and Ron. Linda Hermann is with them."

"Good."

After much ado, I was wheeled into the back of the ambulance and covered with heaps of blankets.

"We are going to drive you to Syracuse," said Ronnie. "I checked, and they have the shortest wait time in their emergency room."

"Okay, Ronnie. Let's go. I have decorations to put up!"

After an hour ride to Syracuse, two hours in the ER, and another half hour getting used to being on crutches, I was heading home in Antoinette Chloe's delivery van from her restaurant, Brown's Four Corners. Her van couldn't be missed. On the side, it sported a colorful salami with a fedora dancing with a chubby ham in jogging shoes and a tennis outfit. Nearby was an assortment of cheeses watching the dancing and clapping to music that only deli items could hear.

I climbed into the van, or rather, shoved my ample butt up and into the seat, with ACB helping me. I plopped into the seat and then tried to position my behemoth of a cast into a comfortable spot.

It didn't help that I had a couple of broken ribs.

"It smells like garlic in here," I said, taking a deep breath.

"Fingers just made a kielbasa run to Utica. Remember?"

"Oh. I forgot."

ACB and I loved this one kind of kielbasa that we could find only at a certain grocery store in Utica. I had turned ACB on to it, but I'd been eating it for years. It was a Matkowski tradition at Christmas and Easter and was complete only with fresh horseradish that I made.

Fingers, who was missing a couple of them, was ACB's cook at Brown's Four Corners Restaurant in downtown Sandy Harbor. ACB was thinking of selling the place to Fingers and opening a year-round drive-in movie theater on land she owned adjacent to mine, but she hadn't figured out the logistics of snow and blizzard conditions on the drive-in screen or on the drive-in goers, especially if they came in snowmobiles or Amish wagons.

That was my pal ACB. Her ideas were as wild as her couture.

I glanced down at her sandaled feet. I had given up nagging her about wearing flip-flops in the dead of winter. She had some kind of aversion to winter boots. She told me that she lined her flip-flops with faux fur to shut me up.

"Do you want to stop for anything in Syracuse?" she asked.

"I'd like to go home and get some sleep, to be honest. It's been a long day."

"While they were putting your cast on, I called Linda Blessler. She's going to work for you until further notice."

"Oh! That's so nice of her, and it's thoughtful of you to call her for me. Thanks, Antoinette Chloe. I'll call her later and tell her that I might be recovering for a while. The doctor said that I did such a number on my ankle that I couldn't have a soft boot. He had to put a cast on it."

"Oh, and I know you have a lot of catering coming up. Of course I'll help you."

"What about your own restaurant?"

"Fingers will shout if he needs me, but he never does. I should just sell the place to him."

"Does he want to buy it?"

"I think so, but we never discussed it seriously," she said. "Maybe we should."

"Yeah." I yawned. "The doc gave me something for the pain. I think I'm falling asleep."

"Go ahead, but first, tell me how to get to the highway."

"Go straight. Down the hill. You should see signs."

"I remember there used to be an Italian bread bakery around here, right?" she asked. "I love their bread."

"Antoinette Chloe, it's ten o'clock at night. It's probably closed." I pointed to the tiny store in an old shingle house by the highway entrance. "See? Closed."

"Too bad. I'm in the mood for warm bread. We could have shared it on the ride home. I'm starving."

As if on cue, my stomach growled.

Antoinette Chloe laughed. "I see a restaurant over there. Are you interested?"

My throbbing ankle yelled, *Are you nuts?* but my stomach screamed, *Let's go!*

"It looks mostly like a bar. Do you think they have anything to go?" I asked, hopeful that I could stay in the van.

We both must have looked in the grimy window at the same time as ACB tried to park her big van in a space fit only for my cook Linda Blessler's red Mini Cooper.

"It's a cowboy bar," ACB said.

The mechanical bull in the window with a cowboy type riding it and ladies in Daisy Dukes cheering for him was our first clue.

"You stay here, and I'll see if they have sandwiches to go," she said, reading my mind.

"Thanks, Antoinette Chloe."

"Yee-haw!" was her response.

I was going to point out that her dancing-salami-and-ham van was only half-parked, but she was already opening the door to the Ride 'Em Cowboy Saloon.

That was our other clue that this was a cowboy bar.

She came back to the car and opened the door. "Oops . . . Trixie, do you have any money?"

I went to reach for my purse but came up with a handful of air. "Oh, no. I don't." It was the second time I'd reached for my purse that wasn't there. The first was to hand the ER intake worker my insurance card. Luckily they already had my insurance information from my recent late-in-life tonsillectomy.

"Don't worry, Trixie. I'll get us some takeout." She slammed the door.

Yikes. We were headed for jail as sure as the snow was falling outside.

The heat was on full blast in the big, empty van, but I still shivered. I closed my eyes for just a moment, and when I opened them, I saw my friend Antoinette Chloe Brown riding the mechanical bull in the window.

I could hear her yee-haws and laughter over the heat blasting and over the highway noise. A couple of street people who were camping next to the highway in boxes and crates came to investigate.

"Someone being stabbed?" I heard one ask the other.

"I think it's that lady in the muumuu riding the bull. She's certainly enjoying herself."

My friend's rhinestone flip-flops caught the glint of the overhead lights surrounding the bull.

I had to get her out of there, or we'd never get home.

I rolled down my window and gave the horn a little tap.

"Excuse me, sir." One of the men pointed to himself, and I nodded. He came over to my side of the van. "I just came from the hospital. I have a cast, and it's hard to walk. Would you mind going in there and telling my friend"—I pointed to ACB in the window—"to come to the van, please?"

"My apologies, but I'm banned from going in there."

"What about your friend?"

He looked at the man standing not four inches from the window, looking at ACB. "He is also not welcome."

"Would you pound on the window, then, and yell to her that Trixie wants her?"

"Who's Trixie?"

"I am."

"Oh. Okay."

They pounded on the window, got ACB's attention,

and pointed to me sitting in the car. Reluctantly, she waved to me, and slid down from the bull as her muu-muu slid up.

Yikes.

I could hear the crowd hoot and holler and Antoi-nette Chloe grinned and waved.

Whatever I had been given in the hospital for pain and nausea was beginning to wear off. My body ached, my head was throbbing, and my leg felt as if I were dragging an anvil. I was hungry enough to search the pockets of my jacket for stray, lint-covered Tic Tacs.

I found one. It was delicious.

Again, I was feeling sorry for myself. But at least I wasn't living in a box by the highway in the middle of winter like my two new friends, who were now staring at a platinum blond woman with a red sequined blouse and shorty shorts now riding the bull.

I looked up at the hospital that I'd just left. It was sprawled on top of a hill overlooking Syracuse and glow-ing like a lighthouse in the crisp, dark night. I was much luckier than most of the people in that hospital, too.

I ached all over, but a lot of people in the hospital wouldn't be coming home for Christmas. I vowed not to whine or complain no matter how I felt.

Making a mental note to contribute to the hospital as my Christmas gift, I beeped the horn to my two street guys. My friend came over.

"Yes, Trixie?"

"Um . . . I don't know your name."

"I'm Jud and this is Dan."

"This is all the money I have right now." Pulling out

all the change from the ashtray, I handed Jud around sixty-two cents. "Jud, if you and Dan ever get to Sandy Harbor, stop at the Silver Bullet and get yourself a nice meal on me. Okay?"

"We sure will." He smiled, and I wished I could get him some dental work.

"Merry Christmas, Jud."

"Merry Christmas, Trixie."

Finally ACB shuffled out of the bar carrying several white bags. She hesitated when she saw Jud and Dan.

Rolling down the window, I shouted, "They're okay."

She plodded to the car. Dan pulled off the navy fisherman's cap from his head and clutched it to his breast.

"You are my kind of woman," Dan said. "May I have the pleasure of knowing your name?"

"Antoinette Chloe."

"Antoinette Chloe," Dan repeated. "It rolls off the tongue like a song . . . or rather a poem by Lord Byron." He cleared his throat. "'She walks in Beauty, like the night / Of cloudless climes and starry skies; And all that's best of dark and bright / Meet in her aspect and her eyes. . . .'"

"Climes?" ACB's eyes grew wide. "Don't you swear at me, mister."

Jud held up his hands. "It means weather. Climates," he said. "Dan and I were both professors of literature until the school we taught at was downsized. Now we are writing a book about living with the homeless."

"That's got to be sad," I said.

He looked over his shoulder to the mess of boxes and crates. "It'll be even sadder as Christmas gets closer."

My heart sank. "I wish I had my pocketbook, but I'll be back as soon as I can."

Antoinette Chloe was busy searching in her cleavage purse. That's what I called the depository in her cleavage, which held just . . . everything. She pulled out a roll of money.

I looked at her in astonishment.

"I won it. Over two hundred bucks. Apparently no one thought a full-figured woman in a muumuu and flip-flops could ride Cowabunga—that's what they call the electric bull."

She handed the money to Dan. "I am counting on you to make sure that they get whatever they need for this *clime*—blankets, soup, coffee . . ."

"You have my word, my lovely Antoinette Chloe." Dan kissed the back of her hand, and she giggled like a fifth grader.

Jud nodded like a bobblehead. "Darling ladies, the charitable goodness you promulgate is beyond reproach."

"Who said that?" ACB asked. "Shakespeare?"

"Judson Volonade."

"Is he famous?"

"Not yet. He's me. I am Judson Volonade."

We waved good-bye to the professors and headed north to Sandy Harbor.

I felt bad for dragging ACB out of the saloon. She was having fun, but I was cranky from pain.

"So, Antoinette Chloe, do you think that Jud and Dan are legitimate?" I asked, taking a bite of a chicken tender. It was still half-frozen, but I could eat around the frozen part.

She shrugged. "I'd like to think so."

"I just hope they are really professors doing research and that we didn't just give them a drinking binge that will last until Christmas," I said.

"Yeah."

"Oh, I'm being negative, and I just vowed to stop whining and not to feel sorry for myself."

"Trixie, you'll still have a great Christmas, and we'll all help you fill your orders and deliver them."

Tears stung my eyes. I knew they'd help, but I was convinced my Christmas season wasn't going to be the same that year.

Though maybe, just maybe, it would be even better!

Chapter 2

*T*y Brisco met us in the parking lot in front of the Big House.

I bought the whole "point" from my aunt Stella when she retired. The point included the Silver Bullet Diner, twelve housekeeping cottages, which now total eleven (but that's another story), and the Big House, all on the sandy shore of Lake Ontario.

Ty was a real cowboy, and he used to be a Texas Ranger until he decided that he wanted to work in a smaller department. Ty had moved there about six months before I did because of fond memories of fishing there when he was a kid and his father rented one of the cottages.

He'd thought he could pace himself in sleepy Sandy Harbor, but he'd been busier than he ever expected with a variety of crimes—mostly petty stuff such as directing traffic during the plethora of parades that Sandy Harbor loved, and some serious stuff during tourist season.

Ty opened the door of ACB's van and held out his hand to help me out.

"Ty, you would have loved the Ride 'Em Cowboy Saloon," Antoinette Chloe said as she leaned over me. A plastic miniature turkey glued onto lime green netting on her fascinator in honor of the holiday fell onto my lap. "I rode an electric bull there named Cowabunga."

I handed her the plastic turkey, and she dropped it into her cleavage purse.

"Um, I gave up riding bulls—electric or otherwise—a long time ago," he said.

I made a move to get out of the van, but suddenly became queasy from the crazy way ACB drove and the half-frozen, greasy chicken tenders from the Ride 'Em Cowboy Saloon.

Ty had better duck at a moment's notice!

"Let me help you, Trixie."

"I'm not feeling all that great."

"I know. Antoinette Chloe called me from the ER. So, your leg and ankle are a mess, huh?"

I shifted on my butt and pivoted in the front seat to get out of the van. Some French fries slid from somewhere and dropped onto the snow.

"Yeah. I'm a mess. And I have a couple of broken ribs." I tried not to complain, but I throbbed in places that I hadn't known I had. "And I'm missing a cap on my front tooth."

I put my hand in his and noticed immediately how warm and strong his grip was. Nice.

Moving my casted leg to the running board of the van, I felt the snow seep through the sock that was keeping my toes semiwarm. When the wind gusted, the right side of my jeans, which the medical personnel had cut for the cast, and which were barely hanging on by a thread near my crotch, flapped in the breeze.

Not one of my best moments.

"I've got you."

He had both arms around me and was about to lift me onto the ground. Was he kidding? Now, Ty was a hunk, more than six feet tall, and studly, but he wasn't immune to hernias.

"Whoa, cowboy! I don't want to visit you in the hospital. I can do it. Just let me get my bearings."

Antoinette Chloe laughed. "Get out backward. That's what I sometimes do. Or maybe we can get you a plastic milk crate as a step."

I could just see myself balancing on that.

As my jeans billowed out, I slowly turned around, putting my good, booted foot on the ground first.

"Wait! I have a plastic bag to put over your sock," ACB said, going around to the driver's side, pulling out our takeout garbage from a plastic bag, and tossing the trash in the back of the van.

She hurried to my side, her flip-flops flopping.

With one foot on the ground and the other still on the running board, she scrunched up the plastic bag, lifted my foot, and pulled the bag on. Then she tied the handles around my cast.

"Perfect," she said.

The scent of onions from ACB's onion rings order wafted up from the bag.

"Thanks, Antoinette Chloe," I replied. "Great idea." And it was.

"Need help getting that leg down from the van?" Ty asked.

"I can do it." I just didn't want to fall.

Slowly I got my foot onto the ground. With Ty's help, I turned around and hobbled a couple of steps away from the van. It was then I noticed that the plastic bag on my foot was as slippery as a greased banana.

As I floundered, Ty gripped my arm.

He was like that. As a friend, not only did he stop me from falling, but he steadied me.

ACB was on my other side. She wasn't everyone's cup of hot chocolate, but she was the whipped cream of my life.

Just ahead was the long sidewalk that led to the Big House. Someone, probably either Max or Clyde, had shoveled and sanded the sidewalk. Just after that, the front stairs loomed ahead.

Remembering my fall, I sighed. Suddenly my ribs hurt even more when I breathed and my ankle throbbed to the tune of "Jingle Bells."

I just had to keep my mind occupied and not think of my fall.

Which reminded me . . . "You know, guys, I have crutches in the van somewhere. I should be getting used to them."

"I'll get 'em!" ACB said, dropping my arm.

"Uh . . . okay." Off she went, and I debated whether Ty could handle all of me.

Ha!

I felt his arm go around my waist and my parka, then compress. The couple of times that he'd had his arm around me, I was always wearing a puffy coat.

What a waste.

"How're you doing, Trixie?"

"Okay. But this sidewalk seems endless, and the plastic bag is really slippery. I don't want to fall again."

"Don't worry. I've got you."

It was time for the stairs, and, holding onto the icy railing, I lifted my good foot. Then the plastic-bagged foot.

Ty was giving my butt a boost, adding extra incentive for me to take my time and relish the experience.

The stairs were easy, but when I opened the door, Blondie came running and dashed between us.

Ty chuckled. "Looks like Blondie needs to use the snow. I should have let her out, but while you were at the hospital I got a call and had to direct traffic in town."

Two more steps brought me inside, and I slid my coat off, then the bag and my wet sock, and tried to put my jeans together.

I needed duct tape, but that was in my kitchen drawer.

Sinking into a recliner, I put an afghan over my legs and yanked the handle back.

Relief.

"What happened in town that you had to direct traffic?" I asked.

"Sylvia Thistle got her husband's Silverado stuck in a snowbank again. She was plowing out their driveway, and a deer jumped across her path. She yanked the wheel and landed across Route 3, and the traffic couldn't get around her. I detoured the traffic down Center Street until Bob Cameron pulled her out with his heavy-duty tow truck."

"Sylvia is my ideal. She plows. She runs a day-care center. She volunteers at the Red Cross. She can fix anything and do just about anything."

"So can you, Trixie. You've proven that time after time."

"Thanks, Ty. That's nice of you to say."

That was high praise indeed from Ty. I found myself in a pink glow for a while. Then Antoinette Chloe walked in with my crutches, and then I remembered all the things on my to-do list—the same to-do list on the end table next to me.

Maybe Sylvia could do everything, but I wasn't sure I was up to the challenge in my condition. How would I get everything done?

Picking up my list, I leafed through it and found the corresponding calendar that ran for the rest of November and through the first two weeks of the New Year.

Catering the pageant rehearsals was an everyday thing. The Sandy Harbor Community Church was paying me for the food, but my time would be my little contribution to the community.

The pageant was going to be on Christmas Eve. After that, I would be catering a sit-down dinner for the performers, their guests, and whoever bought a ticket for the cost of ten dollars per family, or five bucks per person. A festive, spirited crowd always attended, and as the evening progressed, the children's excitement increased as the impending visit from Santa grew nearer.

I had office Christmas and New Year's parties scattered across the calendar that I was supposed to cater, and two wedding receptions—one large, in the basement of the Catholic church, St. Luke's of the Lakes. Then I'd scheduled one small but elegant bridal shower at Larry and Larissa McDowney's house for their daughter, Louise.

Oh my! Louise's bridal shower was Saturday! Two days away.

Then there was my shift at my diner. I hoped that Linda Blessler would be able to work the kitchen for me until this cast came off. I still planned on checking on everything and keeping up with the ordering of food and supplies.

Yikes—I needed help. I couldn't depend on Ty for everything; he had his own job to do. And my pal Antoinette Chloe would do everything she could, but she was only one person, and she had her own restaurant to tend to.

I wasn't finished shopping. I wanted to decorate. I wanted to sing in the choir at St. Luke's. I—I . . .

Ty must have heard my groan. "Would you like me to make you a cup of something warm?"

"I'll do it," ACB volunteered. "I'll make us a pot of coffee—fully caffeinated. You go over Trixie's list with her, and see what she needs us to do."

"Good idea."

"Make a list for me, Trixie. Put on it whatever you'd like me to do to help you out," ACB said. "My brain turns to mush this time of night."

Thanksgiving Day was almost over, and I closed my eyes and said a silent prayer for being lucky enough to have such great friends.

"Trixie, you must be exhausted," Ty said. "It's been a long day for you. First you cooked and served turkey and fixings for half of Sandy Harbor. Then there was the whole hospital thing and the trip home. I know how

Miss Muumuu drives—like the road is a giant pinball machine."

"You forgot the Ride 'Em Cowboy Saloon and waiting for her to ride Cowabunga."

"I'll bet that was an experience."

I grinned. "You have no idea."

There was barking at the front door, and Ty got up to let Blondie back in. She waited until Ty sat down, then she settled at his feet.

"So, Trixie, what do you have scheduled in the near future?" he asked, absentmindedly petting our dog.

"Tomorrow, I have to start catering the practices for the Christmas play at the Community Church. Pastor Fritz Robinson hired me to make sure that everyone is fed, since they will be coming from school and work. Auditions are tomorrow, and I planned a buffet with make-your-own sandwiches. I already bought a couple of hams to slice. I planned on slicing the ham during auditions since the big slicer at the Silver Bullet is out for repairs." I checked my list. "And I bought salami, chicken salad, and bologna. Kids like bologna. I planned on making potato and macaroni salad during my shift tonight at the Silver Bullet in between orders. And I was going to make a chef salad and put out an assortment of cheeses and relishes. That ought to do it." I flipped over the page. "Juanita is making a white sheet cake and decorating it in red and green. I told her to write 'Sandy Harbor Christmas Pageant Auditions' on it. She should have made it today during her shift at the diner, so that's all set."

"What needs to be made, Trixie?" Antoinette Chloe said, returning with a tray. There were three mugs of coffee depicting Pilgrims planting corn in a ditch along with my smiling Pilgrim creamer and sugar bowl.

Aunt Stella had left me twenty-four place settings of the smiling and working Pilgrims, complete with extra pieces.

I'd planned on putting it away that night and bringing out my poinsettia-and-holly Christmas set.

She passed out the mugs and we took turns with the smiling Pilgrims. "I need the potato and mac salads made. I can make the chef salad tomorrow. I can sit down while I do that. And I need everything loaded into my catering van."

With some of the profits from the diner and cottages, I'd purchased a catering van with lots of shelves and a refrigerated area on the left side. On the right side was a heated area to keep things warm. It all ran magically with a special kind of fan.

The advertising on the side was not as flashy as Antoinette Chloe's dancing salami and whatnot. I just simply had SILVER BULLET DINER CATERING, ROUTE 3, SANDY HARBOR, NEW YORK, with my phone number. And there was a line drawing of my diner.

Well, the diner would be mine after several more balloon payments to Aunt Stella or my hundredth birthday, whichever came first.

My mind was wandering. Must be the painkillers from the hospital.

ACB raised an index finger. "Trixie, I can make the salads. Easy peasy."

"And I can load and deliver everything to the church and help set up," Ty added. "All you or Antoinette Chloe have to do is aim me toward the buffet table and direct me where to place things."

"And with a chair, there are things that I can do," I said, thinking of renting a motorized scooter to help me get around.

"You need to rest, and you need to keep your feet up. You should make friends with that recliner and watch the snow fall out your windows. Read a book. Make lists. Check them twice."

"Find out who's naughty or nice," Ty added.

They both burst into "Santa Claus Is Coming to Town," or at least I think it was. I laughed until my broken ribs hurt and I gasped for air. "Stop! You have to stop!"

Uncle Porky's grandfather clock chimed. One o'clock in the morning.

"Let's call this a day—or a morning," Ty said, standing. "Do you need help getting upstairs?"

I couldn't stand the thought of hoisting myself up a flight of stairs right then. "I'm fine right here for the night. Thanks for everything, Ty."

Ty petted Blondie, who was looking up at him adoringly. "See you tomorrow, Trixie. What time shall we reconnoiter?"

Nothing like cop talk. It was like Dinerese, the special language between my waitresses and the chef on duty. Why say *Two eggs over easy on toast with sausage patties* when you can say *Two dead eyes on a raft with pig*?

"I'd like to be unloading at the kitchen in the community room by three o'clock, and ready with the buffet by five o'clock. Auditions start at four o'clock for the kids, and five o'clock for the adults. Liz Fellows gets wacky when her schedule is disrupted. I'll keep the buffet up until six."

ACB grunted. "But not everyone is out of work by five. And then they have to drive to the Community Church's Community Center. Liz must know that."

I chuckled as I remembered my discussion with Liz. "She said that a lot of people have the day after Thanksgiving off and that anyone who is serious about the pageant should take the day off anyway and practice for the part they are trying out for."

Antoinette Chloe rolled her eyes. "At least Margie Grace knew how to be more accommodating to the people. She directed over twelve Christmas pageants until she was unceremoniously dumped. At least Margie was considerate and realistic."

Ty raised an eyebrow. "Realistic? At the Miss Salmon Contest last fall, she had fishermen doing something weird with their salmon."

ACB shook her head. "The fishermen were catching the salmon as the salmon were spawning."

I had to jump into this conversation. "It looked like the fishermen and the salmon were spawning *together*, Antoinette Chloe. Parents covered their children's eyes. Many citizens of Sandy Harbor were appalled."

"Margie is just . . . artistic. She worked on Broadway, you know."

I laughed. "She passed out playbills and seated people at the Uris Theatre back in 1979."

"And she even met Angela Lansbury's understudy

during the run of *Sweeney Todd*," ACB announced. "And she danced in the chorus of *Gams, Guns, and Gangsters*. It ran for three days before it closed. Margie's like Broadway royalty."

Broadway royalty?

I yawned and couldn't keep my eyes open. "Thanks for everything. Good night."

ACB didn't take the hint, but continued on. "Margie is going around telling everyone that Liz was appointed director just because she is Pastor Fritz's secretary, and because it's his church that the pageant's being held at this year. She's convinced that Liz can't run a pageant." ACB shook her head. "I think that Margie is going to cause trouble."

I took a deep breath, wanting to put this conversation to rest so I could sleep. "Margie is just miffed because she was replaced. For years, she's been the go-to person in Sandy Harbor for all things related to plays, performances, and pageants. It's time for someone else to give the Christmas pageant a fresh perspective and not have salmon and trout doing the tango with Santa Claus and the shepherds."

"Margie just loves her fish." ACB laughed. "But I see what you mean."

God bless Ty, who gently herded ACB to the front door so she could exit. He picked up her plaid cape and tried to figure out how to help her into it, but he eventually gave up and handed it to her.

"See you tomorrow, Trixie," Ty said, dodging as ACB twirled the cape over her shoulder like a matador. "Get some sleep."

"Good night, both of you," I repeated. "And thanks for helping me."

Antoinette Chloe was just about to touch a toe to the first step when she abruptly turned around.

"Hold your horses, cowboy. I'm not going anywhere. I'm going to stay with Trixie to help her while she's recovering. I won't leave her side."

Oh, no! Not again! She'd just stayed with me while I was under Ty's recent, ridiculous house arrest, where she was appointed my "warden" by him.

I should have been grateful that Antoinette Chloe wanted to help me out, so I resolved to enjoy her company. After all, 'twas the season to be jolly.

Once again, Ty was spitting out plaid cloth as ACB removed her cape and tossed it on my flowered sofa.

"Trixie, how about if I take Blondie home with me?" he asked.

Blondie was already four paws ahead of him. Apparently she had already planned on moving in with Ty tonight anyway.

"Sure." It would save me from trying to get up to let Blondie out to potty.

Ty got his black cowboy hat, put it on, and gave the top a quick tap. "See you ladies tomorrow. Call me if you need me."

"You got it, Deputy Brisco," ACB said. "But I have everything under control."

I yawned. "Thanks again, Ty."

He tweaked the brim of his hat. Have I mentioned yet how much I loved it when he did that?

After Ty left, ACB turned to me. "Would you like something to drink?"

"No. Thanks anyway, but I could go for a trip to the bathroom. Would you get my crutches?" They were just a hair out of my reach.

"Sure."

Just as she reached for one to hand it to me, rubber side first, she misjudged the length and sent my twelve-inch, beautifully painted, ceramic turkey flying across the room. It landed, minus its head, at my feet.

"Shoot! I'm so sorry, Trixie." ACB looked like she was about to cry. "It was your aunt Stella's, wasn't it? It had to be over sixty years old."

First my special Santa cocoa mug broke, and now my favorite turkey that I remembered as a kid. Aunt Stella would put it out for Thanksgiving, and I named it Thomasina, because I was sure it was a girl.

Thomasina became mine when I bought the point. Each Thanksgiving when I brought her out, I sat with her on my lap, admiring every brushstroke and lamenting how much I liked to eat turkey—not only on Thanksgiving, but throughout the year, too.

Sorry, Thomasina.

I swallowed the lump in my throat. The mug and ceramic turkey were only inanimate objects, after all.

"The turkey can be glued, and it'll be as good as new," I said. "Please don't worry. Just put the pieces in the kitchen, and I'll find the glue. But first, can you help me get up?"

She set both parts of Thomasina on the coffee table and supercarefully handed me the other crutch.

I pulled myself up to my feet—or should I say to my foot—and with Antoinette Chloe's help, I stood. Then dizziness set in just as my stomach churned.

Thinking of the less than delightful takeout from the Ride 'Em Cowboy Saloon, I knew I had to hurry out of the room, go through the sitting room, then the kitchen, then the walk-in pantry, then the laundry room. The bathroom was off the laundry room, out of the way of the kitchen.

I'll spare you the details, but after my mission was completed, I decided to throw in a load of laundry and fold the clothes that had been in the dryer since that morning.

Balancing myself and trying not to breathe because my ribs hurt, I unloaded the dryer and put everything in a laundry basket. Oh, I found a nightgown!

I slipped everything off that I could, stepped out of my cut-up jeans, and let the soft blue flannel of my nightgown warm me.

When I walked out, Antoinette Chloe was at my oak kitchen table with my notebook and calendar, groaning and moaning.

Did you write this in Polish?" she asked. "It's a mess. From what I can tell, you're missing Chet and Lottie Campbell's fiftieth wedding anniversary on the second of December on your calendar. You have a menu in your notebook, though. You do have an entry for Louise McDowney's bridal shower."

Two bookings for one day. "Good catch, Antoinette Chloe, but I'll think about it all tomorrow."

My house phone rang, and I jumped. At two in the morning, it couldn't be good news.

ACB was already up and answering. "Trixie's house. Antoinette Chloe speaking. Oh, hi, Linda. Is everything okay?"

Linda Blessler was subbing for me at the diner on the graveyard shift.

"Uh-huh. Oh, no! Gee, that's really too bad! Uh-huh. Uh-huh."

One more *uh-huh* from ACB, and I was going to scream!

"Sorry to hear that, Linda. Sure, Trixie's right here. I'll tell her. Oh, you already called Juanita? She has an idea? Great! Maybe Juanita could pull a double or I could work graveyard for Trixie. Or maybe some kind of combination. Okay. Have a safe trip. Bye."

"Trip? What happened?"

"Linda saw the light on in the kitchen here, and she felt like she could call without waking you. She said that Ty told her about your accident and she's sorry about—"

"Antoinette Chloe, what trip is Linda taking?"

"She has to fly down to Florida. Her sister, Lulu, needs her help with babysitting."

As I stood there with my ankle throbbing and my ribs aching, my mind was going in a million directions.

"Um . . . Antoinette Chloe, who is going to cook on the graveyard shift? I heard you volunteer, but I think you are going to be busy enough with my catering. And you have your own business to run, and your own Christmas stuff to do . . . and . . . and . . ."

I took a couple of deep breaths. Things would be better in the morning.

ACB stood. "You haven't heard the best part. Juanita is going to contact Bob and tell him that we need him."

"Bob? You mean, *the* Bob?"

Bob—whose last name I didn't know or couldn't remember—was an old army buddy of Uncle Porky and cooked on the graveyard shift. Bob had been missing in action since Uncle Porky died.

I'd never met Bob, but he always checked in with Juanita from various casinos around the U.S. and Canada, claiming that he was too ill to come in to work.

Yeah, right.

Bob? *Ho. Ho. Ho.*

Chapter 3

*W*hen I opened my eyes the next morning, the sun was streaming through my windows. I smelled coffee, and something garlicky cooking—maybe kielbasa or fried bologna.

The clock in the shape of a ship's wheel over the TV told me that it was almost ten thirty.

Ten thirty! Yikes! I had a million things I needed to do.

I pulled the lever on the side of the recliner, and the footrest dropped way too fast.

"Yeow!" I gasped as my casted foot hit the hardwood floor. It rattled my teeth.

"Trixie, are you awake?" ACB yelled from the kitchen.

"Barely."

"Breakfast is ready. Can you make it to the kitchen?"

"Sure," I replied. "First I need to make a pit stop and wash my face and comb my hair."

I hobbled—or should I say crutched?—to the kitchen and saw the big oak farm table set for about ten. I turned to Antoinette Chloe, busy at the stove, who looked over her shoulder and answered my unasked question.

"We're having a 'help Trixie meeting.' Ty's coming

over for breakfast. So are Juanita, Ray, Max, and Clyde. Oh, and your waitresses Nancy and Bettylou are coming, too, just as soon as they cash out their customers. Cindy is cooking and wants to help, but we'll fill her in later. Everyone wants to help you, really. They all do. We're getting a plan of action together."

I smiled, happy to the core. I was surrounded by wonderful friends, and they were coming to breakfast on this pretty day to plan how they could help me.

Ray is a high school senior who is mostly my computer expert. He also busses tables and loads and unloads the dishwasher.

Ty talked me into giving Ray a job when he was caught hacking into a computer at the Sandy Harbor High School a couple of years back and changing grades. I had reservations at first, but as it turned out, Ray has been invaluable to me and a great worker.

I inherited Max and Clyde from Uncle Porky. They're my handymen and were also army buddies of my uncle. They take care of the grounds; I couldn't run the point without them. I inherited Juanita Holgado, too, my day cook and assistant. I don't know what I'd do without Juanita.

Yikes. If all these people were coming over, I'd better make myself look presentable.

I searched the laundry basket for some clothes to wear, because I didn't want to ask Antoinette Chloe to make a clothes run for me upstairs when I could still tap into the basket.

I found a jean skirt that I could just pull on over my cast and a T-shirt that read SANDY HARBOR: SALMON

FISHING CAPITAL OF AMERICA and had a picture of a salmon jumping out of some waves on it. It was a stretch to claim that, but the shirts were the idea of the Sandy Harbor Tourist Bureau, which consisted of Loretta Mitchum and her next-door neighbor Elsie Crom, who ran the tourist bureau out of Elsie's farm stand on Route 3 two days a week from June until September.

I continued to get myself together, glad that Uncle Porky had loved porcelain enough so that the Big House was equipped with several bathrooms, showers, and tubs.

It was way too much house for me, but on several occasions in the past, the rooms were full of guests. I was very glad to welcome them, but was also ecstatic when they left, and Blondie and I had some peace and quiet.

Speaking of guests, they all arrived for breakfast at once and swarmed around me. Juanita helped me to a chair and propped my foot up on a pillow on another chair. It wasn't very conducive for eating at the table unless I twisted.

Eventually I pushed the chair and pillow away and hoisted my cast under the table. I figured that I'd be fine for a while.

Antoinette Chloe handed me a pain pill from the little envelope I'd received at the emergency room. Since my ribs and ankle were throbbing, I took it and washed it down with some orange juice.

Juanita unwrapped a quiche that she must have made during her shift at the Silver Bullet. Antoinette Chloe set out kielbasa, scrambled eggs, bacon, French toast, and breakfast sausage.

"Eat!" she ordered. "Before it gets cold!"

I could remember Uncle Porky always saying that at functions. Then he'd always mutter under his breath that it's nice to be polite, but everything's getting cold.

Everyone got busy passing, reaching, and talking.

ACB stood on the side of me, loading up my plate as if I couldn't do it myself. I raised an eyebrow at Ty as she was trying to shake off a chunk of kielbasa from a fork onto my plate. It landed with a splash in Max's coffee.

Max didn't notice. He was busy teasing Ray about Ray's new girlfriend. ACB fished the kielbasa out with a spoon and plopped it onto my plate as if nothing had happened.

Clyde noticed and took the opportunity to sop up Max's saucer with a napkin and fill up Max's cup.

Clyde elbowed Ty. Ty chuckled. I bit my bottom lip so I wouldn't laugh out loud.

Max took a sip of kielbasa-flavored coffee and grinned. "Good stuff."

Antoinette Chloe Brown was one of a kind.

Juanita Holgado tapped a fork on the side of her coffee cup and everyone became silent.

"Boss Trixie, I speak for everyone here. *Sí.* All your friends. We wish to help you with the catering. And we'll decorate for Christmas at the diner and here at the Big House. We all know how much you love Christmas. And whatever you need, we will do."

Sentimental tears filled my eyes. "Thank you so much. I really appreciate it, but you all have so much to do already. And I'm not completely helpless. I can do most everything—except drive, and carry things to the van, and stand for long periods of time, and walk for any length, and put things in the oven and take them out, and—"

Ty cleared his throat. "You can keep on top of the ordering from your food distributor and you can list every morning what needs to be done. We'll put a duplicate calendar in the Silver Bullet's kitchen. Max, Clyde, Ray, and I will be your loaders, unloaders, and drivers."

Just then there was a knock on the door.

"Come in!" ACB yelled.

Gee, I hoped it wasn't an ax murderer that Antoinette Chloe was letting in, but we did have Deputy Brisco on the scene.

Nancy and Bettylou walked in and kicked off their boots. "What a busy day already!" Nancy said.

"You aren't kidding!" Juanita added. "I have to hurry back and help Cindy, so let's plan."

Nancy and Bettylou didn't want anything but coffee, and ACB motioned for them to help themselves.

We all kept talking, mostly about the catering and delivery to the Christmas pageant rehearsals at the Sandy Harbor Community Church.

My notebook appeared in front of me, courtesy of ACB. "I was thinking mostly about winter comfort food. Things like soups and chili and sandwiches. Pot roast. Roasted chicken with mashed potatoes."

"And gravy," Clyde added.

"Of course," I said. "And spaghetti and meatballs with garlic bread."

"And a chef salad," said Juanita.

"And baked macaroni and cheese," I said, remembering our recent contest for the best mac-and-cheese dish.

"Cream of tomato soup and grilled cheese sandwiches," said ACB. "I always loved it when my mother made that on a cold, winter day."

I nodded. "So did I."

I noticed that Ray Meyerson was awfully silent. "Anything you'd like to add, Ray?"

"I was just thinking. Do you think there would be time for me to try out for the pageant?" he asked.

"Well, of course!" I said. "I hope to be in it, too."

Clyde laughed. "You could always play Tiny Tim."

There was laughter all around, and I joined in. "What a great idea!" I said. "I'll have to tell Liz Fellows that I'm trying out for Tiny Tim. I come with my own crutches, too."

More talking and joking ensued. I didn't want it to end, but little by little everyone started to take their dishes to the dishwasher. ACB rinsed and loaded them in.

"Antoinette Chloe, what are you going to try out for?" Clyde asked.

"The Ghost of Christmas Presents," she replied. "I'm going to help Santa pass out the presents, just like I did last year. I had a ball."

"It's the Ghost of Christmas Present," Ty said. "As in the *present* day, and not like gifts."

"You think of it your way, and I'll think of it my way. I'm going to be the Ghost of Christmas Presents, and I'll be helping Santa distribute gifts after the pageant," she said stubbornly.

"Do we even know what the pageant is going to be about?" I asked. "I mean, Antoinette Chloe, you're planning on a scene from *A Christmas Carol*. What if Liz Fellows has something else in mind? Maybe she's going to do some version of *A Charlie Brown Christmas* or *It's a Wonderful Life*. Or maybe the one with Ralphie and Randy—*A Christmas Story*."

"I love that movie!" Nancy said.

"I laugh and laugh," added Bettylou.

"Humpf." ACB crossed her arms. "We'll see about my part tonight, and I'd better be the Ghost of Christmas Presents—that's *p-r-e-s-e-n-t-s*."

Clyde sniffed. "A theatrical diva is right here in our *p-r-e-s-e-n-c-e*," he spelled, imitating ACB. "As for me, I don't like the limelight. I'm going to volunteer to take tickets at the door."

"And I'll take care of parking everyone," Max said. "As usual."

There was more banter like this, and I sat back and enjoyed it. All catering talk was over, and I knew that my friends would fill in as needed.

There was another knock on the door. I didn't miss the raised eyebrows and the clearing of throats around the table.

Juanita stood and walked over to the door. "I wonder who that could be."

I had a feeling that she already knew.

She opened the door and there stood . . .

Santa Claus?

The man had—*I kid you not*—a round face with rosy cheeks, a big belly, a shock of white hair, and a beard. He wore a red parka and red and black checked pants tucked into shiny black rubber boots, and he was smoking (you won't believe this) a corncob pipe.

And he carried a poinsettia plant.

"This lovely lady must be Trixie," he said. "My dear, it's a delight to see you after all these years. I remember you as a young lady. You've grown into a fine woman."

"Yes. I'm Trixie Matkowski. Pardon me for not getting up."

He handed me the plant. "For you, lovely Trixie. It's a pleasure to finally meet you."

I looked over at Juanita. Her brown eyes were as wide as saucers. It was the same look she had when she worried about snow, the bread rising, a big take-out order, and giving me bad or shocking news.

Then it hit me. "Bob?"

He nodded. "One and the same."

"Where've you been, Bob?"

Legend had it that Bob, one of the primary chefs at the Silver Bullet, had disappeared after my uncle Porky's funeral service at the cemetery. Apparently Bob had kissed and hugged Aunt Stella, gotten into his car, and driven away.

He'd called in "sick" a month later to Juanita. And since I'd taken over three years or so ago, he'd still been calling in sick from various casinos across North America.

He'd never asked for me. He only talked to Juanita, probably because he was afraid I'd tell him to return to the Silver Bullet and get back to work.

"I've been traveling, but I heard you needed me. So I'm here," he said. "I'm ready to help out."

I needed him desperately, especially with Linda not being able to cover for me, but I wasn't going to let Bob off that easily.

"Traveling?" I raised an eyebrow. "I know exactly where you've been traveling."

Looking around the table, I saw the amusement on everyone's face. They all knew him from the old days when he'd worked alongside Porky. They were cooks in the army together. They both had the same stature and the same twinkle in their eyes. And they were both from Brooklyn.

"Ho-ho-ho." He laughed. "I'm going to try out for Santa Claus tonight. It's been a long time since I've played Santa, and I miss the kids." He cleverly changed the subject of his disappearance.

"Speaking of tonight," Antoinette Chloe said, "I hate to cut this reunion short, but we all have things to do to get ready."

"What do you want me to do, Trixie?" Bob asked. "I'm ready to do whatever you need me to."

"Why don't you let Juanita help you get reacquainted with the kitchen? I'm going to need you working the third shift." Then I remembered my manners. "Do you need to get settled in first?"

Juanita nodded. "He drove nonstop from Connecticut to be here this morning."

"Foxwoods Casino or Mohegan Sun Casino?" I asked.

"Foxwoods."

"Where are you staying?" I asked, thinking that I should offer him a guest room here at the Big House.

"He's staying at my house," Juanita answered.

"What?" Clyde sat up straighter in his chair. "At your house?"

Juanita raised an eyebrow at Clyde. "Yes. I am all alone, and Bob can keep me company."

"Bob could stay with me. I'm all alone, too," Clyde said sharply.

"Well, whose fault is that?" Juanita snapped, then glared at Clyde.

I looked at ACB, who was hiding a smile. We both knew that Clyde had a crush on Juanita but was too shy to do anything about it. Juanita had just sent him a little tweak to make him jealous.

Wow! Nice move, Juanita.

Bob chuckled. "I feel so wanted, but I'll stay with Clyde, Juanita. I don't want to start tongues wagging in Sandy Harbor."

Everyone carried their dishes on the counter, helped ACB clean up, and left. Only Ty, ACB, and I remained.

Ty poured himself another cup of coffee. "So that's the infamous Bob."

I laughed. "You know, it's hard to yell at Santa for being missing in action."

Ty stretched out his legs. "Yeah. There's the whole coal-in-the-stocking thing to worry about."

"Bob's here, so that's going to help out a lot," ACB said. "I guess we should get to work. Right, Trixie? Ty, you're excused. You have to go to your real job. Trixie and I will make the salads here. Everything we need is on Trixie's back porch: pots, pans, big boxes of macaroni, bags of potatoes, mayonnaise, veggies, and two huge hams. I figure that we can get everything ready for four o'clock and you can drive the van to auditions tonight."

Ty stood. "I'd better get it all inside before everything freezes."

"Oh, yes!" ACB said. Sometimes she overlooks the big picture.

Ty brought in everything, then headed to work.

I looked at my stove. It was much smaller than the industrial ones at the Silver Bullet and would only accommodate one of the bigger pots at a time, and I wondered whether ACB could lift it by herself.

When cooked, the macaroni and potatoes could cool quickly outside on the porch. I'd keep an eye on it. In the winter, everyone up north here used their porches or garages as additional fridge space.

A few hours later, we were done with the three salads—mac, potato, and chef—and were wondering why we still hadn't run out of conversation.

Ty arrived with Ray and Bob and the three of them loaded everything into the van.

"Uh . . . Trixie, you have two whole hams still on the porch," he said.

I looked at Antoinette Chloe. "I put them there. I figured that we could bake them in the community room kitchen at the church since it's much bigger than yours."

"Juanita could have baked them at the Silver Bullet while we were making the salads," I pointed out. "They would have been ready to load in the van."

She shrugged. "Or we could have done that."

"Actually, Juanita could have cut them up on the slicer

and we could have just heated them up in the steam pans. The hams are already cooked. No sense turning them into jerky with a lot of baking."

"We could have done that, too," ACB said.

"We have to get on the road," I said, checking the time.

The men rode in my van while ACB and I went in my car. It was easier for me to plop into the passenger's seat than to be hoisted into a van.

As we entered through the back door, the sounds of children running and shouting bounced off the walls. I peeked through the door and saw kids were running everywhere while Liz Fellows stood in the front surrounded by parents—mostly mothers.

I heard angry talking and whining. The parents were doing both.

"Liz, Johnny has always been the butt end of the donkey. Can't he be the head for once?"

"Liz, my Cortney wants to lip-sync to 'Shake It Off' by Taylor Swift. Cortney can do all the choreography, too, and has her own costume. I know that this is a Christmas pageant, but Taylor Swift is a year-round personality."

"I want my twins, Tiffany and Tommy, to have a speaking part this year. They only spit a little with their new braces. I don't know why the children in their class complain so much."

"Liz, my Ralphie can play Ralphie from *A Christmas Story*. They look just alike even though my Ralphie is fourteen."

Ty was at my side. "Looks like a three-ring circus in there. Maybe I should help Liz defuse the situation so she can get to work."

He walked into the room, put his fingers to his lips, and let out a loud, shrill whistle.

The room became silent.

"Everyone take a seat and keep quiet, please. I don't know how Ms. Fellows can even think, let alone do her job."

"*I* would never put up with such noise and confusion." That haughty proclamation came from Margie Grace. Yes, the same Margie Grace who gave us the Christmas pageant with the tangoing shepherds and salmon. Oh, and let's not forget the spawning salmon dance at last year's Miss Salmon Contest.

"Margie, I need to start the auditions. Please take a seat along with everyone else," Liz said, flipping pages on her clipboard.

"How dare you! I ran this pageant long before you became Pastor Fritz's secretary!"

There was a gasp from the spectators, and Liz looked like she was going to faint.

Margie held her cell phone in her right hand and was just winding up to throw it at Liz as if it were a baseball and she was a pitcher for the Yankees. Thankfully, Ty grabbed her wrist and held it.

"Knock it off, Margie. The kids are watching. Where's your Christmas spirit?"

But as long as Ty still had a grip on Margie, it was Liz's turn.

"How dare you, you old has-been! I am not a secretary. I am an administrative assistant."

"I don't care what you call yourself; you do not have any experience in putting on plays." Margie paused for dramatic effect and looked out at the spectators, who were now silent and riveted in their pews. "Unlike me."

I heard breathing in my ear. It was ACB glued to my side. "This is like a production of *As the Stomach Turns*."

"I know. Liz would have been really hurt if Ty hadn't stepped in and grabbed Margie's wrist." I shuddered, thinking of what might have happened to Liz's face.

Ty held his hands up like a prisoner surrendering. "Ladies and gentlemen, in the spirit of the Christmas season, can you put your differences aside? Let's move these auditions along so we can start rehearsing. Trixie is here with dinner and dessert for everyone. She's setting up now."

He gave me a pointed glance, and I hurried as fast as I could to the kitchen on my one good leg with one plastered leg, two taped ribs, one uncapped tooth, and two wooden crutches.

"Trixie," Bob said. "I have some bad news. The meat slicer we were going to use for the ham is broken. Apparently the maintenance man used it to cut wood to fix the banister on the front stairs."

ACB shook her head. "The maintenance man should know better than that."

"I guess we'll have to slice the ham by hand," I said, glad that I remembered to bring my favorite knife. "I can sit and slice it."

ACB walked in. "Speaking of bad news, you should see what's happening out in the church. It's mayhem. Apparently there's a rumor going around that a Hollywood talent scout might attend the pageant."

"So that's it." I shook my head. "No wonder the usually lovely people of Sandy Harbor are turning into gargoyles."

Ray was out of breath when he ran in. "Mr. Constelli said that his daughter Daphne would *definitely* be singing 'The Twelve Days of Christmas.' But she can't remember the lines and sounds like a squeaky mouse. When Liz told Daphne to learn the lyrics of the song and try again, her mother threw the sheet music at Liz. Ty had to ask the whole family to leave. He kicked out Margie Grace, too. Daphne started crying and Mr. Constelli says he is going to sue."

"For Pete's sake." Ty walked into the kitchen, and I could swear that steam was coming out of his ears. "I put Vern McCoy in charge of keeping the peace at the auditions. What's gotten into these people?"

"There may be a Hollywood talent scout coming to the pageant," ACB said.

"Seriously?" Ty asked.

"That's the rumor," ACB replied. "I wonder who started it."

"Probably Margie Grace," Ty said. "She seemed the craziest."

"Maybe she figured that the rumor would cause problems for Liz," I suggested. "If so, she was absolutely correct."

"You know, it's hard to believe that Margie and Liz used to be good friends way back. In fact, Margie knew how much Liz loved flowers, and got her involved in the Garden Club." ACB adjusted her fascinator just before it hit the ground. "If I remember correctly, they had words over their rose entries at the state fair. They fought, and

I don't know who did what first, but both of their rose entries ended up on the floor of the horticulture building, decapitated. That put an end to their relationship."

"Decapitated roses, huh?" Ty grunted. "On that note, let's get to work."

I put Ty, Ray, and Bob to work positioning buffet tables, putting on tablecloths, and setting up the buffet with plates and utensils. Whereas Ty and Ray might be rookies, I was happy to see that Bob took charge. In the end, everything looked fabulous.

Ray and Ty put bread and rolls on trays. Then Bob fancied it up. They put out mayonnaise, butter, mustard, ketchup, and horseradish in front of the rolls and salad dressings in front of the salad, then set up the steam pan for the ham. Bob even found some candy canes to put on the tables for decoration. Cold drinks, ice, and cups were set up on a round table. A big urn of coffee was perking on another table set with milk, sugar, spoons, and cups.

"Trixie, where are the napkins?" Bob asked.

"Um . . . uh . . . oh, no . . ." I remembered buying pretty napkins with snowmen on them, but they were nowhere to be found. "I think they are still in my kitchen pantry at the Big House."

Bob opened his wallet, stuffed thick with bills, and handed Ray several of them. "Ray, hustle on over to the grocery store or to the Spend A Buck and buy a bunch of napkins. Pretty ones for Christmas."

"Thanks, Ray. I'll reimburse you, Bob," I said, slicing the ham.

"Don't worry about it," he said. "You can't remember everything."

"But it's my *job* to remember everything," I protested. "I'm the boss."

"Trixie, you broke your ankle and have broken ribs. And you are whistling with that gap in your teeth. You're allowed to be a little forgetful now and then. Give yourself a break."

Word came from the church via Antoinette Chloe, who ducked out of the kitchen to audition for the Ghost of Christmas Presents, to say that Bob could audition for Santa Claus when the children were gone.

"Bob is the perfect Santa Claus. I don't know why Liz is making him audition," ACB complained. "Besides, no one else is signed up to try out. Margie Grace is right. Liz Fellows doesn't know what she's doing."

"Antoinette Chloe," Ty began, "Bob hasn't been around Sandy Harbor for a very long time, and I don't think that Liz even knows him. What if he is the worst Santa this side of the North Pole? That wouldn't be good for the pageant."

"Oh, I suppose you're right." She returned to cutting up dill pickles and putting olives into bowls. "And I almost forgot! Trixie, Liz says you are in as Tiny Tim. No audition necessary."

Everyone laughed at that, and we returned to our festive mood.

Just then Pastor Fritz and his wife, Darlene, walked in. Pastor Fritz was a tall, skinny Ichabod Crane type of guy with an Adam's apple that moved when he spoke or swallowed. I heard that during his sermons, several of the parishioners would fall into a hypnotic trance simply by watching it move. He was bald except for a comb-over of exactly nine pitch-black strands of hair.

Darlene was the opposite of Pastor Fritz. She had huge brassy yellow hair with roots growing in and was about five feet tall. She was as wide as she was tall, always laughed, and loved to have a good time. Everyone said that Darlene was the best thing that ever happened to the church—she added a lot of new programs, the teens loved her, and she had a generous heart.

"I heard from Deputy Brisco that you broke some bones, Trixie," Pastor Fritz said, looking down. "I'm sorry to hear that, but thanks for doing all this work and not leaving us high and dry."

"I'd never do that, Pastor Fritz."

"Of course she wouldn't. You should know better than to say such a thing," said Bob, standing up with a grunt from loading cases of soda into a cooler and grinning.

"Hey, Bob, is that you? What brings you back to Sandy Harbor?" asked Pastor Fritz. They shook hands.

"I got an SOS from Juanita Holgado. She said that Trixie needed a hand," Bob said.

"It's good to see you again," Darlene walked over to Bob, stood on her tiptoes, and lifted her arms to give him a hug. It still wasn't enough height.

Bob bent over and smiled widely. "Hi, Darlene." Then Bob turned to me. "The pastor, Darlene, and I, and a bunch of others built a Habitat for Humanity house together in Syracuse."

Darlene broke away and took her husband by the arm. "Fritz, let's go say hello to everyone else and watch the auditions for a while. I have a couple of announcements to make. I ran into Margie Grace outside. She wants to announce something about a spring trip to see the lilacs in Rochester. I don't know why she insists on talking about it now, when it's Christmas, but I guess she can't let Liz have all the attention. Then we can all eat when Trixie gives us the word."

"I thought you kicked Margie out," I whispered to Ty.

"I did."

Ray came in with the napkins as Fritz and Darlene exited. I asked ACB to take all the ham that I had finally cut up and put it in the steam pan and light the cans of fuel.

"We are done," I said, looking around the room. "Everything is perfect. Thanks so much, everyone. Now, let's all go watch the rest of the auditions, listen to the announcements, and let them know that dinner is served."

"Good idea," ACB said, leading the exodus out of the kitchen. I went the other way.

"Trixie?" Ty asked, holding the door open for me.

"I'm heading to the ladies' room first," I replied. "Go ahead without me."

I hobbled over to the cooler, got an orange soda, and took a long draw of the cold stuff. Mmm . . . icy cold. I put it on the table next to my knife, thinking that as soon as I got back to the kitchen, I should pack the knife away.

It took me longer than usual, with my injuries. And I had to wade through budding Sandy Harbor starlets and their mothers spraying a variety of products into their hair.

"Hold your breath while I spray, Lynette. You don't want to be a flat-haired angel," one mother said.

"Sweetie, I convinced Ms. Fellows that you didn't have to know ballet for the Sugarplum Fairy—you can tap dance instead. Won't that talent scout from Hollywood be impressed?" another one asked.

A little while later, I walked back into the kitchen to do a last-minute check on everything and to make sure that the ham was getting hot.

But I paused in midcrutch. Something—or rather, someone—was lying on the floor, facedown, with my knife sticking out of her back. Blood was on the back of her white blouse, staining it a bright crimson.

Liz Fellows!

I didn't have to check her pulse to know that she was dead.

I felt the room starting to spin, but I didn't dare fall. Been there, done that. Had the cast to prove it.

I heard screaming, then more screaming. High-pitched. Annoying. Loud.

Why wouldn't that woman shut up?

That's when I realized that woman was me. And I just couldn't stop.

Chapter 4

*P*astor Fritz was the first through the door, followed by Darlene, Ty, and then Bob.

Ty immediately went over to Liz, knelt on one knee, and checked for a pulse. Standing, he shook his head and then radioed for an ambulance. He also radioed for Hal Manning, the owner of the Happy Repose Funeral Home and our resident coroner, and the last member of the Sandy Harbor Sheriff's Department, Lou Rutledge, since Vern McCoy was already on the scene, keeping the crowd out of the kitchen.

"Bob, would you go to the other door and keep people out, please?"

"Absolutely, Ty."

Pulling over a chair, Ty guided me to its seat. He took my crutches as I collapsed with a sigh. I glanced at poor Liz and quickly looked away.

"Who would want to kill Liz?" I asked. "She didn't have a mean bone in her body."

No one answered.

Ty instructed the pastor and Darlene to move away "from the body," and they moved behind the stainless steel island, right by the ham—the ham that I'd been slicing.

There was a commotion outside the kitchen, and Deputy McCoy's raised voice echoed throughout the room. "Go back to the auditions, everyone. Please."

Ty turned to Pastor Fritz and Darlene. "On second thought, would you two mind going back to the church and telling everyone to sit and wait for further instructions from me? Don't say anything more just yet."

"Certainly, Deputy Brisco. Whatever we can do to help," said Darlene, wide-eyed. She turned and just about ran to get out of the kitchen. I could relate to that.

Pastor Fritz lagged behind. "I'd like to say a short prayer for Liz first, if that's okay."

"Sure. Go right ahead, pastor," Ty said, shifting on his feet.

We all bowed our heads and Pastor Fritz made a big sweep of his arms and clasped his hands together. "God bless our sister, Elizabeth Fellows, and welcome her into heaven, for she was a kind and loving person. Amen."

"Amen," Ty and I said in unison.

"Someone didn't think she was a kind and loving person, Pastor Fritz," I pointed out.

"Then they didn't know Liz like I did. She was a savior to the church office. So organized. So helpful. She was putting our bookkeeping records into the computer on a spreadsheet. Amazing. She could do anything. And what attention to detail! She kept ahead on the ordering, and she jumped at the chance to direct the Christmas pageant." He thought for a moment. "Now who's going to direct the pageant? Maybe we should cancel it. . . ."

"Don't cancel the pageant. I'll direct it," I heard myself saying.

What? Like I didn't have enough to do these days?

My heart beat wildly in my chest at the thought of taking on more things, but I couldn't let the kids down.

I took a deep breath. "The kids will be crushed if the pageant is canceled. Besides, it's a Sandy Harbor tradition. I'll do it. I'll fit it in my schedule somehow . . . some way."

Pastor Fritz nodded solemnly. "Thanks for volunteering, Trixie. The Sandy Harbor residents appreciate it, and the Sandy Harbor Community Church appreciates it." He looked at the body of Liz on the floor and shook his head. "Maybe now is not the right time to discuss it, but I'm glad we got it settled. Let me join Darlene in talking to everyone."

I just sat stupefied for a while. "What just happened?" I finally asked Ty.

"Looks like you're the new pageant director." He grinned. "I distinctly heard you volunteer."

Just then, Hal Manning walked in. "That's quite a knife in her back," he said, bending over the body. "Anyone take pictures yet?"

"My equipment is in my car. I wanted to preserve the crime scene, so I didn't leave to get it," Ty said.

"Now would be a good time," Hal said.

Ty hurried out the back door.

"Hal, that's my knife," I said. "I was slicing that ham

over there." I pointed to the table. "I left the knife on the table when I went to the ladies' room. When I came back, I saw . . . I saw . . . Liz like that." Tears flooded my yes. "It's all my fault."

"It's not your fault. Unless you stabbed her. Did you?"

"Don't be ridiculous."

"Then it's not your fault, Trixie. Don't ever think it was."

"Do you mind if I leave?" I asked. "I'm just going to hobble into the church and get out of here."

"Sure. Go ahead. But don't go far. Ty will probably want to take your statement later."

It was going to be a long night because Ty typed about three words a minute. Maybe he'd let me just type it up to save us both time.

Until then, I had a pageant to run and tons of food ready to put out—just as soon as the crime scene was cleared.

It wasn't as if I was being callous, but I had to feed these people somewhere . . . somehow. Didn't I? It seemed horrible moving everything to the back of the church—maybe the children's room—but it seemed even more awful moving Liz out and then eating where she was killed.

Maybe ACB had an idea as to what could be done. Or maybe Pastor Fritz and Darlene might have one.

But this volunteer might talk about pageant auditions just to distract everyone. I didn't have a clue what to say or what to do first, though.

All I could picture was Liz lying on the black-and-white linoleum floor, covered in her own blood, with my carving knife sticking out of her back.

Pastor Fritz was leading everyone in a prayer for Liz.

Afterward, there were numerous questions, but the pastor said that Deputy Ty Brisco would address everyone later.

It seemed like I was having an out-of-body experience. I was sitting in a pew and listening and watching everyone, but I couldn't believe that we were talking about the pageant with Liz lying dead in the room across the hall.

But like ACB said, there were a lot of kids there who were excited to audition for the either fictitious or real talent scout. We might as well talk about it—rather than talk about Liz in front of the kids.

As I looked around at all the hopefuls who wanted to be in the pageant, I wanted to split. Then I remembered what ACB had said earlier: Anyone who tried out could be in it.

It wasn't as if this was Broadway, no matter what the backstage mothers and fathers thought. If little Junior or Juniorette couldn't sing or dance or act, he or she had to be the butt end of a camel!

Or didn't we care about talent?

I whispered to Antoinette Chloe, "Is this a variety show? Is it a play?"

"It's both, from what I can tell."

"Did Liz have any notes?" I asked hopefully.

"She has—had—a laptop. It's somewhere around here." ACB looked around in the pews and found it.

Thank goodness. I'd have to look at her plans thoroughly later, when I got home.

I stood when I heard Pastor Fritz introduce me. "I'm the new pageant director because . . . uh . . . Liz is no longer able to do it. For you who don't know me, my name is Trixie Matkowski, and I'm also catering the auditions and the practices, and then the Christmas Eve community dinner. However, as you can see, I have a broken leg, and other people have stepped in to help me. So I thought I should help out with the pageant." I gave ACB a pointed look and motioned for her to come so I could talk to her.

I whispered, "Ask Vern to let me know when I can let everyone out of this room." The kids and their parents didn't need to see Liz in a body bag being transported to the Happy Repose Funeral Home in Hal Manning's hearse.

ACB flip-flopped out of the church, and I answered questions.

Finally Vern opened the side door and gave me the thumbs-up sign.

"I am canceling auditions for today. Please return Tuesday at the same time. By then, I should be organized. However, before you go, please take out a piece of paper and write down your name, address, and at least two phone numbers where you can be reached. Also, list your children's names and what they'd like to be in the pageant. Antoinette Chloe will collect them on your way out. Thank you, and I'll see you Tuesday at six o'clock."

I figured that we could refrigerate the food and bring it back out for Tuesday.

Sitting on a chair that ACB brought me with my leg

stretched out, lost in thought, I probably discouraged the backstage mothers from approaching me.

Finally the church was empty, with the exception of ACB and me. She sat down and showed me a stack of papers. "That's all of them. I think that the parents figured that Liz passed away—maybe from a heart attack or stroke—but they don't know that she was murdered."

I nodded. "I figure that we can put the food away and serve it Tuesday. It'll be fine."

"We'll take care of it as soon as everyone is done in the kitchen."

"What are they doing in there?" I was getting tired—or maybe I was just adrenaline dumping.

ACB looked off in the distance. "They're taking pictures and measuring things, but I think they are getting ready to move Liz."

"Do you know much about her?" I asked.

"Not really. Just what I'd heard about the rose decapitation, and she quit the Garden Club after that. Liz is fairly new to the area. Maybe three years now. She came to Sandy Harbor about the same time you did. She lives alone in that really cute cottage on Daffodil Street. I'm sure you've noticed it. It's buttercup yellow and surrounded by a white picket fence. In the summer the whole yard is loaded with flowers. For Christmas, she has white icicle lights hanging from the eaves."

"I love that house! And Liz is quite the gardener. I wonder why she never came to the Silver Bullet."

ACB shrugged. "Probably because she didn't drive much. She frequented my place because she could walk to it."

Just then Ty Brisco entered the church. "Where's everyone? I was going to start interviewing people about Liz Fellows."

"I sent them all home. It's not right being in the middle of a crime scene, especially for the kids," I said.

"Good idea, but I wanted to ask if anyone saw anything strange or saw anyone leave the room at the time of Liz's murder."

"We have everyone's name and contact information for you. And you know this town: In about an hour, everyone in Sandy Harbor will have heard about Liz, and anyone who might have seen anything strange is bound to come forward."

"Yeah." Ty looked at me. "Sorry you had to see that."

I swallowed the lump in my throat. "I'm glad it was me and not a little kid."

He put his hand on my shoulder as if to comfort me. It helped. "What about all the food?" he asked quietly.

"As soon as you'll allow us into the kitchen, Antoinette Chloe and I will wrap it all up and put it in the fridge."

"You can come in now. Hal Manning cleaned up the couple of spots of blood from the floor. Everyone is gone. I'll help you, and we'll get out of here faster."

"Come to think of it, where are Bob and Ray?" I asked.

"They are sitting in the van now. When you discovered Liz, Bob took Ray out of the kitchen and plopped him in the van with a couple of U2 CDs."

"Good idea."

"I'll go get them," Ty said. "We could use their help in packing up everything."

"No. Leave them. The three of us can handle it. It won't

take long. But let's get moving. Pastor Fritz is waiting to lock up."

I pointed to Liz's things. "Ty, these are some of Liz's personal things—like her coat, purse, and tote bag. Would you like me to pack them up for you? Maybe they'll help you find her next of kin."

Ty nodded. "Thanks. That'd be great."

I should have mentioned Liz's laptop, but I wanted it. Liz had notes on the laptop for the pageant; I had seen her checking it. And maybe it might have clues on it as to who the murderer could be. I intended on seeing what I could find. It would only be stored in a locker at the sheriff's department until they got around to finding tech experts anyway.

Ty helped me out of the chair and handed me my crutches. I took a deep breath, but that was a mistake. My ribs protested.

ACB, bless her heart, was rolling up Liz's coat and stuffing it into her tote bag. She tossed Liz's purse over her shoulder and winked at me.

I knew exactly what she was up to. She was going to walk out with Liz's purse and laptop, hoping that Ty wouldn't notice.

That's my friend!

Back at the Big House, we could check out Liz's purse and her computer. Maybe it would give us a clue as to who had a grudge against her.

I had a stake in trying to find out what happened to Liz. After all, my carving knife was the murder weapon, but Ty would order me to mind my own business and leave the investigating to him, a trained professional.

Yeah, right. He worked within the confines of his job title and the law.

ACB and I had no such problem. We both were in the food business. I owned the Silver Bullet, eleven cottages, and a big farmhouse. ACB owned a restaurant in town and had an old Victorian house in a historic part of the village where Victorians were the staple. But ACB's house was more than a "painted lady," as ornately painted Victorians were called. ACB's house was a painted lady on an LSD trip.

We went to work, wrapping the ham, salads, and whatnot. We put everything we needed to in the industrial fridge. I avoided looking at the area where I'd found Liz, and soon we were done and out of there.

Tuesday's catering would be a snap.

I hobbled out to the van. Bob and Ray jumped out to open the front door for me and help me into the passenger's side.

Ty, ACB, and Ray climbed into the backseat. Bob started up the van, and we drove away into the darkness, back to the Big House.

We barely talked on the ride home, each of us lost in thought. But ACB hated silence, and asked, "How long did Liz work in the church office?"

"About three years," Ty answered. "Pastor Fritz told me that Liz was working on computerizing the church's records. She organized the cemetery records and the weekly bulletin, and she was working on the accounts and the bookkeeping. Seems like Liz was bringing the Sandy Harbor Community Church into the twenty-first century."

"Sounds pretty routine," I said.

ACB sighed. "Who on earth would kill her? All I can think of is that some of the parents might have gotten crazy mad at her because she didn't give their darlings a good part in the play. But I don't know if anyone would be so upset that they'd kill her."

"I noticed that, too," I said. "And then there's Margie Grace. Who would have thought that sweet Margie Grace would have turned into such a fruitcake? And she was absent from the church when Liz's body was discovered. Ty kicked her out due to the cell phone incident. Remember?"

ACB chuckled. "I never would have expected that Margie would attempt to throw a cell phone at anyone. She's such a sweet lady. And she's no spring chicken either. She's old enough to remember when Joshua Bilten's wagon threw a wheel, and he founded Sandy Harbor."

"Shush, Antoinette Chloe! Here she comes," I said.

"So, Trixie Matkowski, I hear that you are going to take over directing the pageant."

"Yes. I am, Margie."

"And what are your credentials?" she asked.

"I was present when they were looking for volunteers, and I volunteered."

"But what are your credentials?" she asked again, and I thought for a second she was going to fling a fox fur over her shoulder like a twenties movie star.

"I was in the chorus of *South Pacific* in the fifth grade. We all had on green crepe skirts and danced the hula. We didn't have any coconuts, though. We had to wear white blouses instead." If that wasn't a satisfactory credential for Margie, I could always mention that I was a lonely goatherd in sixth grade in *The Sound of Music.* I still wasn't sure what a goatherd was.

"Another outrage!" Margie yelled. "What is Sandy Harbor coming to? How do they expect to see a quality show when amateurs are directors?"

"Margie, Steven Spielberg had to start somewhere." I should have just changed the subject, but I couldn't help myself. "This pageant is for the kids, so I'm going to try my best. I have to be here anyway, since I'm catering the auditions and practices, so I might as well help out. I hope that there won't be any hard feelings between us."

"Humpf. That remains to be seen," she said, turning around, ready to exit, stage left. "Margie, wait! One more thing. Have you been telling everyone that a Hollywood talent scout is going to come to the pageant?"

She squinted at me. "I might have said that. You never know who might be in the audience."

"Margie," I said calmly. "How about stifling that rumor? Let's go back to peace on earth—or at least peace in our little slice of the earth. The mere mention of Hollywood has everyone acting a little strange. Things need to calm down, Margie. Know what I mean?"

I think I got my message to Margie. She looked a little embarrassed. Moving my leg to a better spot, I got more comfortable in the seat and watched Margie as she walked away.

Ty and Margie crossed paths, and before Ty could say

something to her, Margie scampered out like a church mouse.

"Are you doing okay, Trixie?" Ty asked me. "I hope that Margie didn't upset you. You've had a bad day."

"I can handle Margie. But I'm fine, Ty. Just moving around a bit. This cast must weigh five hundred pounds." I took a deep breath and asked, "Did you interview Pastor Fritz and Darlene?"

"I spoke with them informally, but I'll talk to them more back at the sheriff's department."

"What did they have to say?" ACB asked, sitting down next to me.

"I can't answer that, Antoinette Chloe, but if I did, I'd tell you that, according to them, Liz Fellows was a model employee and a good friend."

"That tells me nothing," ACB snapped.

"And that's just what I'm going to tell you—nothing." Ty grinned.

Ugh! What a cunning play on words. I exchanged eye rolling with ACB, and vowed that I'd solve the case before Ty—just because.

"And I want to remind you two to stay away from this case. It's my job to find the murderer. It's Trixie's job to direct the play, and it's Antoinette Chloe's job to, well, to do whatever it is that she does. Stay away from this case. Got it?"

I could have set my watch by Ty's *butt out* lectures.

"Trixie? Do we have an understanding?"

I smiled. "Of course, Deputy Brisco."

"What about you, Antoinette Chloe?"

"Why, certainly, Ty," ACB was sitting behind Bob. I couldn't see her hands, but I'd bet the change in my car's cup holder that her fingers were crossed.

Just like mine.

Ty took Blondie, our mutually shared dog, out for an evening jog. Ty said he needed to think.

Antoinette Chloe and I immediately sprang into action and got out Liz's purse and laptop and started snooping.

We started with her purse. It didn't have anything exciting in it. It could have been anyone's purse, because it had a wallet, credit cards, makeup, tissues, keys, a checkbook, and a cell phone.

I looked at her cell phone. Nothing jumped out at me except for several calls made to Buffalo, New York, and several to the church's office.

The calls made to the church's office were probably pertaining to her job. And she probably had friends in Buffalo. But I wrote down the numbers anyway. I'd call them later if I thought they were important.

"Did you find anything on the computer?" I asked ACB.

She gave me a thumbs-up. "There's a list of the people who auditioned so far. She gave them a plus or a minus sign. I think we both know what those stand for."

"Yeah, either they had some talent or they were going to be the camel's butt."

We laughed, fixed some tea, and then went back to work.

"I do see some plans for the pageant. Oh, she was doing scenes, so it's like a variety show. She planned on a scene or two from *It's a Wonderful Life* and a scene from *The Nutcracker*. Here's one from *A Christmas Story*—it's the one where Ralphie and Randy are visiting Santa, and Ralphie asks for a Red Ryder BB gun." ACB laughed. "And then there's my scene. She jotted down a line of dialogue I gave her: 'If you're not good boys and girls, you aren't going to get a present from the Ghost of Christmas Presents.' Brilliant, huh?"

"Definitely brilliant." I chuckled. "What else did she have planned?"

"A nativity scene with a children's chorus singing 'O Little Town of Bethlehem.'"

"That sounds wonderful." There wouldn't be a dry eye in the church, and I'd be the first to get sentimental.

"And—get this—she planned on an adult chorus. That would quiet down all the stage mothers and dads and keep them busy."

"Another great idea! I'm going to keep those ideas. What else?"

"That's about it, but I'll keep looking."

"You know, Antoinette Chloe, it seems pretty heartless that we are continuing on with everything when Liz Fellows has just been murdered."

She nodded. "I know, but that's one of the reasons that we are going to find out who killed her and get him or her arrested. Then everything can return to normal, and we can all enjoy the season."

"Let's hurry and find the killer, okay? Then I can put my whole heart into this pageant. We can dedicate it to Liz."

"Excellent idea, Trixie. Let's see what else is on her laptop. Maybe we can find something that gives us a clue as to where to start."

Instead of searching, ACB pushed the laptop over to me. Then she got up, filled our two mugs with water and fresh tea bags, and put them both in the microwave.

She tapped on the counter with her long acrylic nails as she waited.

I looked at the "recent documents" section. She was working on something called Buff, but it looked like the folder was on a removable drive, like a flash drive. Matter of fact, there were a lot of Buffs and a lot of Bings.

Looking though her black laptop case, I unzipped all the compartments and checked all the pockets, searching for a flash drive, but no luck. "Antoinette Chloe, did you happen to find a little flash drive in Liz's purse?"

"No, but I'll look again. Why do you ask?"

"Looks like she was working on something called Buff and Bing quite a lot. They might be important."

"I wonder what it means," she said. "Buff . . . as in no clothes?"

"I didn't know Liz very well, but I doubt if she meant *buff* as in no clothes. I don't have a clue what it stands for. But maybe Bing means Bing Crosby and 'White Christmas.'"

She brought over the mugs and set them down. "I'll go through her purse again."

Dumping everything on the table, she turned the lining inside out and felt the cloth, then the leather. "Nothing here."

The two of us searched everything. Then I sat back and took a sip of tea. "Maybe it's in her house. Or it could be in her office at the church."

"We're going to have to look in both places, Trixie."

"In case you haven't noticed, I can't get around all that great."

"I'll help you."

"And I can't run," I said. "Not that I ever really could."

"Then I'll roll you."

I tried not to laugh. My ribs were still hurting, and I hated to open my mouth due to my missing front tooth. Speaking of which . . .

"Antoinette Chloe, I wanted to remind you that I need a ride to the dentist's office tomorrow. Hopefully he can glue something on temporarily so I don't look like a Halloween pumpkin."

We both heard a shuffling on the porch outside the kitchen.

"It's Ty!" ACB said jumping up. "He's back with Blondie."

I pulled the sleeve of her magnolia muumuu to get her to sit back down. "Toss everything back into Liz's purse. Hurry!"

While she did that, I put Liz's laptop back into the case and put it under the table.

When Ty walked in, all he saw were two friends having a cup of tea.

After he got done wiping Blondie's paws with a towel that I keep by the door, he looked up. "You both look guilty. What are you two cooking up?"

"Why, nothing, Ty," ACB batted her eyelashes, feigning innocence. Ty didn't buy it.

"I know guilty looks when I see them. Spill," he said.

"You're mistaking guilt for sadness. We were talking about Liz's murder." I wasn't lying. We *were* doing that in a roundabout way.

"And I was reminding Antoinette Chloe that I have to go to the dentist tomorrow. She's going to take me."

He turned to ACB. "I can drive Trixie if you can't."

"No, I'm free. It'll be my pleasure. Would you like some tea, Ty?"

"No, thanks. I'd better get home. It's been a long day, and tomorrow will be even longer," he said. "I have to find Liz's next of kin."

"Pastor Fritz should know. Or his wife, Darlene," ACB said.

"They don't seem to. They said that Liz was kind of quiet and never spoke about any family members."

"Maybe there's a will in her papers," ACB suggested.

"If we can find one. Or if someone steps forward," Ty said. "Speaking of that, where's Liz's purse?"

"Here you go." ACB lifted it up and handed it to him. It was a little more lumpy and sloppy than when we'd gotten it from the church. He narrowed his eyes but didn't say anything.

"Is there anything in the purse that might help me with finding Liz's next of kin?"

"My goodness, Deputy Ty Brisco. How on this snowy earth would we know?" ACB put a hand on her throat and looked appalled. "Do you think we'd purposely dig through a woman's purse?"

"In a New York minute!" he said.

"Well, maybe, but in this case there was nothing in it of interest." ACB tried not to smile.

"See you tomorrow, ladies."

"See you, Ty. And thanks for all your help," I said.

He nodded and headed out the door. Ty lived across my lawn, past the diner, past the boat ramp, and up the stairs above the Sandy Harbor Bait Shop. Uncle Porky had helped the owner of the bait shop, Mr. Farnsworth, build the extra room. It was going to be used for over-flow guests of the cottages, but then they both offered it to Ty when he moved down here from Houston.

"He's a good guy," ACB said.

I took another sip of tea. "And he's a *smart* guy. If he catches us meddling in this case, he'll have our heads."

"He'll lock us up. That's what he always threatens us with."

"We're going to have to be really careful this time," I said, thinking that with a cast and broken ribs, I'd be a handicap.

"I know," ACB said. "Great minds think alike."

"First thing in the morning, we'll head to Liz Fellows's house. Oh, crap! We should have lifted her keys from her purse."

ACB dangled a key chain loaded with keys in front of my face. "Who said I didn't?"

"Antoinette Chloe Brown, you are magnificent, just magnificent."

"I realize that your senses are not up to par consider-ing your problems, but tomorrow you'll have a tooth fill-ing that gap of yours, so you won't look like the Wicked Witch of Sandy Harbor."

"Let's get to sleep early, Antoinette Chloe. We have a lot of things to do tomorrow."

But the microwave bell dinged, signaling that our tea was ready. Instead of going to bed early, we talked about our plans to break into Liz's house tomorrow.

And we both hoped that her house would give up Liz's secrets.

Chapter 5

*A*t the crack of dawn, after Antoinette Chloe made us a breakfast of fried bologna, sourdough toast, scrambled eggs, and a couple of donuts, we headed to Liz's house in her van.

I questioned the sanity of going in the daylight in her very distinguishable van, but we both agreed that the longer we waited, the quicker Ty would be on our trail.

ACB hit a pothole, and my teeth rattled and my ribs screamed. As we passed Margie Grace's forest green cottage, I started to worry. "You know, despite our conversation last night, I don't think Margie Grace is going to be happy with my directing the pageant. With Liz gone, I'm sure Margie thought that she'd be asked."

"You're right. Anyone who would think of throwing a phone at Liz needs to be watched. I'll keep an eye on Margie," ACB said.

"Do you think that Margie was mad enough to kill Liz? And what about the lady who threw sheet music at her? There're probably a half dozen other wacky stage-door parents who ordered Liz to give their progeny good parts. But would they kill her over a Christmas pageant?"

ACB snorted. "I think people kill over a lot less. You'd better watch your back!"

"Or someone might thrust a knife into it?"

"Oh! I didn't mean that, Trixie. I mean . . . I . . . I really . . ."

"I was only joking. Relax."

She chuckled. "Oh, good."

"Antoinette Chloe, we need to go over our plan, or lack thereof. How are we going to get into Liz's house in daylight with me on crutches?"

"I thought of that already. Look in back."

I turned around as much as my broken ribs would allow. "I don't see anything other than a dolly! You're going to roll me on a dolly?"

"Yeah. Isn't that a brilliant idea? You can stand on that little platform, and I'll tip you back and roll you in. I can even get you up the stairs that way."

Oh my!

"I think you should park on a side street, not in front of Liz's house. Drive around the block and park," I said.

She did, and we found the perfect parking space on a side street behind Liz's house, but not too close. It might appear that Brown's Four Corners Restaurant was making a delivery to another house.

True to her plan, ACB got out the dolly and made me stand on it. Why didn't they make those little platforms larger? "I'm going to tip you back now."

"I'm going to die."

"Nah, but you just might slide off."

Instead of worrying about falling off, I tried to concentrate on the blue sky with pretty, fluffy clouds.

Oh, look! One's in the shape of a bunny.

ACB rolled me through Liz's backyard. She had a nice brick walkway, which must have reflected the sun and melted the snow, because it was clear rolling.

Poor ACB tried to yank the dolly up the stairs, which were loaded with snow and ice, but her grunts and heavy breathing told me that she just couldn't do it.

"I'll walk now, Antoinette Chloe. I don't want you to have a heart attack."

I got up the stairs by using my crutches and the railing and pulled Liz's keys out of my coat pocket. Much to my surprise, I picked the right key and the door squeaked open.

Suddenly I didn't want to do this.

"Umm . . . I'm not so sure I think that this is a good idea anymore. Maybe we shouldn't—" I found myself whispering.

"Get your butt in there, and start snooping. The neighbors have probably called 911 already and reported that a body has been seen on a dolly with a woman pushing it wearing a stunning rose-covered muumuu with sequined flip-flops, a Christmas-themed fascinator, and exquisite seashell jewelry."

I grinned. "You're probably right. And that gives us about five minutes before Ty rushes in and puts us in the stocks in the village square so the seagulls can peck out our eyes as the kids throw snowballs at us."

With a quick prayer to whatever patron saint protected diner owners, I pushed the door open wider, got my crutches into place, and crutched in.

I stopped in my tracks. "Unless Liz Fellows was a

complete slob or a hoarder in training, someone beat us here."

ACB looked around, her mouth open. "No way."

"Way."

"Should we clean this mess up?" she asked.

"No way. Start looking for something important and let's get out of here."

"Trixie, it's obvious that we're the second string. Someone already beat us to the important stuff."

"I didn't take that state fair ride on your dolly for nothing. So start looking."

ACB moved some clothes and books and, at the same time, we noticed Liz's old-fashioned answering machine lying on a red-and-green Christmas sweater. The machine had to be put back together and the little cassette rewound, so I'm guessing that the burglars couldn't handle ancient technology and just tossed it on the floor, disemboweled.

I left ACB to get the machine working as I clomped around looking for a flash drive or something important.

Moving things out of my path with a crutch, I noticed the twisted remnants of a metal-and-glass computer desk by a bay window. Looking intently at the area around it, I didn't see a flash drive.

She didn't have a computer on the desk, and I looked on the floor under office supplies, file folders, paper, and heaps of paper clips, pens, and highlighters.

What a mess!

I went into Liz's bedroom. It was pretty, or it must have been at one time. I could see that the bedspread, now torn from the bed and heaped on the floor, was covered with botanical-labeled flowers. Only now it looked like lawn mower clippings because someone had taken a knife to it and slashed the stuffing out of it.

Drawers were opened, the contents discarded, and everything was haphazardly tossed on the floor.

Perfume bottles, makeup, and jewelry were lying everywhere.

Liz's possessions, her special things, were discarded like yesterday's birdcage liner. This was more than sad. It was horrible.

And it obviously wasn't a professional burglary, because it seemed as though valuable pieces of jewelry weren't taken.

So what was the amateur burglar looking for?

Maybe it was the same thing that we were looking for. A little flash drive.

"Trixie, I got the answering machine working!" ACB yelled from the other part of the house.

"Be right there."

I crutched out and stood next to ACB. She hit play.

"You have reached Liz Fellows. I can't come to the phone right now. Please leave a message, and I'll get back to you as soon as possible."

Beep. *"You have three new messages and no saved messages."*

"Liz, this is Sally from Harry's Snow Removal and Lawn Care. I'm calling you at home because Darlene isn't answering at the church's main number. Anyway, the check you wrote to cover our snow removal of Sandy Harbor Community Church's parking lot in the amount of three hundred and twenty-five dollars has bounced. The returned check fee is

fifty dollars. Please write us another check—one that won't bounce (snort, chuckle)—and add that amount into the balance. Thank you."

Beep.

"Hey, Liz! It's Lorraine from Lorraine's Hairdo It Your Way. Darlene Robinson, you know . . . Pastor Fritz's wife, owes my salon a chunk of change. Four hundred and fifty dollars, to be exact. She keeps writing checks and they keep bouncing. Half of that amount is fees. The other half is what she really owes me. I am at the end of my hair roots, so I decided to call you for help. It takes a village—I mean a hair salon—to keep Darlene's hair dry and frizzy with Brass Glow number two-one-three-one (laugh) that I can't talk her out of. I'm going to have to refuse service to her soon. Can you imagine her hair then? Can you help me out? And, by the way, your appointment is scheduled for Tuesday at five. See you then, and no Brass Glow two-one-three-one for you!"

ACB shuddered. "Lorraine uses Posey Purple four-four-two-two on me. But when my roots grow out, it's a horror. I can't imagine Darlene's hair if Lorraine bans her from Hairdo It Your Way."

Beep.

"Liz, Pastor Fritz here. Would you mind coming in an hour early tomorrow morning? I have several very important things to discuss with you, and it's for your ears only. I don't want my wife or Roger to get wind of it. Thank you, Liz."

Beep.

"End of messages."

I wonder if Liz had attended her meeting with Pastor Fritz. It would have been the morning of the auditions. The same day she died.

And who was Roger?

"Antoinette Chloe, these messages show that Darlene isn't paying the bills. Their creditors must be desperate for them to ask Liz for payment. If there are two on the machine, there are probably a lot more who haven't called yet," I said.

I needed to sit down, but where? I didn't want to touch anything since I was smack-dab in the middle of another crime scene. So I kept looking for something—anything—that would help us find Liz's killer.

What I did see was a Sandy Harbor Sheriff's car drive very slowly down Daffodil Street and pull over in front of Liz's house. I knew immediately who was driving.

"Oh crap! Double crap! Antoinette Chloe, it's Ty. I think he's coming here. He can't catch us! Let's roll!"

She looked as panicked as I felt. We both hurried to the back door. She flip-flopped as I crutched.

ACB locked the door as I hopped down the stairs as if it were an Olympic event and assumed my position on the dolly.

"Hurry, Antoinette Chloe!"

In her haste, she lost a flip-flop on the stairs, and it seemed like she was going to leave it there and go barefoot on one foot.

"What? Are you channeling Cinderella?" I said through gritted teeth. "Pick that up and let's go!"

She did, and for once I didn't nag her about wearing boots, although boots would have made a world of sense.

"Wait!" I yelled, looking at the overstuffed mailbox on the side of the back door. "There's mail in Liz's mailbox! Grab it!"

She ran back up the stairs, pulled the mail out of the mailbox, and stuffed it into her cleavage purse. Sliding into the errant flip-flop, she hurried back down the stairs.

I took a deep breath as she tipped me back and rolled me up the brick walkway, then across a sidewalk, took a shortcut through a snowbank, and then finally we reached her van.

She opened the door and shoved my butt into the passenger's seat. I had barely sat down when she heaved the dolly through the back door, pulled herself into the driver's side, and took off down the street.

I struggled to get my seat belt on. ACB was driving like we were at the Indy 500.

"Slow down, Antoinette Chloe, before you tip us over. We made our getaway. I don't think Ty saw us."

"That was a close call!"

"I know. You tipped me over so fast on that dolly, I think I swallowed my necklace!"

"I lost my flip-flop again somewhere!"

My mouth went dry. If Ty found the glittery, sequined rubber flip-flop with the sunflower glued to it, it would lead him right to ACB and me.

We might as well pack our toothbrushes and get ready for our cell at the Sandy Harbor Jail. At least when ACB was incarcerated before, she'd decorated with a cabbage rose theme, and added plush lime green toilet seat covers and matching shag rugs.

ACB was one impressive decorator when it came to jail couture.

As we raced through downtown Sandy Harbor, which consisted of a half block of stores, restaurants, the Spend

A Buck discount store, a Laundromat, a bar, and a hair salon, she zoomed into a parking spot in front of her restaurant, Brown's Four Corners.

"Do you have to check on your restaurant?" I asked.

"Nah. Fingers is doing a great job. I have a few dozen spare flip-flops there. I'll go in and get them. Besides, I just wanted to see if anyone is following us."

Is this CSI: Sandy Harbor? If anyone was following us, it'd be Ty, and he could find us anywhere.

"Remember, I have a dentist appointment," I said, checking my watch. "In twenty minutes."

"I forgot about that. I'll be quick."

While waiting for ACB, I got my crutch and fished for my purse, which had slid under the dolly. ACB really should have strapped the dolly in, so it wouldn't turn into a projectile in case we had to stop fast.

Finally ACB rounded the corner, looking more presentable. She now wore zebra-striped flip-flops and her holiday fascinator was back in place instead of hovering over her chin.

"You've got to take this," she said, getting into the van. She pulled Liz's mail out of her cleavage and handed it to me.

"Whew! That feels better. The points of the envelopes were poking into my boobs."

"What else have you got stored there?" I wondered.

"The usual. My wallet, tissues, some makeup, another fascinator . . ."

"And why don't you carry a purse?" I asked.

"Too bulky."

"I see." But I really didn't.

ACB held up a lumpy yellow envelope that obviously contained something. "This feels like a flash drive, Trixie!" She set it down on her lap. "People send themselves important things in the mail all the time, mostly to get a date stamped on it for proof of . . . uh . . . the date and maybe location."

"Do we dare open it?" I asked.

"And go to federal prison?"

"As opposed to state prison for breaking into Liz's house?"

"We didn't break in. We had a key," she pointed out.

"That we stole from her purse!"

"Good point."

The rest of Liz's mail was the usual run-of-the-mill junk, so that was a disappointment.

"Trixie, I have a brilliant idea how we can find out what's in the envelope."

"What's that?"

"Well, we are going to the dentist, right?" ACB asked, driving way too close to the guardrail on my side.

"Yes."

"And the dentist has an X-ray machine," she said.

Oh, I suddenly knew where she was going with this. "What am I supposed to do? Stuff the envelope into my mouth?"

"Trixie, you have to think more like a criminal, for heaven's sake. We take an X-ray of the envelope when the dentist isn't around."

"Oh, I see." I was more than a little sarcastic. "Do you know how to take an X-ray of an envelope with a dental X-ray machine?"

"How hard can it be? Marie Elaine Caluzzio works for Dr. Covey, and she's not the brightest bulb in the movie marquee. We went to Sandy Harbor High School together. She was voted Most Likely to Marry Someone Rich. She did."

"Who'd she marry?" I asked.

"*Rich* Covey."

"Rich?" I shook my head. "Oh, I get it now. I fell for that, didn't I?"

"Marie and Rich started going out together in freshman year." She grinned, still enjoying her joke. "Maybe I'll just ask Marie to X-ray it. She might ask questions, but she probably wouldn't remember the answers."

ACB pulled into Dr. Richard Covey's driveway. It had a big molar-shaped mailbox with a six-foot-tall toothbrush as a post. I always chuckled when I drove by it.

No one was in the lavender and green waiting room when we walked in. In fact, there wasn't any receptionist either.

"Hello?" I asked. "Anyone here?"

Marie Elaine Covey came out from another room, munching on an English muffin. I could smell the peanut butter on it. "Oh, I think that our receptionist has the day off. Come with me, Antoinette Chloe."

"Marie, it's Trixie who has the appointment, not me."

"Oh, yeah. Come with me, Trixie." She crammed what was left of the muffin into her mouth and licked her fingers.

"Maybe I'll come, too," ACB said. "We can talk about old times."

"What old times?" Marie Elaine asked.

"You know, old times in high school. When we were in Gamma Gamma Gamma sorority."

Marie looked blank.

"The Tri-Gams, Marie. You must remember the Tri-Gams."

"Oh sure, but I don't remember Trixie."

"She didn't go to high school here."

"Then why did you say that she was in the Tri-Gams?"

I raised an eyebrow at Antoinette Chloe. "Yeah, Antoinette Chloe. Why did you say that I was a member of the Tri-Gams in high school?" I chuckled.

ACB looked as though she was going to pull off her fascinator and toss it at me. I really liked that one, too. It had two real candy canes sticking up out of a wreath of plastic holly berries and red netting. ACB would wear Christmas-themed fascinators until Christmas Day; then she'd switch to something pertaining to the New Year.

I sat down in the banana-shaped yellow chair and stretched out as Marie clipped a paper bib around my neck.

"Hey, Marie, would you mind taking an X-ray of what's inside this envelope?"

"What is it?"

"Um . . . well . . . I think it could be Trixie's tooth that someone found. If we open it, we can't send it back, so could you just X-ray it and tell us what it is?"

That made absolutely no sense, but Marie thought it did. She clipped it to a plastic stick, and held it up to something on a big X-ray arm.

The image came up on a computer screen on a counter next to my banana chair.

"It looks like a tiny ice scraper," ACB said, squinting.

"On a chain," I added. *A tiny ice scraper on a chain?*

"It's not a tooth," Marie proclaimed. "It's one of those scrapers that you get from some lottery places to scrape off the silver coating that's on the tickets."

"Really?" I asked. I guess that made some sense. What else would you use a tiny ice scraper for?

I was a little disappointed. It had felt like a flash drive through the envelope. But I guessed it was just a dead end.

Marie puffed up her blond flip. "I got one from Gus's Gutters and Snow Removal when he sent me my bill. Here, I have it hanging from my purse."

And she did.

I held out my hand for ACB to give me the envelope. She did. Looking at the return address, I read: "'Gus's Gutters and Snow Removal. Our thirtieth year in serving Sandy Harbor, New York. Call us for an estimate!'"

"Oh," ACB said quietly. "I guess we should've read the envelope."

Just then Dr. Covey walked in, and I handed the envelope back to ACB.

He looked at me, then at the computer screen, then he scratched his head.

"It's a little scraper," Marie said. "For lottery tickets. That's not Trixie's tooth, so she doesn't have to send it back."

If he thought that Marie was talking nonsense, he

was probably used to it and didn't want to pursue it, so I changed the subject.

"Hi, Dr. Covey! I'm so glad you could fit me in. I fell down the stairs and my cap came off. I don't have it with me because it fell somewhere in the snow, and I couldn't find it, but maybe you could give me a temporary one so I don't look so . . . awful."

"I can do that. Certainly."

For the next hour, he worked on my tooth and squirted gunk in my mouth to take impressions for a new cap. Midway through the procedure, he kicked out Marie and ACB because their endless chatter was distracting.

"Much better," he said.

He was a man of few words, whereas Marie talked about as much as ACB did. We could still hear the two of them in the waiting room.

Finally he finished up. Dr. Covey handed me my crutches, and I stood, then hobbled out to the waiting room.

ACB handed me my purse, and when I opened it to get my checkbook, I saw all of Liz Fellows's mail.

Guilt shrouded me like fog off Lake Ontario, and I tried to shrug it off. If I was going to find out who murdered Liz and why, I'd better stop feeling guilty about bending the rules to do it.

Yeah, right.

Saying good-bye to Marie and Dr. Covey, ACB and I walked down the stairs and through the parking lot. I was glad to be going back home after the morning from hell. I had a million things to do, including preparing for Tuesday's auditions and the weekend's catering events.

The sound of a siren shattered the silence of the countryside under snow. Then revolving red lights caught my eye.

A green and white Sandy Harbor Sheriff's Department car came into sight, flew into Dr. Covey's driveway, and stopped between us and ACB's white van.

Deputy Sheriff Ty Brisco exited the vehicle, plopped his hat on his head, and hurried toward us.

"Ladies, is there anything you'd like to tell me about before I take you both to jail?"

Chapter 6

*T*y didn't have a slight smile tweaking the edges of his mouth. Nor did he have a merry twinkle in his eyes. His one dimple that appeared on his right cheek when he was joking stayed hidden.

This could be serious.

"Get into the backseat of my car, please."

ACB giggled nervously. "Oh, Ty. You can't be serious."

"I told you both, over and over again, to stay out of this case. To stay out of all cases, actually. Because you'll ruin evidence. You'll ruin clues."

"Ty, we're very careful, and—" I started to explain, but didn't have a chance.

"Like at Liz Fellows's house just now?" he shouted. "Antoinette Chloe's flip-flop prints are all over the place. Trixie, I saw one boot print from you and your two crutch tip prints. Am I wrong?"

"No. We were there, but—" I began.

"No *buts*. This isn't a game!"

"Ty, listen to me, and then you can take me in. This was my idea, not Antoinette Chloe's."

ACB grunted, then waved her hand. "It was my idea,

too. In fact, think I thought of it first. We'll share the blame."

"And I'm thinking that you both share one *brain*," Ty said. "So get in the car. You can share the backseat."

"Deputy Brisco," I said formally. "I have a million things to do. I have to prepare to audition kids for the Christmas pageant and place orders for more food."

"Then you'd better get into the car, so I can get you both charged, and then arraigned if I can find Judge Frazier. Maybe you'll be able to make bail before tonight."

"But, Ty—" ACB and I both protested together. Maybe we did share one brain.

"Get in! Don't make me handcuff you."

We got into his car before Wyatt Earp's head exploded.

I'd never seen Ty so mad. He was usually easygoing in a laid-back cowboy way. People usually mistook his relaxed temperament as being lenient and tried to take advantage of him, but then he'd spring to action and the cop side of him would take over.

Like now.

Believe it or not, ACB and I didn't say a word for the whole ten-minute drive to the sheriff's department. Instead, ACB fussed with her candy cane fascinator, put on another layer of makeup, and changed her earrings twice.

I wondered if she might have a bottle of water in her cleavage purse. My throat was dry, and my heart was beating crazy fast.

I was going to jail, and Ty Brisco was taking me there.

Ty was the man who shared my beloved Blondie. He was the man who ate every meal at my diner, and most of the time I joined him. I'd revealed some of my deepest secrets to him. Like how I couldn't seem to have kids when I was married to Deputy Doug and how he found a twentysomething while we were married who gave him twin girls. And how sometimes I thought I'd let down my parents because I could never measure up to my sister and brother.

"We're here," Ty said, breaking the silence. "Your new residence for a while."

Nothing like rubbing it in. He was enjoying this way too much.

He offered ACB his hand, and she took it. I didn't. I handed my crutches to him instead.

Setting my crutches against his car, he offered me his hand again. "I can do it myself."

The lone dimple appeared.

"This isn't funny, Ty. Like I said, I have a million things to do."

"You should have thought of that before you broke into Liz's house."

"We didn't break in. We had her keys," I said, echoing what ACB had pointed out to me earlier.

"Save it for Judge Frazier. If he isn't ice fishing, he'll be at his fly-tying shop. I'll try to locate him. If not, there's always tomorrow. Oh, before I forget to tell you, there's going to be a memorial service for Liz Fellows tonight."

"Ty, I have a perfect idea. The food that's there . . . Everything can be for a reception after Liz's service!"

"That is a fabulous idea. I'll let Pastor Fritz know about your generous offer. I'm on my way to see him now."

"I have a party to cater tomorrow night. It's going to

be very elegant, and I have to make fancy appetizers and cook a prime rib and the side dishes. It'll take Antoinette Chloe and me all day to prepare everything and then some. So we have to leave—right now."

Ty put his hand on my back to herd me to the sheriff's department. At another time, I might have enjoyed the volts of heat spreading through me.

But I couldn't enjoy it. Not at all.

"I'll let you call Bob and Juanita," he finally said. "You can set something up with them."

ACB burst into tears. "'Tis the season of peace on earth and good will to all men . . . and women."

Ty snorted. "'Tis the season to leave investigating to the professionals and not disturb the victim's house."

"Wait a minute!" I said. "Do you think that we were the ones who trashed Liz's house? Oh, no! It was like that when we walked in. Someone else made all that mess."

Ty shook his head. "I never thought you two trashed her house. You wouldn't do that, but you walked over any other footprints that might have given us something to go by. You picked things up, and probably moved them, and—I can't believe this, but—I think you took her mail, as well."

He unlocked the door with a key. Must be that the two deputies were on patrol. The 911 operator, Fanny Fowler, was way in the back of the long office in a glassed-in room with low lighting.

Ty flicked the lights on and waved to Fanny. She waved back.

ACB and I waved to her and she blew us a kiss. *Merry Christmas*, she mouthed, standing.

If I remembered correctly, Fanny, who was about twenty years old and five feet tall, with a blond ponytail and big blue eyes, wanted to be Mrs. Cratchit in the pageant. If I was going to be Tiny Tim, she'd be my mother. I'm not going to tell you my age, but let's just say she could be my daughter.

What casting! I'd have to think of something else for Fanny. She'd be perfect as Cindy Lou Who.

One thing I knew for sure—Ty Brisco would be perfect for Ebenezer Scrooge! Or maybe the Grinch.

"So there's a memorial service at the church tonight?" I asked.

"Yes."

Ty slid over two uncomfortable-looking metal chairs and motioned for us to sit down. "I am going to type up your official charges. Then you can tell your story in an affidavit, and I'll type it all up on the computer."

I took a deep breath. "Ty, no offense, but you can't type to save your life. You use one thumb and one finger. We'll be here until next Tuesday. Let me type it for you," I said. "In the meantime, please try to find Judge Frazier, and ask him if he'll arraign us here instead of at his fly-tying shop, so we can get out of here really fast!"

Ty closed his eyes and shook his head. Not a good sign.

"You are not running this show, Beatrix Matkowski. I am. And for your information, I can type at least six words a minute, without mistakes. None. No mistakes."

He called me Beatrix! No one calls me Beatrix, but I decided to let it go, considering the circumstances.

"Who cares about mistakes?" I asked. "They can be

fixed easily on a computer! Ty, let's get this show on the road so we can get out of here."

"And you will have learned nothing from this experience. Correct?" He chewed on a bright yellow pencil, and looked like he was going to bite it in half.

"Oh!" Antoinette Chloe repositioned her fascinator, which was making an escape attempt via her shoulder. "This is like *Scared Straight*. You know, that TV show where kids are scared by prison inmates, so they don't commit any more crimes."

Ty's mouth gaped open. "No, Antoinette Chloe, that's not what I'm trying to do." He stood. "Come with me. I'm going to put you into a cell, and I'll take care of the paperwork at my own pace: six perfect, meaningful, profound words a minute. When I need you, I'll let you out, one at a time. Let's go to jail, ladies."

"Ty, I can't go to jail. Not now. I'll go in April before the cottages open. I promise," I said.

Ty raked his fingers through his black, shiny hair, which usually had a groove in it due to his cowboy hat. That's what he always did whenever he was frustrated, usually by me.

Not that I'd noticed.

I took a couple of deep breaths, figured that I'd just write everything down that needed to be done and beg him to allow me to take my cell phone into the cell.

After all, this was Sandy Harbor, not Attica.

"Okay, Ty. Let's go," I whispered, trying to find my voice. "I just can't stand the thought of sitting idle in a jail cell when I have so much to do."

ACB's candy canes on her fascinator were pointing

down and her Midnight Tryst mascara was running in several small rivulets down her cheeks. Each had a touch of gold eye shadow shimmering in them. Just like how I imagined the rivers of Sutter's Mill would have looked.

I took her hand and held on to it. She didn't want to go to jail either, particularly not at Christmas. "We'll get through this, Antoinette Chloe. It's okay."

I turned to Ty. "Okay, Deputy Brisco, lock us up. Just let me keep my cell phone, paper and pen, and calendar. I have a lot of calls to make and food to order."

"Okay, listen to me, ladies," he said. "I won't lock the door to the cell. You can do your business in there. I'll call Judge Frazier and ask him to drive over here. But what I want you to get through your heads is that there is a killer on the loose who stabbed Liz Fellows. I don't know the motivation or the reason or anything else at all at this time. I do know that now *you*"—he pointed at me—"now, you, Trixie, are the pageant director, just like Liz was. I don't want to scare you. I just want you to be aware. But I don't know if her murder had anything to do with the pageant yet because instead of investigating, I find myself one step away from having to hog-tie the two of you."

"We're sorry, Ty. We *really* are," ACB said, wiping her face on the sleeve of her muumuu. "We won't go back to Liz's house."

She looked at me to make sure that was okay. I gave a slight nod.

"And, Ty, we'll give you all of Liz's mail. There's a little lottery scraper in one of the envelopes. We know that because we got the envelope X-rayed at the dentist's office."

"You did *what*?" he asked.

"Uh . . . um . . . we didn't want to open her mail because that's a federal offense," I explained.

"For heaven's sake, so is taking someone else's mail!"

Ty held out his hand, and I reached for my purse, pulled out Liz's mail, and placed it in his hand. "It's not exciting. Just some bills and that tiny ice scraper from Gus's Gutters and Snow Removal."

"It's Gus's thirtieth year in serving Sandy Harbor," ACB said. "We figure that he put the little scrapers in his bills for his customers. It has his address and phone number on the little thing."

Ty paused in the middle of looking at Liz's mail and looked up. "Good to know," he deadpanned.

"It's not a clue or anything," ACB said. "So don't worry about that. Unless you want to worry about it, but I don't think you need to."

Ty looked at me for help. But since he was the one who'd arrested us, he could just handle ACB on his own.

"That's the one." ACB pointed to the yellow envelope. "That one. Right there. It's Liz's bill from Gus's Gutters and Snow Removal."

Ty looked at me. "What were you two hoping that this little ice scraper was?"

Oh crap! Should I answer that? We could be all wrong, and Ty might ask for a two-physician commitment for mental health services for us.

"Well, Trixie?" he pushed, staring at me with those darn blue eyes.

"We thought it might be a flash drive. It was kind of the right size and felt like it might be just that."

"A flash drive for Liz's laptop? The same laptop that you took from the church? That laptop?"

"The very same," I said. "If you want the laptop, I'll certainly give it to you. I just gathered up all of Liz's things that were left in the church and thought I'd keep them until you told me otherwise."

"Otherwise," he said.

"Huh?"

"Otherwise. I'm telling you to give me all of Liz's property."

"Why didn't you just say so?"

Steam was coming out of his ears. He was fun to tease, but I knew I was pushing him.

"Did you find anything on the laptop?" he asked.

"Yes. I was looking for pageant help—lists, names, what she had in mind for the pageant—and I found pretty much what I needed."

"Nothing else?"

"Nothing exciting. Maybe Ray Meyerson could find something important, or some wizard at the State Police, but I couldn't."

"What about you, Antoinette Chloe?" Ty asked.

"I'm about on Trixie's level. I'd still be keeping my restaurant accounts on paper, but Fingers has all kinds of programs for keeping track of things, so I let him. He can tell right down to the stick of butter how much to order and the cost."

At least ACB knew that flash drives existed—maybe because Fingers usually sported two on a lanyard around his neck.

"Whoever beat you to Liz's house, what do you think they were looking for?" Ty asked.

"Are you asking for our help?" I couldn't believe it.

A vein pumped in his temple. "I'm just asking a question."

I nodded. "We don't really know. We're just guessing that the killer might be looking for Liz's flash drive, too, if she was using one. It's just a big, fat guess—a shot in the dark."

"I'll be picking up Liz's laptop tonight. Where is it?"

"On my kitchen table."

"I'll let myself in," he said. "And I'll take Blondie home with me."

ACB adjusted her bra straps. "You're still going to charge us?"

"Yeah, but you can take your cell phones and whatever else you need. Call for takeout. I'm buying."

"Darn right you are, Ty Brisco," I said. "Who do you want to interview first?"

"Antoinette Chloe can go first. And don't forget, I have to take your statements from yesterday, too."

I sighed. "Remember to call Judge Frazier and get him down here. If you don't I will ban you from being served at the Silver Bullet for the rest of your lifetime or mine, whichever comes first."

He slapped his hands on his heart. "You wouldn't dare!"

"I dare."

He reached into his desk and threw me a set of keys. "Let yourself into the jail. Leave the door open, so I can make sure you're okay."

The Sandy Harbor jail cells were through a double door. A left turn led to the men's cell—a right led to the women's. I turned right and had to smile when I came to ACB's creation. It looked like a fabric store had exploded.

I opened the cell door and hesitated for a moment before I walked in. Slumping into a Queen Anne chair decorated with colorful climbing roses, I leaned my crutches against a writing desk that looked like an antique. Too bad it was painted in bright pink.

Digging out my cell phone from my purse, I decided to call the Silver Bullet for takeout.

Only in small-town Sandy Harbor would I be given the keys to let myself into my own cell—a cell decorated by Antoinette Chloe, fashion and décor maven—and be able to keep my purse and phone and have the deputy pay for lunch.

Sitting quietly for a while, I could hear the muted conversation of ACB and Ty. I wondered what was happening, but I'd find out soon when it was my turn.

So Ty was going to go through with charging us with a crime. Trespassing, I presumed. Probably not burglary because we didn't break in or take anything—well, other than mail. I didn't know if Ty could charge us with federal offenses, or if that had to be someone else, but I didn't want to find out.

Maybe he'd forget about the mail thing.

All this thinking was making me hungry.

I called the Silver Bullet.

"The Silver Bullet Diner, serving since 1952. How can I assist you?"

"Bob?"

"You're speaking with him."

"Bob, it's Trixie. I have some strange news. Antoinette Chloe and I have been arrested by Ty and are at the sheriff's department. I don't know when we're going to get out of here, and I'm so worried that I'm not going to get everything done, but I'm going to try. I can do the organizing, but not the cooking. I'm so sorry, Bob."

"What are you in for? Bank robbery?" He laughed.

"I don't particularly know yet. Ty's working on our charges, but I'm really worried about all my catering."

"Look, Trixie, with you and Antoinette Chloe out of the picture, it's going to be difficult, but not impossible. We need more help cooking. I know you have a fancy party tomorrow night."

"It's at the McDowneys'. I'm worried about the appetizers," I said.

"I haven't had much experience with fancy appetizers. There wasn't too much call for fancy things as an army cook. But Juanita has a talent for it. I can cover for her, and she can fuss with that stuff. What else?"

I read my notes. "Prime rib, loaded baked potatoes, creamed cauliflower, cheese biscuits, baby carrots, relish platter, horseradish—both plain and with mayonnaise—and au jus sauce. The McDowneys are going to take care of the serving pieces, the table settings, and the drinks. So it's just the food that we're responsible for."

"I can handle it. Will you take care of the ordering?"

"It's already done and should be delivered by Sunshine Foods any time now."

"Perfect."

"I hope we'll be out of here soon, Bob."

"Was it a misunderstanding on Ty's part?"

"Nope. Guilty as charged." I laughed. "Or just as soon as Ty figures out the charges, I'm guilty. He's not the fastest typist in the typist pool."

"Don't worry, Trixie. I'm on it."

What a surprise! For someone who hadn't been there to do his job for the past three years, he was amazing me.

That said a lot for Bob's character.

"Bob, one more thing: Please pack up three specials to go along with a couple of liters of soda and ask Ray to drive them over to the sheriff's department. Oh, and throw in several fruit hand pies. I know that Sarah Stolfus made a delivery today. The bill goes to Ty Brisco."

He laughed. "You got it!"

"Thanks for everything, Bob. I mean it."

"Don't mention it."

I was lucky to have such a great staff and great friends. I still considered Ty a great friend. Even though he deserved coal in his stocking, he was only doing his job.

I reached over to the pink desk, pulled on the knob, and found a spiral notebook and a pen. Instead of taking care of catering orders or the pageant, I decided to write out my two statements—my discovery of Liz and our foray into crime. Maybe it would save time.

"Ty, for heaven's sake, let Trixie type for you!" I heard ACB shout. "We're going to miss New Year's Eve the way you type—New Year's Eve two years from this one!"

Less than an hour later, our food arrived. Ty and ACB brought everything to my cell. It was the meat loaf special, my favorite. Juanita made a great meat loaf by draining mild salsa and mixing it into the ground beef. Fabulous.

Her mashed potatoes were perfect, and so was the beef gravy ladled over everything. Peas were the veggie, and we got fresh Italian rolls. Yum.

We sat around talking and eating as if we were dining at the Ritz instead of in a jail cell.

"Ty, did you get ahold of Judge Frazier?" I asked.

"I did. He's up in Alexandria Bay doing some ice fishing. He's packing up and will be on his way."

"That'll take at least two hours," I said. "If he hurries. Is the paperwork done?"

"Nope."

"Do you at least have the paperwork ready so he can arraign us?"

"I'm still typing."

I squirted a ketchup packet on my meat loaf. "Please let me help you. I'm not threatening your masculinity or your cop-ness, but I can type fast and you know it."

"Yeah, okay. After we eat, you can have at it," he said.

"Finally!" ACB shouted, her fist pumping the air.

After we ate, I was at Ty's desk typing on his computer. Only in Sandy Harbor would a deputy sheriff let a civilian have access to unlimited law enforcement data. If I knew how to hack, I could run anyone's rap sheet or put out a warrant for someone's arrest. I could even delete records.

I wish I could delete this afternoon.

When the judge walked through the door, everything was ready. Ty did charge us with trespassing, a violation of the law, which, Ty told me, could result in a sentence of fifteen days.

Judge Frazier wore army gear and a hat with fishing lures dangling from it.

I expected nothing less.

"Trixie Matkowski!" He grabbed me into a bear hug, and since he was considerably shorter than I was, his hat rested on my boobs. I hoped that the lures would stay in place and not stab me. "How good to see you!"

"Hello, Judge Frazier."

"And Antoinette Chloe!" He took his hat off to her and scrunched it in his hands. "The sweetheart of Grange three forty-five." He hugged her, too.

ACB grinned. "Glennie and I were the King and Queen of Grange three forty-five's New Year's Eve Gala, 1959. Those were the days, huh, Glennie?"

"Yes, they were, my queen." He kissed her hand, and she fluttered her eyelashes at him.

I looked at Ty. I think he knew that he was going to lose this one.

"Have you ladies been bad?" the judge asked, index finger wagging.

"Well, Glennie, we did go into Liz Fellows's house. And my flip-flop prints where there and Trixie's crutch prints, but we weren't the ones who trashed the place. But Ty said, and he was right, that we might have ruined clues, but we were very careful. And the little thing in the envelope that we had X-rayed at the dentist was a little ice scraper, but we thought it was a computer thing. I should have looked at the return address. Anyway, that's what we did. Oh, the ice scraper was from Gus's

Gutters and Snow Removal, and it was in Liz's mail that we took."

"Oh," the judge said, clearly confused. "Deputy Brisco, may I speak to you in private?"

"Yes, sir."

They walked through the double doors to the jail, but we could hear everything.

"Are you serious about this, Ty?"

"Definitely. Those two are an accident waiting to happen. I don't want them to get hurt, and I want to drive home the point that they need to leave the investigating to the professionals."

"Well, okay. If you insist. Let's arraign them."

When they walked back out, ACB pointed to the pack of paper—white on top, then blue, pink, and yellow—copies for the players in the criminal justice system. "Trixie typed this all up. She's a fabulous typist."

"She typed her own charges?" Judge Frazier looked at Ty.

"Yes, and didn't she do a beautiful job?" ACB asked.

"She sure did. It's a pleasure to arraign you with a document like this."

"And it's a pleasure to get reacquainted with you, Glennie." ACB was still batting her eyelashes.

Only in small-town Sandy Harbor.

I stepped forward. "Your Honor, why don't we waive the reading of the charges, since I typed them and Antoinette Chloe read them as I worked? Can you just set bail?" I gave him my best smile, but he had eyes only for ACB.

"Sure, Trixie. How much bail would work for you?"

"Gee, I don't know. How much would bail be set for a trespass charge?"

Thank goodness Ty hadn't pursued the mail stuff.

"Let's say fifty bucks each," he said.

"Fifty bucks?" ACB nudged him on the arm. "C'mon, Glennie, we don't carry that much money around. We are good citizens and have contributed a lot to this community. Why, Trixie is even the Christmas pageant director, and she's looking for someone to play the judge at the end of *Miracle on 34th Street*. You know, where the judge finds Santa Claus not guilty. That's not guilty! Oh, my stars! It's the perfect part for you, Glennie." She turned to me and winked. "Right, Trixie?"

"Oh . . . absolutely. Right. You'd be perfect for the part of the judge, Judge."

If we weren't doing something from *Miracle on 34th Street* before, we were now.

"Okay, bail is set at twenty-five dollars each," Judge Frazier said.

I looked at Ty. He knew when he was defeated.

"Oh, Glennie, honey, just dismiss the charges already, and let's go to the Silver Bullet and catch up on old times. It's been so long, and I've been meaning to get reacquainted with you since we are both single now." She ran her index finger around the collar of his jacket, and a red flush started on his neck and shot to his cheeks.

Sheesh. She was good.

"But the district attorney is the only one who can make a motion to dismiss charges," he said.

"Oh, Glennie, just tear them up. The district attorney

isn't here and what he doesn't know won't hurt him."
She picked up the papers and stepped closer to him.

Judge Glennie's eyes were directly on ACB's ample
bosom. She took a deep breath, and I swear if he hadn't
moved back, she would have given him two black eyes.

He was mesmerized with ACB and, magically, he
now had the papers in his hand.

I was impressed. Ty was not.

"Just tear them up, Glennie, and let's get out of here.
It's just not a fit place for two . . . ladies to be," she said
in a singsong voice.

I looked at Ty. If he'd had a white flag, he would have
waved it.

Judge Glennie tore up the papers, tossed them in a
wastebasket, and left arm in arm with Antoinette Chloe.

She turned to me. "Trixie, are you coming?"

"Oh. Um . . . yes. Of course."

I hurried to put my coat on, tossed my purse over my
shoulder, and positioned my crutches for a quick escape.

"This isn't over, Trixie," Ty said.

"I know."

Chapter 7

The Honorable Judge Glen "Glennie" Frazier followed us to the Silver Bullet in an ancient, camo-painted pickup dotted with all kinds of colorful stickers containing hunting and fishing slogans. The glue from the stickers was probably holding the rusty truck together.

I let the two potential lovebirds sit in a back booth by themselves as I sat at the counter eying the freshly brewing coffee and some Christmas-frosted cupcakes that someone had made.

Nancy and Bettylou, the day waitresses, had about an hour left on the day shift, and Chelsea and JoAnn were due to come in. So was Cindy, the second-shift cook.

I felt a hug from behind. "Good to see you, Trixie," Bettylou said.

"Yeah, boss, you getting around okay?" Chelsea walked around to serve me at the counter.

"I'm managing. I'm really sore under my arms, but my coat gives me padding. Other than that, I'm feeling kind of useless."

I hoped it didn't sound like I was whining. I was just stating fact. Okay, maybe I was whining a little.

"Don't you worry one bit." Nancy took a seat on the side of me. "Bob, Juanita, and Cindy have everything under control."

"I'm making cheese-olive puffs for the bridal shower," Chelsea said.

"And I'm making sausage stars," Nancy added. "We volunteered."

"You did?" I felt all mushy as Nancy poured me a cup of coffee and slid a cupcake decorated with red icing and sprinkles over to me on a small plate without my asking.

The waitresses knew me so well.

"Yeah. We volunteered to help," Chelsea said. "The three chefs all are making fancier things, but the two of us can handle the easier stuff."

"I'm so grateful—to everyone!"

As soon as I could check my books, my staff was going to get a Christmas bonus the size of the North Pole. Well, it'd probably be the size of a small snowflake, but it'd be every penny I could afford.

Ray plowed through the double doors pushing a cart with a gray tub on top. He was the best dishwasher and computer genius I'd ever hired. In fact, he was the *only* one I'd ever hired.

"Hey, boss! Good to see you!"

Ray was a high school senior who was scheduled to graduate in June. His folks had contacted me when Ray was a junior and asked to hold his party on the "party deck" outside the Silver Bullet on the Sunday after graduation.

They planned on inviting the entire Sandy Harbor senior class and their families.

On Saturday evenings in the summer, I throw dances on the party deck, just like Aunt Stella and Uncle Porky did back in the day. There's always a live band—usually Frankie Rudinski and the Polka Dots—and a huge buffet and bonfire.

"Good to see you, too, Ray."

I motioned for him to come over. "Are you doing the books for me?" It was his spreadsheet program that had brought me into the computer age. "Actually, I could do them."

He shook his head. "Don't worry. I'm on the scene."

"Thanks, Ray."

The doors swung open again and out walked . . .

Aunt Stella?

"Aunt Stella!"

I almost fell off the stool.

"Trixie, you poor dear! Breaking your leg at Christmastime. And so much to do!"

I just adored Aunt Stella. She was just the perfect aunt—sweet, caring, loving—and I was like the daughter she never had. That's why she'd waited to sell the diner to me and turned down several fabulous offers. She'd wanted to keep it in the family, and that's why "the point" means so much to me. It's my legacy, as well as my aunt's.

But my payments on the diner and cottages were up-to-date, so what was she doing here instead of traveling with her friends who all lived in the same condo complex down in Boca Raton?

Aunt Stella came around the counter, wearing a bright, white apron, and I swiveled to face her. We hugged and kissed and I could smell the scent of gardenias, her favorite perfume.

"It's so good to see you, but what are you doing here?"

"I'm going to help you out."

"But how did you know I needed help?"

"Bob called me." When she said his name, I swear she blushed under her pale makeup.

"Bob called you?"

She nodded. "And he flew his plane to pick me up. I was in North Carolina at the time. My friends and I went to the Rodanthe Inn on Hatteras Island because Hattie McDougal saw the movie *Nights in Rodanthe* starring Richard Gere and Diane Lane, and wanted to find romance. I think maybe she thought Richard Gere was still there hanging out. Anyway, Hattie talked us into going, so we did. But it was too cold to do very much. All we did was stay in the inn and watch the movie over and over again and act out some scenes in the various rooms. Oh, and we played dominoes."

"I see," I said, making a mental note to see the movie. "So, did Mr. Gere ever check in?"

Aunt Stella grinned. "No, but Hattie had a good time."

"That's all that matters," I said. "Now, let's get back to the plane that Bob sent for you."

"It was his private plane. He flew it and he picked me up." She shook her head. "You should have seen my friends' faces when he walked out of that plane and gave me a big hug."

"But I talked to him on the phone not too long ago! I thought he was at the Silver Bullet."

She sat down next to me, and Bettylou handed her a

cup of coffee and a cherry hand pie. "I know. He somehow had the diner's calls forwarded to him, and he answered while he was picking me up. He didn't say anything because we wanted to surprise you."

I couldn't have been more surprised. "Let me get this straight. Bob's a pilot. Flew to North Carolina himself. You were there because of Hattie and Richard Gere. I have to watch *Nights in Rodanthe*. And you are going to help me out with my catering and the diner."

"Exactly."

"Well, that's crystal clear." I rubbed my forehead. "I'm amazed by Bob. He has a private plane?"

"He told me that he won it in Reno from some billionaire in a big-stakes, backroom game of Texas Hold'em. Bob said he never would have taken the plane, but the man was a jerk."

I laughed. "I'm glad that he has standards."

"Bob is a kind soul and he's very thoughtful. I've almost forgiven him for leaving right after Porky's funeral."

"I wonder why he did that."

"If you want to know, you'll have to ask him yourself."

"Well, Aunt Stella, what else is new?" She was a wealth of information.

"I heard about Liz Fellows. That's downright shameful. What's going on here in Sandy Harbor? It almost makes a soul want to lock her doors at night."

"Liz was killed with one of my knives, and I hate that fact, Aunt Stella."

She put an arm around me. "Things happen, honey.

It's not your fault. If someone wanted her dead—and I can't understand why—they would have found a way."

"Did you know Liz well?"

"We were both on the church revitalization committee. Not the Sandy Harbor Community Church one, but the one at St. Luke's of the Lake, the Catholic Church."

I raised an eyebrow, and Aunt Stella said, "Liz always told me that God is everywhere, so it doesn't matter what church you belong to or where you pray. She said that the Community Church needed her, so she went to work for them."

"I wish I'd known her better." I felt so sad for Liz. It felt as if someone were squeezing my heart. "Did she have any family?"

Aunt Stella took a sip of coffee. "As far as I know, she didn't. She said that she always did a lot of volunteer work to meet people and keep from being lonely. I do know that she had a lot of friends, some near and some far."

"The Community Church needed her, huh? I was told that she wrote the church bulletin and did some computerization of their records, but had a lot more to go."

"Good for her," Aunt Stella said. "Now, who made these fruit pies? Juanita?"

"Sarah Stolfus. She an Amish friend of mine who moved here about the same time I did. A whole community of Amish settled here and bought up a lot of the abandoned farms. Sarah is such a great baker, so I feature her goods at the diner."

"Brilliant. I also see that you have some healthier additions to the menu, and have kept the Polish entrees."

"Who doesn't like a dry kale salad?" I rolled my eyes. "And who doesn't like potato and cheese pierogi fried in onions with a side of kielbasa?" I laughed.

She squeezed my hand. "You've done many wonderful things with the diner. I'm proud, and your uncle Porky would have been proud, too."

I bit my lip so I wouldn't get misty. "Thanks. That means a lot to me."

"So, I'm here to help, and I brought my friends. We call ourselves the Busy Babes of Boca."

"Just how many Busy Babes of Boca did you bring?" I hoped that I could accommodate all of them in the Big House.

"Eight. Nine, counting me. They all wanted to ride in Bob's plane and come up north for a white Christmas. And they wanted to help."

"What a nice surprise! I could certainly use the help."

"Don't worry about a thing. The Babes will take care of it. You just rest and take care of the Christmas pageant. You need to enjoy Christmas. I know how much you love it!"

"Where are all the Babes now?"

"In the dining room eating meat loaf. They are raving about it. Salsa, right?" She waved, and eight ladies waved back. A couple blew kisses.

I blew kisses back. "Yes. I drain salsa and add it to the meat loaf. We all go by Uncle Porky's recipe here at the diner."

"Delicious."

"I'm going to join them. Later tonight we'll have a meeting at the farmhouse. Oh, I hear you call it the

Big House now," she laughed. "You're right. It *is* quite big!"

"Antoinette Chloe is staying with me, too. Bob is staying with Clyde."

Her eyes went to the pass-through window, where we could see Bob cooking with Juanita. She smiled slightly.

Hmm . . . I'd never noticed it before, but as much as Bob resembled Santa, my aunt Stella resembled Mrs. Claus. And Stella Claus seemed to be interested in Bob Claus.

Uncle Porky had been gone for almost four years. Maybe it was time for someone special in her life again.

I glanced over at ACB and Glennie. They were deep in conversation and a rosy glow seemed to radiate from them. Aunt Stella went back into the kitchen.

Christmas romance was in the air. Or maybe it was Christmas magic.

Thinking of Christmas reminded me of the pageant and the fact that I needed to get back to investigating Liz's murder.

Yes, call me crazy. Call me certifiable, even. I wasn't looking to antagonize Ty or ruin any clues or trample any crime scenes, but I couldn't get the image of poor Liz out of my head. She was lying on the kitchen floor with my knife sticking out of her back, her blouse stained with blood.

I flipped my place mat over, found a pen in my coat pocket, and started making notes.

Now, I knew that Liz volunteered her time at various agencies. Liz was worried about being lonely. Liz had a lot of friends. She retired and moved to Sandy Harbor about three years ago, about the same time as I did. She was helping the Sandy Harbor Community Church get computerized. She was in charge of the community's Christmas pageant and the stage-door parents were giving her a sleigh-load of crap.

And Margie Grace was number one on my suspect list. She just wasn't coping appropriately with someone else taking over the Christmas pageant. It was as if she'd lost her whole identity as—what had Antoinette Chloe called her? Oh, yes. Broadway royalty.

Sweet little Margie suddenly seemed like Sweeney Todd.

I shuddered.

Margie and Liz had a rocky history together. And where was Margie when Liz was murdered?

Margie might have been in her golden years, but she didn't seem frail to me. And I thought that in a rage, she could easily plunge a knife into Liz's back.

The door opened, and Ty walked in. I yanked the place mat from the counter and shoved it into my coat pocket. If he saw me still mulling over the case, he'd break my other leg.

No, he wouldn't. He'd take me to jail, find a judge that wouldn't drool over Antoinette Chloe, and throw the book at me.

So I'd just have to be sneakier this time around. With all this help, I wouldn't be needed in the kitchen. And I wasn't going to get ACB involved unless I needed a ride.

Darn. I was going to need a ride everywhere. It wasn't as if there were subways and a fleet of taxis in little Sandy

Harbor. There were snowmobiles, pickups, ATVs, and SUVs, but I couldn't drive any of those either.

Ty took the seat next to me that had just been vacated by Aunt Stella. No one had cleaned up her area just yet.

"Was someone sitting here?" he asked.

"Believe it or not, my aunt Stella was. Now she's talking to her friends—the Busy Boca Babes."

"I see . . . I guess."

"Bob flew them all up in his—get this—private plane. Apparently he won it in a card game in Reno."

"Wow. That's impressive."

I nodded. I was still ticked at Ty. Although deep down, I knew he was right, but sheesh, we were only trying to help.

"Listen, Trixie, about my taking you down to the station—"

I held up my hand. I just didn't want to discuss it anymore. "We're good."

"I just—"

"I get it, Ty. Let's not rehash the rehash. And since you already had the meat loaf special when ACB and I were incarcerated, I suggest you try the spaghetti and meatballs. It comes with a small antipasto and garlic toast."

"Trixie, I want to explain. Just sit and listen for a second. I wanted to really impress on you that you two are in over your heads. You're putting yourself right in Liz's place in the pageant, and if you're going to snoop around . . . why don't you just paint a target on your back?"

"Whoever killed Liz didn't need a target painted on her back. The coward just waited for her to turn around."

"Exactly my point. And I don't want you two contaminating my crime scene. At Liz's house, you might have trampled on evidence that would have been important."

"Did we?" I asked.

"Not that I can tell—yet."

I was relieved about that. "We were pretty careful, Ty. But the place was a mess. And all we discovered was a tiny ice scraper instead of a—"

"Flash drive?" he asked. "I think that the burglar was looking for a flash drive, too."

"Okay, Ty. We're good. I know that you arrested us to prove a point. Point proven. Now get something to eat."

I made a motion to Nancy with my head. She rushed right over. She always hurried to wait on Ty.

I took that opportunity to crutch into the kitchen to see how Juanita and Bob were doing.

They were busy, and it seemed like they were doing the Silver Bullet Shuffle as if they were on *Dancing with the Stars*. The Silver Bullet Shuffle is what I call the ballet of the diner chef—a twirl to the fridge, a twirl back to the grill. A leap to the toaster Ferris wheel, another leap back to the fryer.

"Hi, Bob . . . Juanita. How is everything going?"

"Couldn't be better, boss Trixie," Juanita said. "We have lots of help with *las chicas* here."

"*Las chicas de la Boca Raton?*" My Spanish was hit-or-miss. "I think I just said 'the girls from the mouth of the rat.'"

Juanita and Bob chuckled.

"Sí. *Boca Raton*. Mouth of the rat," Juanita nodded. "Very good, boss Trixie."

"How is everything going for the shower tomorrow night?" I asked Bob.

"We have help making the appetizers, you ordered everything that we needed, and Ray, Stella, and I and the Boca Babes are going to make the delivery, set up, and serve. Louise McDowney and the kid she's marrying will have a bridal shower better than White House dinners for heads of state."

Bob flipped the page on my calendar. "I see you have Chet and Lottie Campbell's fiftieth wedding anniversary. That's on December second. We'll have to get ready for that, too."

"I already ordered the food for it while I was in jail," I said. "They want prime rib, chicken parmesan, and broiled haddock. Everything should arrive tomorrow." I was relieved that I was on top of things. "Tomorrow there's a Christmas party for the library workers and the library volunteers. That's from two to six. They want finger foods, various cheeses, wine and beer, and my rum cake for dessert."

"That sounds easy enough," Bob said. "We'll be ready. If it starts at two at the library, we'll leave here at noon, with the van loaded. I'll handle it, Trixie."

"Perfect," I said. "I'll make up a couple of cheese platters right here. You can add the crackers, pita, and sliced baguettes later. Juanita or Cindy can make the cake. We're probably going to need four of them. And we'll want to make some Christmas cookies. Maybe we can put the Boca Babes and ACB on that."

"Got it."

"Who's going to help you for the library party?" I asked.

"Stella, Ray, and the Babes."

"I have the Christmas tablecloths, cups, paper goods, and plastic utensils ready to go. We had better take two cars. Aunt Stella can drive my car."

He whirled around Juanita and got a handful of hamburgers from the fridge and put them on the grill like he was dealing a deck of cards. After a perfectly executed pirouette, he had a tray of freshly baked hamburger rolls and placed six on the Ferris wheel toaster. Another twist later, he was setting up plates with lettuce, sliced tomato, and sliced onion, a handful of carrot curls, and some radish roses.

Beautiful.

In the meantime, Juanita was preparing plates of spaghetti, ziti, and Spanish rice.

One of the plates of spaghetti must be Ty's. At any other time, I'd grab a tray and serve him. But not now. It was hard to serve with crutches, and even if I could, I think we needed some distance from each other for a while.

Speaking of Ty . . .

"Bob, is Ty Brisco helping you tomorrow?"

"Nope. I told him about the Boca Babes and Stella when I was flying us from Hatteras. He said that he and the other two deputies were going to concentrate on interviewing everyone who was at the church when Liz was killed."

"Oh! The church! Tonight is the memorial service for

Liz. I'd like to attend." I checked the clock on the wall. "It starts in an hour. I'll see if Antoinette Chloe wants to go, along with Aunt Stella. Juanita, how about you?"

"Oh, *sí*. I'd like to go, too." She wiped her hands on her apron and looked down at her chef's outfit: red and green chili peppers on her pants and a red blouse monogrammed with her name and SILVER BULLET DINER under it. "But I don't look so good."

"You'll have a coat on. Don't worry about it."

The memorial service would be a good opportunity to watch and learn, and to pay my respects to Liz, of course. And I could do this all without being scrutinized by Wyatt Earp, who was at the counter right this minute eating spaghetti and meatballs.

I didn't count on the fact that he was going to attend also, and was going to take as many as could fit in the Sandy Harbor Sheriff's Department paddy wagon.

Pastor Fritz looked appropriately serious, overly pious, and very pompous. But it struck me that his tribute to Liz was pretty generic, like he didn't know her very well.

Darlene had more to say about Liz. "Liz was a hard worker and had the sweetest disposition of anyone that I'd ever met. She was brilliant with computers and was bringing our bookkeeping methods into the modern age. I'm afraid that all of Liz's progress will be halted now. But most of all, when Liz saw an injustice, she strove to correct it. And that is the mark of a genuine person and a true friend. God bless you, my friend."

Now, that was a curious thing to say. Did Darlene or someone close to Liz suffer an injustice? A friend? How was Liz trying to correct it? I filed this in my brain for future consideration.

"Now, Margie Grace would like to say a few words," Pastor Fritz said as Darlene sat down.

"What?" ACB nudged me in the ribs, and I gasped from the pain. Margie stopped in her tracks, gave me a scathing look, then continued to the podium.

"It's no secret that I didn't like Liz Fellows and that we fought over the Christmas pageant. It was her fault that I was unceremoniously dumped as director and she took over."

Ty sat up straighter next to me. Was Margie confessing?

Margie continued. "I had a wonderful vision for the pageant this year. Santa's sleigh was going to be pulled by a team of salmon with red noses, and the elves were going to be trout. I believe in showcasing the resources of Sandy Harbor, but my vision wasn't shared by Liz."

Someone ought to get the hook and get Margie off the podium.

But Margie didn't stop. "Now, I understand that Trixie Matkowski is going to be in charge of the pageant, but this individual is also new to our community. She's only been here three years, whereas I grew up here and know all the talented members of our community. Again I was shunned. And she can't even teach the dance numbers with her broken leg—that is, if she even knows how to dance, which I doubt."

ACB grunted. "Why isn't someone getting her off the podium?"

"I am here to tell you that maybe Liz was a nice person, but not in my experience, and maybe she was murdered for a good reason, and—"

"That's it!" both Antoinette Chloe and Ty said at the same time. Muumuu flying and flip-flops slapping, ACB raced up the aisle, followed by Ty.

Ty held her back, walked up to Margie, gently put his arm around her, and escorted her out of the room. Vern McCoy hurried out to assist.

Pastor Fritz called for a moment of silence for everyone to regroup. Then he called upon several more people, who told some wonderful stories about Liz.

Then it hit me. Liz and I had been in town for about the same amount of time. Whereas Liz had made such an impact on others, all I'd done was cook at my diner and rent out my cottages.

She worked at two churches and volunteered where she saw the need. And anyone who had a glorious garden like Liz had the magic touch.

Liz had left a positive impact on the people of Sandy Harbor—with the exception of her killer. I just added calories to their daily diet.

Okay. No more feeling sorry for myself. It was Christmas. It was time to find poor Liz's killer.

ACB leaned over to me and whispered, "We have to find Liz's murderer."

"Just what I was thinking."

"I think that Margie is crazy enough to kill her."

I nodded. "Maybe Ty will get a confession from her."

"Shhh!" Josephine Piranelli turned and rolled her eyes at us. I remembered from Liz's notes that Josephine's daughter and son were auditioning for the pageant.

They were both singing and playing kazoos to "White Christmas."

I couldn't wait to hear that—not!

Pastor Fritz announced that everyone should gather in the community room for a reception.

I'd decided to donate all the food that we'd prepared for the first audition. Because I couldn't bear to go into the kitchen just yet, I turned it all over to the members of the Elks Lodge. They did a wonderful job getting everything ready and setting it out.

Most everyone who attended church came to the reception. I couldn't help but think that just as she had during life, Liz would have enjoyed all the camaraderie and friendship from the people of Sandy Harbor. Several people attended whose lives she'd touched: the pastor and some parishioners from St. Luke's, a shut-in who she shopped for, a Girl Scout troop that she led when their leader got sick . . .

What a wonderful legacy.

But even then it wasn't enough to stop someone from plunging a knife into this lovely woman's back.

I took a seat as far away as I could from where I'd found Liz, and leaned my crutches against the table. Slipping out of my coat, I let it scrunch down behind me.

Then I watched everyone, hoping for some kind of clue.

Hal Manning, the owner of the Happy Repose Funeral Home and our resident coroner, sat down across from me. Hal loved to talk about his latest case, and usually spilled more beans than Ty ever would. All I had to do was ask leading questions.

"Been busy, Hal?"

"You know it. This thing with Liz has everyone stumped."

"What do you mean?"

Hal shook his head. "Liz was a pillar of the community. Everyone loved her. She had a clean rap sheet. And when she was killed, it seems that everyone was in the church at auditions or in the rest rooms with the exception of Margie Grace. Ty told me that he escorted her out of the church."

"I was one of those in the ladies' room," I said. "Me, some mothers, some girls, and a lot of hairspray."

"And what about that Margie Grace?" He whistled. "She's the number one suspect in my book. I don't know about Ty's book. I think Margie's cheese has slipped off her cracker. You be careful, Trixie. Ty's worried that you might be next. He wants to cancel the pageant."

"Yeah, I know. Ty told me that I may as well paint a target on my back. But I can handle myself, and I won't cancel the pageant. No way. It's for the kids, Hal. They love the pageant, and everyone loves the community dinner after it. And the visit from Santa. It'd break their little hearts. I'll talk to Ty about it and convince him that it shouldn't be canceled."

"I knew Liz, and she'd want the festivities to go on."

"Hal, what do you think about some of the stage mothers and fathers? Do you think that any of them are on Ty's radar?"

"Definitely. Especially some of the more vocal ones."

"I don't know. I don't think any of the parents are killers."

Hal took a big bite of a ham sandwich. "As the investigation continues, there will be more suspects. The big project will be to figure out who disappeared from auditions long enough to sneak into the kitchen, get the knife, and off Liz."

"Yes. That would be difficult. The window of opportunity isn't that big. I think that I was only gone for ten minutes or so. It would have been shorter, but I had to wait a bit, and I had to crutch back and forth." I hated to point a finger at Margie Grace again, so I kept my mouth shut this time.

Antoinette Chloe joined us. "How have you been, Hal?"

"Busy."

Knowing Hal, he'd start all over again, so I gave ACB an eye. She got the hint.

"Where's Joan?" ACB asked.

Joan Paris was Hal's girlfriend. They lived together over the Happy Repose, and Joan was a good friend of mine.

Hal took a long draw of punch. "Joan's busy getting tomorrow's edition of the *Lure* out. She's doing a mini-biography of Liz, but it's been difficult for her to write because Liz didn't have any relatives."

Pastor Fritz and Darlene walked by the table, and ACB motioned for them to join us. Another man was with them, whom I didn't recognize. He shot us a side glance and kept on walking.

"Your friend can join us, too," I said, pointing to his departing form.

"He's not very social," Darlene said.

"Who is he?" ACB said. "I don't recognize him."

"The church's maintenance man," Pastor Fritz said. "He's fairly new."

"Oh. That's nice. Is he from around here?" ACB pushed.

"No," Darlene said. "He's from the west."

"He must have known Liz," I said, "since they both worked at the church."

Darlene's eyes narrowed. "Yes. I believe they knew each other."

ACB pulled on Darlene's sleeve. "Darlene, are you going to hire anyone to take Liz's place? You still must need office help."

What was Antoinette Chloe up to?

"We don't need any office help," Darlene snapped.

Whew! What was that about?

"We probably don't," Pastor Fritz said. "Darlene can finish what Liz was working on. It'll save us some money."

My heart was pounding. I was about to get in even more over my head. "But, Pastor Fritz, I can volunteer to work in the office free of charge. I have a lot of help for my catering business, and I have some free time. I can assist the church. And if I say so myself, I'm not all that bad with computers."

Actually, I am hideous with computers, and I'm lying to a pastor!

Darlene raised an eyebrow. "It's not necessary, Trixie."

"You said so in the eulogy that what Liz had started might grind to a halt. We can't let her work go unfinished, can we?"

Darlene's mouth opened, but nothing came out. Pastor Fritz had a tight smile on his face, and his Adam's apple was working overtime.

"Thank you." Pastor Fritz shook his head. "That's not necessary, Trixie. Your aunt is here. You must want to visit with her."

"Oh, I insist," I said. "It'll be my Christmas present to you."

Pastor Fritz clasped his hands together. "I am speechless."

"That's a first, my husband." Darlene laughed. "When do you want to start, Trixie?"

I felt as though I might as well jump right in. The sooner I could check out Liz's work computer and look for a flash drive, the sooner I could quit.

"Tomorrow."

Chapter 8

*A*ntoinette Chloe dropped me off at the church's office and helped me up the five stone steps that led to a set of double doors.

She opened them for me, told me that she was meeting Judge Glennie for breakfast, and quickly flip-flopped away.

"Hello?" I said. "Anyone here?"

I heard steps echoing from a long marble hallway, coming closer. "Good morning, Trixie. You're right on time."

Darlene Robinson opened a glass door for me, turned on the lights, pointed to a dark wood desk, and quickly left.

"I'll be back later to show you what to do. I have a group session with the Teen Talkers," she said.

I was sitting at what used to be Liz's desk. I knew it was hers because there was a picture of her with the Robinsons, along with a picture of her getting some kind of plaque.

Poor Liz. She looked so happy in both pictures.

The look on her face made me even more determined to find her killer.

The plaque depicted in the picture was hanging on the wall. I read, "'Elizabeth Anne Fellows. For service to the Sandy Harbor Literacy Initiative. Volunteer of the Year. 2014.'"

That was very nice.

But if she didn't have any relatives, who would get all of her things? Little things, such as this award and picture. Big things, such as her house. Another big thing was her car. When ACB had dropped me off that morning, I'd noticed that Liz's light green Honda Civic was still in the parking lot behind the church.

I returned her picture to where she had placed it on the desk. I was in a sunporch type of place, and there was film on the window where I could look out, but no one could see in.

There was a similar desk opposite me. I think it was Darlene's because shopping bags and boxes were heaped all over it. There were piles of mail—which looked mostly like bills—doing a landslide on her desk. I went over to tidy the piles before they hit the ground. They were *all* bills. And there was a big checkbook, the kind with four checks on one page and set up for duplicates. I flipped it open and looked at the last date. Darlene hadn't written a check in more than a month!

Why not?

Each desk had a computer approximately the size of a corn silo on it. I'd have to move my chair around it to see any visitors.

Liz's personal laptop was state-of-the-art, and Ty had come over to the Big House, snatched it, and taken it home last night.

That was just after the Busy Boca Babes fussed all over him for an hour.

But back to me at the church office.

I should explain that the Community Church looks more like an office building than a church. It used to be the local cable office until they moved to Oswego. But it was enormous, and no matter how churchy everyone tried to make it, it was still a tomb of a building.

Darlene would be gone an hour with the Teen Talkers. She had twelve girls, she'd told me before, and they met every Sunday morning.

It was obvious that Darlene loved heading this group. She said that they kept her young, and that she could show them a thing or two about living.

I wondered what she meant by that.

I took a stroll down the hallway to the ladies' room. On the way, I peeked through the kitchen window on the left. Everything was dark and quiet. My eyes traveled to the place where I'd found Liz's body, and goose bumps made an appearance on my arms. I said a quick prayer for her.

Right across from the kitchen was the church. That was mostly dark, except for some strategically placed lights, giving those who wanted to pray or just a quiet place to think, some privacy.

I came to the bathrooms and the meeting room where Darlene was leading her teen group. Chairs were arranged in a circle, and there was an animated discussion in progress. I could hear Darlene's armful of bangle bracelets tinkling from there.

Pastor Fritz's office was on the right. He was on the phone and had a desk piled high with papers and ledgers.

I waved through the window, but he didn't seem to notice me.

I crutched back to the office and caught the less than delightful maintenance person rifling through Liz's desk. All the drawers were open, and he was mumbling. His head snapped up when he heard me clear my throat, and I swear his top lip curled. He slammed all the drawers shut. *Sheesh.*

"Uh . . . and you are?" I didn't know his name.

"Roger," he snapped.

Oh! He was the infamous Roger! I remembered hearing his name mentioned on Liz's answering machine by Pastor Fritz. What had the pastor said? Something about how he didn't want Liz to mention their potential meeting to Roger or Darlene.

I wondered whether the meeting had ever transpired and what the reason was for the secrecy.

"Nice to meet you, Roger," I finally said, trying to be friendlier than I felt toward this guy. "We'll be working together here."

No answer, but he was well on his way out.

That went well!

I made a pot of coffee and turned on Liz's computer. It asked for a username and password. I played with guessing some combinations, but no luck.

Unless Liz had her password and username written somewhere, I didn't have a chance to get in. *Hmm . . . I could always use Darlene's.* I'd ask her later.

I took the opportunity of being alone to look through Liz's desk and files. I saw that there was a small index-card-size cassette player, complete with earbuds. That had to be ancient, although when I pushed the Play button, the wheels turned. I absently wondered why on earth Liz might have needed a cassette player. But I couldn't think of anything, so I pushed it to the back of my mind.

There was nothing else exciting in the least, although I didn't exactly know what I was looking for.

I looked through a folder marked QUARTERLY RAFFLE REPORTS. I wondered why there wasn't anything in the folder. There was nothing in BINGO RECEIPTS AND DISBURSEMENTS either, and nothing in a dozen others.

Remembering that Liz had been working on getting things computerized, I decided that the papers must be somewhere else.

I made a note on a small notepad to ask Darlene or Reverend Fritz to give me a list of things to do. I had to keep myself busy, or I'd go crazy with boredom.

The phone rang. "Sandy Harbor Community Church. Trixie Matkowski speaking."

"Trixie, it's Antoinette Chloe. How's it going there? Find anything?"

"Nope. Just a lot of empty folders. I went through Liz's desk. There's no hate mail that I can find; there are no hideous messages on the answering machine. Her desk is a study in efficiency and organization."

"How about a personal phone book?"

"She has one. There are some numbers with the Buffalo area code. I'll make a copy of it. We can both look at it together later tonight. Maybe we can check out who Liz had been calling."

Looking out at the sidewalk, I saw—

"Oh, crap, Antoinette Chloe, it's Ty! Ty's here."

"I was calling to warn you."

"What's he doing here? Does he know that I'm volunteering?" My mouth went dry, and I gulped down some coffee.

"He has an appointment with Pastor Fritz and Darlene. And no, he doesn't know you're working there—not yet anyway."

"He'll find out in less than five seconds. Gotta go."

I dove under the desk before I realized that both my cast and I wouldn't fit.

Ouch. That hurt.

"Hello?" he said.

I tried to disguise my voice, but my British accent left a lot to be desired. Downton Abbey wouldn't even put me to work cleaning the stables.

"Uh . . . um . . . take a seat in Pastor Fritz's parlor, sir. It's down the hall to the left. I'll tell him you're here."

"Miss, are you okay? Wait just a minute! *Trixie?* Trixie Matkowski, is that you?"

"No. Uh . . . my name is Marilyn. Marilyn . . . um . . ." I spotted a box of bond paper in the corner of the room. "Marilyn Bond."

I could see his wet boots in front of me tucked into navy blue cargo pants. He bent over and stared.

His face was hard to read. Maybe amusement and . . . annoyance?

"Well, Marilyn Bond, fancy meeting you here. Would you like some help getting up?"

I struggled to stand, but all that did was hike up my skirt to my cellulite zone. Yanking it down, I mumbled a humble "Yes."

It took a while, and some grunting from both of us, but eventually I was returned to Liz's chair.

"Ty, before you get cranky, I volunteered to help out here as my Christmas present to the Robinsons. With all the elves that arrived with Aunt Stella, and since I can't stand, I might as well make myself useful here."

That was half-true.

He raised a perfect black eyebrow. "I was under the impression that Pastor Fritz and Darlene didn't want any help. Darlene said she could finish what Liz started by herself."

"I guess they changed their minds when I told them that I'd do it for free. You know, my Christmas present to them," I repeated, hoping that he'd go for the Christmas-present angle.

"Why don't I trust you?" he asked.

"Because it's the nature of your job?"

"Maybe. And right now my gut is telling me that you're up to something again."

"Ty, really! What trouble can I get into sitting in this office?"

"You'll think of something. And by the way, don't even think of touching either computer. I'm taking them with me."

Shoot.

"Do the Robinsons know you're taking their computers?"

"That's one of the things I'll be discussing with them."

"I think that Darlene is in a group meeting with teenage girls, but she should be done soon."

"Tell her to meet me in the—what did the British

Marilyn Bond call it?—oh, yes, the parlor. Do you have any relation to Bond, James Bond? And, I say, old girl, would you mind being a love and ringing for tea?"

I made a face at him. Juvenile, I knew, but he deserved no less.

"Ty?" I said seriously. I did want to ask him a question, but I didn't know if he'd tell me the answer.

"Yes?"

"There's something that I'd like to share with you."

"Should I sit down for this?" he asked, his bright blue eyes looking right through me.

"No. It's just . . . something. Or should I say someone?"

He placed the palms of his hands on the desk and leaned toward me. "I'm listening."

"It's the maintenance man for the grounds. His name is Roger. He's not the friendliest guy in town. I saw him last night and a bit this morning, rifling through Liz's desk. And he worked with Liz, so he might have information."

"And?"

"They must have known each other."

He nodded. "His name is Roger Southwick. And just because he doesn't chitchat over coffee and hand pies like you and Antoinette Chloe doesn't mean he's a killer."

"Does he have a record?" I asked.

"Now, that, my dear Miss Bond, is none of your business."

"Go to h—" No. I wasn't going to say it. "Go to . . . the parlor!"

"Remember, don't touch those computers."

"Anything worth finding out has probably been wiped clean already," I snapped.

"We have our ways," he said, making like he was twirling a moustache. Then he turned, disappeared down the hall, and I could breathe easily once again.

Immediately, I called Antoinette Chloe. "We need to find out about Roger Southwick, the maintenance guy. I just have an eerie feeling about him. He was going through Liz's desk this morning, and I think he's up to something."

"Take a picture of him, and I'll ask around when I go to church at St. Luke's. Someone there might know him, and be willing to talk."

"You want me to take a picture of Mr. Congeniality?"

The thought had entered my mind, but I wanted to live to pay off the point.

"Just do it with your cell phone. Make like you're talking on it or something."

"Okay. I'll do it." I took a deep breath. "What's going on with the Boca Babes?" The noise was unbearable that morning, and I had been hoping for some quiet time just to think. "Are they busy?"

"They're all in the kitchen at the Big House making appetizers for tonight. Then they're moving on to Christmas cookies. Juanita took over the rum cake assignment since you're volunteering at the church. Then they are prepping for the fiftieth anniversary party and the library event. They're rocking and rolling, Trixie!"

"The Babes are a miracle, and I appreciate each and every one of them. But I have to ask you something, Antoinette Chloe. Have you noticed anything going on between Bob and Aunt Stella?"

"No, but I'll try to keep my eyes open. It's hard

because I bought this new mascara called Lucky in Vegas, and with my false eyelashes, it's sticking like glue. I can't seem to keep my eyes open, and I—"

"Antoinette Chloe, I gotta go. Roger Southwick is shoveling the sidewalk; maybe I can get a picture."

"Okay. See ya later. I'm picking you up."

I dug out my cell phone and crutched over to the window, trying to get a good picture of his face.

It was impossible with the hood from his coat tied under his chin and reflective sunglasses on.

Yikes! He was staring back at me. He tossed the shovel into a snowbank and stomped up the walkway, swung the door open, and appeared in front of me.

"What do you think you're doing?" he asked standing way too close to me as I hobbled back to my seat.

"Just taking a picture of the snow," I said.

"You were taking a picture of me. I want to know why."

How could he see me? I thought that was a one-way window!

Wrong again, Trixie.

He kept flexing his hands into fists. Because he wore black leather gloves, it looked like he had on boxing mitts. I could smell cigarette smoke clinging to him and his clothes, and his teeth were yellow. It looked as though he hadn't shaved in a couple of days.

I swore, if he punched me and my temporary cap flew off . . .

"Look, Roger, I love the snow, and the sun was glinting off the snow just right, so I thought I'd take a picture," I lied.

"There's no sun out there."

"There was for a while." More lies, and during the holiday season, too.

He swore under his breath. "Look, I don't want to get involved with another . . . I mean, I . . ."

He shook his head and turned with a squeak of his boots, and I let what he'd said sink in. Roger must've been involved with Liz! I wondered what he meant by "involved," though. Romantically? Business-wise?

I guessed I'd have to find another way to get a picture of Mr. Congeniality and find out how involved he and Liz actually had been.

As I looked around for something to do—anything—I decided to take a little stroll down the hall to the ladies' room and eavesdrop at the parlor door. Why not see if I could hear what Ty was talking to the Robinsons about?

I was extra-careful to make sure that my crutches didn't make any noise, so slowly I went down the hall, stopping at the thick brown oak door.

I could hear Ty's deep voice. "I'm impounding Liz's car. Someone from Clem's Garage will hook it and take it to the impound lot. They're apparently short of help, so I don't know when they'll move it. I'm going to be taking her computer with me when I leave. Now, what about yours, Darlene?"

"Oh, no! Liz never, ever used my computer." She sounded stressed and a little too loud. "It only has my things on it, and I need it all."

"Sorry, Darlene. I'll bring it back as soon as possible," Ty said.

"But I have a church to run!" said Darlene.

"My dearest, don't you mean that *we* have a church to run?"

"Of course, Fritz," she shouted, then lowered her voice. "Of course that's what I meant."

The usually good-natured Darlene was showing another side of her personality, and I wondered what about Ty's taking her computer was making her so anxious.

"Pastor Fritz, what about your computer?" Ty asked.

"I don't own one."

"Thank goodness for Liz when you had her! Right, Pastor?" Ty asked.

Pastor Fritz chuckled. "Exactly."

"I'd also like to talk to Roger," Ty said. "Is he around?"

"No. He's not," Darlene said quickly. "He went to the hardware store for a few things he needed."

It was on the tip of my tongue to yell that he was out front shoveling snow, but that would give away my spying.

I meant my accidental overhearing.

"I think that's all for now. Thank you for your time. See you tomorrow for auditions."

Oops. I knew I needed to disappear. I made my way farther up the hall to the ladies' room, then turned when I heard the parlor door opening. That way, it would look like I was returning from the ladies' room.

"Hello, Trixie," Pastor Fritz gushed over me, shaking my hand and then hugging me to him. "Here's my sweet volunteer!"

I didn't think anyone had ever called me *sweet* in my entire life.

Ty raised his eyebrows. I could tell he suspected I was eavesdropping.

Darlene shooed away Pastor Fritz. "Let her walk, Fritz. You'll knock her over."

We all walked to the front of the building. I turned left and the Robinsons saw Ty out.

Missing in action was Mr. Congeniality as well as the church's van.

As I sat back down in my chair and waited for Darlene to return to give me something to do, I couldn't help wondering whether Darlene actually thought that Roger was at the hardware store or if she was lying to Ty for some reason.

If she was lying, what, if anything, did Roger know that Darlene didn't want Ty to know?

Just after Ty packed up the two corn silos, the Robinsons sent me packing, too. Ty volunteered to drop me off at the Big House.

"If you can stand being in the same car as me," he said. "I might arrest you again."

"Seems like I don't have a choice, since I'm being kicked to the curb by the Robinsons."

But I was over Ty's arresting me. Well, maybe not.

The only one at the Big House was Antoinette Chloe. She was cleaning the kitchen, which looked like a flour factory explosion.

According to her, Aunt Stella, the Boca Babes, Ray, and Bob had left to set up the bridal shower for Louise McDowney.

"How did everything turn out?" I asked.

"Perfect. The appetizers turned out beautiful, and Bob certainly knows what he's doing with the roast. The

Christmas cookies looked . . . well, Christmasy, and Juanita decorated the rum cakes with red and green maraschino cherries, dusted grapes, and whipped cream. You should have seen it. I took pictures."

"Got any extra cookies?" Ty asked, bending over to pet Blondie, who had swooned at his feet, turning over on her back for him to rub her belly.

For heaven's sake, Blondie!

ACB crossed her arms. "I don't know if we have extra cookies. Are we speaking to you?"

Ty nodded, grinning. "Yes, you are."

She looked at me for clarification, and I shrugged, deciding to continue the teasing. "Well, he's a neighbor, and we've been friends a long time. He's also my best customer at the Silver Bullet. I guess we can feed and water him. We've done it forever. Why stop now?"

"It still goes against my better judgment." ACB unstuck her eyelashes with an index finger. "Anyway, we have dozens and dozens of cookies left, Ty. The Boca Babes got carried away. Finally I had to unplug the mixers." She laughed. "Both of you, sit down, and I'll get them. The coffee is fresh, too."

"I wish I could do something to help you," I said, collapsing into an oak chair at the table. It felt good to sit down after the exhausting walk from the car on a snowy sidewalk and up the slippery stairs.

Still, it was difficult for me to sit while someone waited on me, and I didn't realize I'd sighed until Ty called me on it.

"Hard day at work, Trixie?" Ty asked sarcastically.

"The two hours I was there? Yes, it was grueling."

"Are you going back tomorrow?"

"Of course. I should be busy," I said confidently, even though there weren't any computers there.

"I don't know about that. Pastor Fritz told me to let you know that you won't be needed."

"He did?"

Ty helped ACB by bringing the coffee mugs to the table, and sat down opposite me. "Uh-huh. When we were loading the computers into my car."

"Why didn't he tell me himself?"

He chuckled. "I think he's scared of you."

"Very funny, Deputy Brisco."

ACB set down a Christmas platter piled high with an extraordinary assortment of beautifully decorated cookies. Sitting down, she crossed her arms. "Tell me, Ty, how was *your* day?"

"Passable."

"Did you make any headway on your investigation?" she asked.

"Not really."

"Are you going to check further into Roger Southwick? I just have a bad feeling about that guy," I said.

"Yes. I know your feelings about him. He isn't sociable, and that is a capital crime in your book."

"He doesn't take off his boots either. He should have a working knowledge of winter etiquette, unless he's not from New York." I baited Ty to see if he'd tell me if Roger was a native New Yorker.

"Doesn't take off his boots?" Ty snorted. "That's a hanging offense in Sandy Harbor!"

"It shows politeness, and Roger Southwick just isn't polite."

"Yeah, but can you see him plunging a knife into Liz Fellows?" ACB asked.

I thought for a while, then nodded. "If she ticked him off enough. The man seems to have a short fuse."

Ty looked thoughtful.

"I don't know if he seems to be the type to toss Liz's home. Is he?" I knew that Ty would have run a rap sheet by now.

"You know I can't tell you that," he said.

"Did Roger and Liz have a relationship?" I asked.

"You know I can't tell you that either."

"Are you going to search his residence?" I asked.

He took another cookie and studied it. "I have no reason to get a search warrant on anyone's residence at this time."

That sounded like a press release.

"Ty, he was on the grounds shoveling when Darlene told you he was at the hardware store. It crossed my mind that she didn't want you talking to him."

"Were you eavesdropping, Trixie?" Ty asked. "I don't remember you being present when this was discussed."

"I must have been," I mumbled, "or how else would I know this?"

"Just what I was wondering myself." He raised both eyebrows.

Roger was going to be my next project. I was going to find out if he had a relationship with Liz or not.

First, I was going to find out where Roger Southwick

lived and where he came from. He wasn't from Sandy Harbor.

I knew that there were at least three apartments located near where the Robinsons lived. They were built for visiting religious dignitaries or for people in need. I also knew that there was a separate door leading to this area off the back entrance.

I would've bet my recipe for rum cake that Roger lived in one of those apartments.

If I could find the right opportunity, I might just find the key and check out Roger Southwick's apartment.

And I'd had a scathingly brilliant idea earlier. The Community Church needed a couple of laptops as a donation, and I was going to donate them. That would get Darlene back on the project Liz started and give me an excuse to hang around and help.

I'd phone Ray when Ty wasn't around, give him my credit card, and tell him to get two laptops that were just like Liz's. Thank goodness I remembered to take down the make and other details before Ty had taken it away.

There was banging on the door, and Antoinette Chloe jumped up to answer it, still talking to Ty as she walked to the door.

"Oh my!" I heard her say. "Won't Trixie be surprised?"

"What? Who?"

There was a lot of shushing and whispering, and I was on the edge of my seat.

When they walked into my kitchen, I burst into tears.

It was Rose and Jack Matkowski.

My parents!

Chapter 9

"Mom . . . Dad . . . what are you doing here?" I asked, giving and receiving hugs.

"We got a call that you needed some help," Mom said. "How are you feeling, honey?"

"I'm okay. I wish I could do more, but luckily I have help. Aunt Stella is here with her friends from Boca, and my staff is doing double and triple duty. And the missing Bob has returned. He's been invaluable."

"Fabulous! It'll be great to see Stella," my dad said. Aunt Stella was his sister-in-law.

I was glad to see them but hated that they'd interrupted their retirement in Tucson. They were entrenched in the culture of the over-fifty-five crowd in Cactus Wheels, a motor home community: golf, pickle ball, rallies, potluck dinners, dances, and more.

They loved it there.

"Who called you?" I asked.

"Clyde," Dad said. "We have an agreement that if anything happens to you, he will call me."

"Oh? I hope he's not calling you a lot," I said.

"Let me just say that you've been very busy!" He

wagged his finger at me. "How about some introductions, Trix?"

"Where are my manners? I was just so excited to see you both!" I hadn't seen them since Uncle Porky's funeral about three years ago.

"You might remember Ty Brisco. He's a deputy sheriff here. He used to camp in cottage six with his father and grandfather and fish nonstop."

They both shook hands. "I couldn't pick you out of a lineup, Ty. You've grown a bit!"

My mother reached up to hug him. "I remember you. You loved root beer and pepperoni."

He laughed. "That was me."

"And, Mom and Dad, you remember Antoinette Chloe Brownelli. She goes by the name of Brown now. Since I moved here, she's been a great friend."

"I know your mom and dad. Sal, my ex, and I used to double-date with them all the time," ACB said.

I'd forgotten that ACB and my parents were about the same age.

"I am sorry about Sal's incarceration," Mom said.

ACB grunted. "Don't be. He tried to kill me."

Thank goodness she hadn't mentioned that Sal had tried to kill me, too, or my folks would never leave my side, no matter what my age was.

My mom put her arm around Antoinette Chloe. "I heard about that. I'm so sorry."

"It's okay." She sniffed. "But I'm getting along fine. Trixie and I have had many fun adventures together."

"Too many," Ty added sarcastically.

ACB gave him a pointed look that meant *not in front*

of her parents. Then she turned to me. "I'll clear my things out of the front bedroom and get the room ready for your parents."

I'd never thought of that! With the Busy Boca Babes staying there and Aunt Stella, where was I going to put my parents?

"We won't hear of it!" Mom said. "We drove up in our motor home. We'll stay in that."

Dad nodded. "Forty-five feet of bliss with all the conveniences of home on eight wheels. It's parked in the parking lot in front of the house. Is that all right, Trixie?"

I remembered another motor home parked out there not too long ago. I shuddered, but then dismissed the thought.

"Perfectly fine, Dad."

"Great. Now what can we do to help you out?" he asked.

"Nothing right now. Aunt Stella and the Busy Boca Babes are at a bridal shower that I had scheduled. The only thing that needs to be done, and we can do it tomorrow night, would be fresh salads and an entrée for the ongoing Christmas pageant auditions at the Community Church."

I looked at my mother. "It was already prepared once, but it went to another event."

"Why? What do you mean?" Mom asked.

"I'll tell you over some tea and Christmas cookies," I said. "If there are any left after Ty gets through."

I put on a stern expression, but I actually loved it that he enjoyed coming over and eating. They say that the way to a man's heart is through his stomach, and

Ty's stomach was flat. And when he ran without his shirt on, I could see rock-hard abs. And then there were the muscles in his arms, and when he . . .

But I didn't notice.

Ty stood. "That's my cue to leave. I have a lot of things to do. Nice to meet you both." He shook hands with my father and gave my mother a kiss on the cheek. "See you both later."

My mother watched him go, and I just knew what she was thinking. "He's a nice young man, Trixie. Is he available? I didn't see a ring."

Of course my mother would notice that.

I shook my head. I was still shell-shocked from my divorce from Deputy Doug of the Philly sheriff's department.

"We're just friends," I said.

My mother looked at ACB for verification, but she was busy slathering on Entrenched in Scarlet, a new lipstick that she'd wanted me to try, but it was way too . . . scarlet.

"They're just good friends," she said as she wiped some lipstick off her teeth. "But sometimes I think that Ty wants to be more."

Since when did she think that?

Was it true? My heart did a little flip in my chest, or maybe it was just too much coffee.

But ACB's statement was like waving a checkered flag at Indy. My mother was off and running.

"Isn't that nice?" Mom said, practically singing the words. "A new relationship would be good for you, Trixie."

"Antoinette Chloe," I said to change the subject. "Can I bother you to put on another pot of coffee for my parents?" I turned to them. "Would you like something to eat? I could order from the diner and have Ray bring it over. I need to talk to him anyway."

"Sounds lovely. I've been dying for Juanita's meat loaf," Mom said.

"So have I," Dad added. "For three years."

"Consider it done." I reached for my cell phone. "How about you, Antoinette Chloe?"

"Just a chef salad with Thousand Island dressing and crumbly blue on top. Oh, and have them add ham and chicken to the salad. No, have them put the ham and chicken into a long roll with the dressing and lettuce, tomato, and onions. And skip the salad."

That was ACB.

I phoned in the order, I added the same sandwich for myself, and asked that Ray bring it over.

A half hour later, after we got into the Christmas cookies, there was a knocking on the back door. As expected, it was Ray with our order.

I introduced him to my parents, and they shook hands.

"Ray, can you join us for a while?" I asked.

"I can't, boss. The Silver Bullet is packed. Some snowmobile club is there—about fifty of them. Juanita and Bob said that I should stay at the diner and help there, and that I wasn't needed at the shower, since the Babes were on it."

That was a good decision. I would have done the

same thing. It made me feel more relaxed that my diner was functioning perfectly fine without me.

"Okay, Ray. Here's the deal," I said, handing him one of my credit cards. "Buy two laptops for me, as soon as you can. I'm donating them to the church. And here's what I'd like." I handed him a sheet of paper with Liz's make and model number on it. "Tomorrow, if you could. Oh, and get two flash drives. And, Ray, you'll be on the clock."

"Don't worry about that," he said. "I can probably drive over to Oswego tonight and get them. It depends on how busy the diner gets."

He was such a good kid, and he worked like a rented mule. I was so glad that I'd given him a chance to prove himself.

During the next three hours, we all ate, talked, and laughed. It was so good to see my parents again.

"Have you heard anything from John or Sue?"

"They both called not too long ago. They're really busy," my father said. "But they're both happy doing what they do."

My sister and brother were in the Red Cross and moved around from place to place as needed. We always joked that they followed the disasters, but what they did was serious business.

Sue was a nurse by trade, but now was an administrator and coordinator of nursing for them. John was a doctor.

And I was a diner owner . . . or would be after I paid Aunt Stella in full.

Sometimes I had the feeling that I was a major

underachiever. What was I doing to save the world like
Sue and John were?

Well, I was going to save my little corner of it by finding out who killed Liz.

It was going to be difficult to do the things I needed
to with my parents there because I wanted to visit
with them, but I did have a job at the church and was
in charge of the pageant.

They just had to keep themselves occupied. Or else
they'd have to audition for the pageant, too.

If I was going to be Tiny Tim, my parents could be
Mr. and Mrs. Cratchit.

Yes!

An hour later, there was an impromptu party at the Big
House when Aunt Stella returned with the Babes and
Bob. Clyde and Max stopped over as well, bringing hot
pizza and wings. Ray came over with the two laptops
and the new flash drives and stayed for some pizza and
wings. Then Bob left to cook and Juanita arrived after her
shift.

Around midnight, the party broke up.

My parents left for their cozy motor home, Clyde,
Max, and Juanita went home, and everyone from Boca
went upstairs to their bedrooms.

Just ACB and I were left. She was wiping off the
counter, and I was sitting as I wiped off the table.

I whispered to ACB, "I think I'm going to break into
Roger Southwick's apartment. I'm pretty sure he's living
above the church, where the Robinsons are living."

"How? When?" ACB asked with a gleam in her eye.

She was ready to help, but it probably would be better if I did it myself.

"Preferably when the three of them aren't around, if there's ever a time like that. And I hope to find a set of keys somewhere that would let me open the door to the upstairs. From what I can figure out, keys are kept in the top drawer of Darlene's desk. Hopefully they're labeled."

"Liz was so organized. I'll bet they're labeled," ACB said.

ACB handed me my crutches. "Liz's flash drive would be the thing to look for. Oh, and remember she was working on something called 'Buff'? Well, in her personal phone book are phone numbers all with the Buffalo area code. *Buff* has to mean *Buffalo*." I pulled out a copy of Liz's phone book from my purse. "Next to the first one, she wrote in 'B.N.'"

"Let's call some of the numbers and see if we can figure it out," ACB said.

"Just what I was thinking." I punched in the first set of numbers.

"Hello, *Buffalo News*. How can I help you?"

"I'm sorry. I have the wrong number," I said, then turned to ACB. "It's *Buffalo News*."

"The next one is labeled 'BVS-CH,'" ACB said. "I don't have a clue."

I dialed and apologized for calling the wrong number again. "It's the Bureau of Vital Statistics in the courthouse."

The next was the Erie County Department of Corrections, Buffalo, New York.

"I wonder who or what Liz was checking into," I said.

The next was the New York State Parole Department.

My first guess was Roger. Just because he'd acted suspiciously. Maybe he acted suspiciously toward Liz, too, and she'd decided to check him out. But Roger had let it slip that he had some kind of relationship with Liz. Maybe it was a negative one. I could see that.

"This is really good, Trixie. We at least know that Liz was snooping around Buffalo. Remember how Ty said that we're not law enforcement professionals?" ACB asked.

"Yes, I do. And it bothered me. Just because we don't have a degree in it, we can't figure things out?"

"Someday he'll discover that we *are* professionals." She laughed. "Now let's figure out a plan for breaking into Roger's apartment like the pros we are."

"Didn't Ty Brisco tell you that we wouldn't need you today?" Pastor Fritz asked on Sunday, before services. He'd been trying to get rid of me since I'd started volunteering.

I was about to lie to a pastor again. I surely was going to hell.

"Gee, no. . . . I don't remember. . . . But I'm here now and my ride left, so I can help all day if you need me. I'll answer the phone while you, Darlene, and Roger are in church. Right?" I'd found out during the week that Roger passed the collection basket, so he'd be occupied while ACB and I did our snooping.

"No. That isn't necessary. We have an answering machine, and—"

"Pastor Fritz, it's no trouble at all. Really. People love it when they get a real person. Don't worry about a thing. I am happy to help. I really am."

"But—"

"I just love this room. It's so cheery and bright. Will Roger be passing the basket today?"

"Roger?"

"Roger the maintenance man."

He looked at me like I had two heads. "He usually does, I guess."

"Fine. Then I won't look for him."

"Look for him? Why would you look for him?"

"You know, give him things to do," I said, babbling. "I can always find things to do around the point. I certainly can find things to do around here."

"But it's a Sunday."

"Of course! He has the day off." I picked up a pen and notebook. "I'll make a list for him for tomorrow."

"He'll love that," Pastor Fritz said, shaking his head. "Trixie, see if you can get a ride home early. There is really nothing to do here. If you can't, I'll drive you home after services."

"Okay, Pastor Fritz, but take your time. I have a lot of things to do. I bought these laptops for the office, and I'm going to set them up."

"That's very generous of you. Thank you so very much."

"You know what they say about computers: Can't live with them; can't live without them," I said. "And you're welcome, very much."

"Well, I'd better get going. My parishioners will be coming in soon."

"Yes." I said, checking the clock on the wall. "It's almost time for the services."

I should be over at St. Luke's of the Lake. St. Luke's was my and ACB's church. She was there now for the nine-o'clock Mass. At the coffee and cake gathering after the mass, ACB was going to ask about Roger Southwick and show the grainy picture that I took. Then she was going to meet me back here.

I had already checked out Darlene's desk and found a set of keys with a small tag labeled DOOR TO APART-MENTS. On another tag was a set of eight keys that read APARTMENTS.

I was one happy snoop.

This should be as easy as baking a cake.

My plan had to be executed with perfect timing. The Robinsons would be in church and so would Roger Southwick starting about eleven o'clock. We had a good hour to snoop around Roger's apartment without being seen.

Now, if only Antoinette Chloe would call from the back parking lot.

I took the laptops out of the box and plugged them in to charge. That was about the extent of my setup knowledge. I'd pay Ray to come down here. Or maybe Darlene knew how to set them up.

I passed the rest of the time scratching under my cast with a yardstick. I couldn't wait for that thing to come off. I'd had it on for only a handful of days, but it felt like decades, and I was tired of wearing skirts. The bright Christmas socks that I chose to wear were a minor con-solation because they made me laugh.

Speaking of my cast, I needed more time to get around than ACB, and I wanted to make sure we could make a quick getaway if necessary.

As I'd told Ty, I didn't have time for jail. So we couldn't get caught. We just couldn't.

My cell rang, and my heart began to race. "Trixie here."

"Antoinette Chloe here. I'm parked way out back by the tree line, half in a snowbank. I hope I don't get stuck."

"Why did you park way back there, then?"

"I thought it was a good idea at the time. And, by the way, none of the Catholics knew Roger. He's not from around here."

"Okay. Thanks for trying. Now, let's get our plan under way. You sure you want to do this?" I asked. "I can do it alone."

"We're in this together. I liked Liz, even though I understood where Margie was coming from. Besides, Liz doesn't have anybody else."

"Meet you inside. By the door to the apartments. It's opposite the kitchen door."

"Got it."

I wore my coat and slung my purse across my body. After this, I was going to go home with ACB, just as Pastor Fritz wanted.

Leaving a note that read *I'm going home after all. All my best, Trixie,* I crutched my way to the back door.

On my way, I paused at one of the small windows to look into the church. Pastor Fritz was greeting everyone. Darlene was next to him. But where was Roger?

There he was. By the collection baskets and the big metal money hopper. It seemed as though he was either guarding the contributions with his life or was about to line his pockets. I hoped that someone was watching him.

I caught up to ACB, and, heart racing, I opened the steel door to the apartments.

"Let's do it," I said.

Her flip-flops left a trail of water and small stones up the clean and dry stairs. My crutches and the boot I wore on my left foot left more prints. *Uh-oh.*

Maybe we needed to wipe down the stairs before we left. I'd never thought of it.

By the time I reached the top landing and looked down a long, shiny hall, I didn't have any air left in my lungs. I handed ACB the other ring of keys as I tried to catch my breath.

"Can you make it down this hallway, Trixie?"

"Yes," I said, looking at a couple of doors. "But how do we tell which apartment is Roger's? There are eight doors here. It's like a hotel. And there's nothing on any of the doors except numbers. So what do we do?"

"We get the keys out," ACB said, holding a massive amount of metal in her hand.

She tried the first door and every key on the ring. The second to the last key worked.

"Here goes!" She opened the door and we both looked in.

"Nothing," I said. "There's no sign of anyone living here. Let's try across the hall."

The fourth key worked on that door. "Someone's living here."

I swallowed hard. "Let's do it," I whispered.

We walked in quietly. I started for the pack of mail

on the coffee table, but then I noticed all the . . . huge trash bags. They were clear plastic bags, stacked tall and loaded to the brim with colorful little papers.

"Look at this, Antoinette Chloe. What on earth?" We both inspected the tower of bags.

"They're pull tabs," I announced. "Like the ones they sell during bingo. You know, you pull the little tabs to see if you win . . . maybe get three cherries or bars . . . you know, like a slot machine. But these are all open!"

"Maybe these are the old ones from bingo," ACB said.

"Why are they here, then, and not put out with the bingo trash?"

ACB snapped her fingers. "Roger Southwick must have an addiction to pull tabs. He sits here on the couch, gets a fresh order right from the vendor, and starts pulling."

"Wow! That's a real addict! I wonder how much those towers of pull tabs cost Roger to buy."

"Not a clue. I know at bingo here at the Community Church, they sell for a dollar each or six for five dollars. It all depends. They're probably more at bars."

I shook my head and went to the kitchen, where there was a cute built-in desk with shelves above it. The shelves contained dozens of cookbooks. The desk was loaded with coupons, Frank Sinatra CDs, and fancy flowered stationery with *Darlene* lettered in tiny purple buds. I noticed a stack of mail on the desk and looked at the addressees.

"Uh . . . um . . . Antoinette Chloe, this apartment is Pastor Fritz's and Darlene's, not Roger's. These are all bills. A lot of bills—personal ones and what looks like church bills on Darlene's desk." I took a peek at one, and it was stamped THIRD NOTICE. Another was marked SENT FOR COLLECTION.

I wondered why Darlene wasn't paying the bills. I remembered the messages on Liz's ancient answering machine. The merchants were obviously desperate enough to call Liz for payment instead of dealing with Darlene again, who was obviously avoiding them. This seemed to have been going on for a long time.

Why wasn't Darlene cutting checks and sending them out?

"Let's get out of here, Antoinette Chloe, and find Roger's place."

She was still staring at all the pull tabs, mesmerized.

I pulled on the sleeve of her muumuu. "C'mon."

I checked over my shoulder to make sure that everything was in place, and we locked the door and went across the hall.

We were in on the first try. I opened the door slowly. "I think this is his place. It smells like oil and gas. It's probably from those gloves on the floor."

"I can smell it."

"I think he was working on the snowplow," I said.

"Other than the smell, the place is immaculate."

I looked at the clock on his stove. "We have to hurry. Let's look for a flash drive."

We opened drawers, looked in his underwear drawer and in a small desk full of military fiction books. There was more military fiction on shelves in his bedroom and stacked in the bathroom.

"I think he was a marine," ACB yelled from a small

second bedroom. "He has all kinds of marine memorabilia. But I don't see a flash drive anywhere."

"Me neither, but I think I found something even better."

ACB flip-flopped toward me. "What?"

"Look!" I did a double take and picked up a picture in a fancy silver frame. "It's a picture of Roger Southwick with his arm around Darlene Robinson!"

"She doesn't seem his type."

"That miserable man is no one's type," I said. "I wonder what their relationship is."

"Brother and sister? Cousins? Friends?"

I put the picture back and adjusted it so it was in the exact same spot.

"Let's go," I said. "We're cutting this too close."

We couldn't get the door locked for some reason. We tried with the key and with the button on the doorknob.

"Leave it," ACB said. "Maybe he won't notice."

"Oh, he'll notice all right."

Finally we got it to work, and we hurried out of there. I sat down on the stairs and mostly slid down on my butt. It was quick . . . but painful. One good thing—I was cleaning our dirty footprints off the steps.

ACB waited for me and then bent over to lock the big steel door.

"What the hell are you two doing?" said a deep, gnarly voice.

It was Roger Southwick.

I moved to cover ACB, who was now done with the door. "My friend's flip-flop came off her foot, and she was just putting it back on. Why are you flipping out? And why are you swearing in church?"

He had the good sense to look uncomfortable.

"Uh . . . sorry . . . I thought you were going into the apartments."

"Why on earth would you think that, Mr. Southwick? We have no reason to go up there," I said, glaring at him. "Do you have something to hide?"

I loved seeing bullies back down, and he backed down.

"I have nothing to hide," he said.

"Then let my friend put on her flip-flop so we can leave. Apparently I'm not needed in the office today," I said, teeth gritted.

"Um . . . okay. See ya."

I nodded and we made a quick exit.

When we got outside, I took several breaths of the crisp, cold air. "That was a close call."

"I can't catch my breath, and I need a drink of water. Maybe it's an adrenaline dump," ACB said.

I gulped the air. "One more second and we would have been caught by Roger."

"And three more seconds, Ty would have caught us, too," ACB pointed to the sheriff's car driving into the lot. "Angels are protecting us."

We hurried to ACB's van and slid in.

Safe!

Or so I thought.

Ty pulled his car to a stop in front of ACB's van and shouted out the window, "What are you two doing now?"

Chapter 10

Oh my! Was there a silent alarm upstairs, or what?

My heart began to race and my face flamed.

"Oh crap." Antoinette Chloe summed up my feelings perfectly.

"Um . . . uh . . ." I said eloquently. "We aren't doing a thing, Ty. Not a thing. Antoinette Chloe is just picking me up from work, and we're headed back to the Big House. We have a couple of salads to make for the auditions—a big chef and a fruit salad. No ham this time. I think we'll do baked ziti and meatball sandwiches."

Ty probably didn't care what I was serving for the auditions—he'd eat anything. This was just a verbal checklist for my benefit as well as ACB's.

"Your aunt Stella told me you were here, Trixie. I know that I gave you the message from Pastor Fritz yesterday that you weren't needed today."

"Did you? It must have slipped my mind." I hoped that the dumb look on my face was convincing.

The look on his face was skeptical.

"Were you looking for me?" I asked him. "Or just patrolling the area?"

"I was looking for you," he said, as my heart was going to leap from my chest.

"What for?" I squeaked out, but I wanted to yell, *Don't arrest me!*

"I wanted to tell you that Margie Grace was released from the hospital this morning, and her husband took her home. Unfortunately she was still ranting about how she should have been asked to direct the pageant, and how she was overlooked when Liz was appointed director. And now she was overlooked again due to you. Her anger was directed at you, Trixie, and I wanted to warn you to be careful of her."

"That woman doesn't know when to quit," ACB said. "Poor thing. It's like she lost her identity as Sandy Harbor's First Lady of the Theater, or at least the First Lady of the Sandy Harbor High School Gymnasium."

"Or the Community Church's . . . church!" I added.

"I'd like to think that she just has hurt feelings, but it seems to be more than that," Ty said.

I sighed. "Ty, I think that we, or I, need to give Margie Grace something important to do in the Christmas pageant. Or Pastor Fritz can just appoint her as the director, and I can be her assistant and keep an eye on her."

"How do you keep an eye on your back, Trixie?" ACB spewed. "If Margie gets distraught enough, her anger can escalate from throwing a cell phone—like she tried to at Liz—to maybe something more."

"She's right." Ty nodded. "I'll be keeping an eye on Margie, too, and so will the other deputies, but there's not enough manpower to put a guard on you, Trixie."

"A guard? Because of Margie Grace?" I shook my

head. "Aren't you both overreacting? I can take care of myself. I'm not afraid of her."

"You never know what people can do when they get mad enough," Ty said.

"Is Margie a suspect, Ty?" ACB asked.

Ty gave a slight nod. That was all we were going to get from him, and he was loath to give that much up.

"Trixie?" ACB rubbed her forehead.

"Yeah?"

"I think you're right. I think that giving Margie some job at the pageant would calm her down. And that way, we both can keep an eye on her."

That was ACB's way of saying that she had my back.

"Just be careful" was Ty's warning as he got back into his car and drove away.

When we got back to the Big House, I found the Boca Babes, my parents, and Clyde and Max doing some kind of Zumba—or was it yoga?—in my living room. I'll just call it Zuga.

And lo, Margie Grace was leading the Zuga!

"Looks like they're having a good time," ACB said. "And nothing seems to be broken yet."

Crash!

Everyone froze in place.

First my Santa Claus mug. Then my turkey. Now my Lenox crystal bowl.

All my traditions. My favorite things for the holidays were falling apart. And I suddenly wanted to burst into tears. While I realized that these were all material things, they meant something to me.

I bent over to take off my one boot, but mostly I was trying to hide my watery eyes and get myself together.

"Pass the hat," Antoinette Chloe said, removing her plaid cape. "Trixie should be reimbursed for the bowl so she can buy another one to replace it."

Aunt Stella helped me take off my coat. "Don't worry, honey. We'll make it good."

"It's okay. It really is," I said. "Excuse me a minute."

I crutched to the bathroom off the laundry room and splashed cold water onto my face. What was wrong with me? Normally three broken things wouldn't send me over the edge. Oh yeah, *four* broken things—I forgot my broken leg.

"Honey?"

My mother. She could always read me.

"Honey, are you okay?"

"I'm fine, Mom. Just give me a moment." I filled the sink up with cold water, then dunked my face into it.

I was not going to feel sorry for myself. No way. A lot of people had it much worse than four broken things.

All these wonderful people had come to help me. I planned to put them to work and keep them busy.

When I finally came out of the bathroom, they were all sitting around the big oak kitchen table.

My father took my hand. "I know you won't take money from us, but the Babes and your mother will go shopping and replace your bowl. They will also look for the turkey decoration that Antoinette Chloe broke and the Santa Claus mug that you broke."

ACB must have told them about everything.

He hugged me close to him and kissed me on the cheek. "We can't replace your broken leg."

"Thank you, everyone. I appreciate it. And I appreciate that you came to help me. I do have some things I need help with."

"Just tell us, Trixie, and consider it done," Aunt Stella said. "I know you always decorate the diner and the house. I know where the decorations are, so we'll take care of it."

"And you need a tree in both places," Clyde said. "Max and I will chop two down at Christmas Tree Acres."

"Can we help?" one of the Babes said. I think her name was Marilyn. "I haven't chopped down a tree since I was a kid."

"Sure. We'll make a day of it," Max said. "Anyone who wants to go, meet here at noon tomorrow."

Judging by the reaction, the entire room was going. I wanted to go, too, but there was no way I could walk around the field.

"So let's decorate the Silver Bullet now!" Mom said.

Everyone got up and migrated to the closet to put on their coats and boots. The men went downstairs to lug up the decorations.

After a while they were all out the door. Everyone except ACB, Margie Grace, and me.

"I'll be leaving now," Margie Grace said. "But first I owe you an apology, Trixie."

"Why's that, Margie?"

"Well, I realized that I may have said some callous things earlier, because I was angry."

"Oh?"

"I did say that you were going to suck as pageant

director, and I did say that you were going to be even worse than Liz Fellows. And I said that I couldn't wait until you were eliminated. . . ."

I wasn't going to play games with her. "Are you going to eliminate me, Margie?"

"I just meant gone from the pageant, not eliminated, as in . . ."

"Murdered?" I asked.

She grabbed at her throat. "Heavens, no!"

ACB grunted. "But Liz was murdered and now she's gone from the pageant. That should have made you happy, until Trixie was asked to run it."

"No matter what our local law enforcement thinks, I didn't have anything to do with Liz's death. That's what I came here to tell you, but then we got to exercising. I had such a good time! I need to keep busy. That's why I wanted to direct the pageant. I realize that I miss people my own age."

"Then move to Boca, Margie. Or run exercise classes for the seniors at the center. That would be wonderful."

"It would be!"

Suddenly I felt sorry for her. She was just a lonely person and felt overlooked by the pageant committee. The plays and pageants were her universe—they made her feel good, and now she was just adrift on Lake Ontario in a boat with no oars.

"Margie, I was going to ask you something. Do you think you could spare the time to help me with the pageant? It just seems so . . . overwhelming. I could use your help."

Her face lit up, then darkened. "I'd love to help you,

but do you really think anyone would want me around?" She shook her head. "Everyone thinks I killed Liz, but I couldn't kill anyone, Trixie. I just couldn't!"

"You think about it and let me know if you'd like to assist me." Margie was getting teary. "How about if we call your husband to take you home?"

"Freddie is over at the Silver Bullet, so he's not far away. I'll walk over and join him."

"I'll give you a ride over, Margie. It's icy," ACB said.

"That's so nice of you!" She sniffed. "I guess I really do have friends."

"Of course you do, Margie, so knock off the drama. And no throwing cell phones at Trixie!" ACB ordered.

"Yes, Antoinette Chloe." She managed a little smile.

"And tell her that you'll help her out with the darn pageant already. You know you're dying to do it!"

"Yes, I am." Margie laughed.

"But no salmon," I added. "No salmon pulling Santa's sleigh. No salmon spawning or dancing. I know it's the official fish of Sandy Harbor, but there are no salmon at the North Pole and there were none in Bethlehem. . . . At least I don't think so."

We all laughed together, and it cleared the air.

I didn't know whether Margie Grace could have killed Liz Fellows, but after this, I didn't think so.

When Antoinette Chloe returned, we started working on the salads and cooking ziti for those of us catering the auditions.

The kitchen was so humid and hot that we were wilting, so we opened some windows a bit.

"I keep thinking of that picture we found in Roger's apartment," I said, taking a break with a Christmas cookie or ten. "The one with him in his marine dress clothes alongside Darlene."

"Darlene looked so young back then." ACB stirred the ziti noodles. "I like her with dark hair instead of that yellowish orange color she wears."

"I am going to do an Internet search on his name," I said. "Maybe there was some kind of article written when he went into the marines."

"I'll get your laptop," ACB said. "We can figure out how to do it together."

"I think I can do it. Ray taught me. It seems to be logical."

ACB walked over the several steps to the large office off the kitchen. It was Aunt Stella and Uncle Porky's office, and most everything still in it was theirs. I'd just added more clutter and a laptop.

She got the laptop, mouse, and mouse pad and set them in front of me on the table.

I knew we should be able to get the Internet, as Ray had set up a network for me. There was one in the diner, too, and my customers loved it, especially when they couldn't get the Internet at their homes.

I remembered back around Valentine's Day how a bunch of reporters had set up shop at my diner so they could get the Internet and send in their reports. The place was hopping day and night.

Turning it on, I waited until it booted up. Then I double clicked the icon that Ray had told me to double click. The blue box showed, and I typed in "Roger Southwick."

Amazing.

A miniature of the same picture was there along with the first few lines of a story. I clicked on that.

Easy peasy.

"And here he is!" I said, just awestruck at how far technology had come.

ACB looked over my shoulder and read, "'The *Buffalo News*, Buffalo, New York: Local resident Roger James Southwick, twenty, recently graduated from the Marine Corps Recruit Depot, Parris Island, South Carolina. Roger is a graduate of Buffalo High School, where he took business courses and was on the varsity football team. He resides with his parents, David and Julie Southwick, and has a sister, Darlene.'"

"Darlene!" we shouted together.

"Not a common name," I added. "And, of course, this is a picture of her. She's obviously younger than he is." I was getting excited. "That's probably how he got the job. With his personality, no one else in their right mind would hire him."

"Yes, but he did back down when you told him off."

I looked for more information on Roger Southwick, but that was it. "You're right. All hot air and attitude, but, you know, a marine could have easily thrust that knife into Liz's back."

"That's why we have to find out if Liz had something on him. That's why we have to find that flash drive!"

"And, my dear friend, let's talk about all those trash bags full of pull tabs in the Robinsons' apartment. And all those unpaid bills! Do you think one or both of them have a gambling problem?"

Antoinette Chloe shrugged. "Maybe all those used pull tabs were just recyclable paper that the Robinsons could get money for to put toward the church."

I didn't want to think anything bad about the Robinsons, but then I thought about it more. "But what about all those unpaid bills?"

"Maybe Darlene just hasn't gotten around to paying them," ACB suggested. "It is Christmastime, after all, and it's very busy at the church."

We weren't getting anywhere.

"At least we know that Roger and Darlene are brother and sister," I pointed out. "Although I don't know what that proves."

"Me neither, but maybe it'll come in handy."

"I wonder if Ty knows," I said.

"That man knows everything."

"I hope he doesn't know we broke into their apartments," I said.

"I hope not, too," ACB said.

"Well, I think we'd better finish getting everything ready. Bob and Ray are taking everything to the church's kitchen at about two, and I have to work tomorrow in the office, so I want to get a head start on everything."

Aunt Stella returned without the Boca Babes, and she helped to make the chef and the fruit salads. Then everyone returned and started decorating the Big House outside. That was fine, but it was only a matter of time until everyone came in.

"I think I'll suggest that they go over to the Silver Bullet to eat dinner," I said. "There's nothing to eat here."

"That's another thing we can do for you—go to the store," Aunt Stella said. "Is the Gas and Grab still operating?"

"Yes. It is, and they even expanded and added a really nice deli."

"Make a list. I'll check it twice," Aunt Stella said with a twinkle in her eye. "And we'll go to the store for you tomorrow. It's on us. So don't skimp."

"But tomorrow is the tree chopping," I pointed out.

"Oh! There's just so much to do!" Aunt Stella said.

"Tell me about it," I said, closing my laptop. I really wanted to look up Darlene, but now wasn't the right time.

The next day, I'd talk to Darlene and Pastor Fritz and insist that we work on getting the two laptops operational for the business of the church. And I'd insist that we work on whatever Liz had been working on.

Yes!

Two hours later, the Busy Boca Babes returned. They raved about how beautiful the Silver Bullet looked. They even reported that some of my customers had gotten into the spirit and helped, knowing that I was incapacitated.

"Everyone asked about you, Trixie," said Barbara, a Babe.

Another Babe, Diane, giggled. "Ty was there, too. He helped us reach the high places. That man is beyond handsome."

"Yes, but he asked *me* if I wanted a cup of coffee," Elaine added. She was probably the loudest Boca Babe.

"He asked all of us, Elaine!" said Ann, who was the sweetest Babe.

"My goodness, ladies! What are you thinking?" said Aunt Stella. "He could be our grandson!"

"Only our *son*. We're not that old," Marilyn said.

"Yes, we are!" Clara added, laughing.

Finally they adjourned to the dining room for pinochle and highballs, and their screams and laughter could be heard in Watertown.

Mom phoned me from the motor home. "Your dad and I are calling it a night. See you tomorrow."

"Do you need anything?"

"No. We're all set. Good night, honey."

"Good night, Mom."

"Do you want me to help you up the stairs?" ACB asked. "You must be sick of the recliner."

My bed was calling my name, but I couldn't stand the thought of climbing the stairs. I was pooped.

"Tomorrow. For sure. But you go ahead, Antoinette Chloe. Get some sleep."

"Don't you dare touch that laptop without me," she said.

Oh, fudge! She knew that I was dying to explore the Internet more. "Um . . . uh . . ."

"Cross your heart and hope to die?"

"No!"

"Will you wait for me?" she asked. "I'd do it for you. Besides, we're sisters in crime. I went to jail with you."

"What are we, in fourth grade?" I asked. "Oh, all right. I'll wait for you."

"Good. Nighty night," she said. "I'll drive you tomorrow."

I crutched to my front room, grabbed the afghan that had cornucopias on it, and sank into the recliner.

Then there was a knock on the door.

After midnight? Who on earth would visit after midnight? *It might be an emergency.*

"Coming!" I said, struggling to my feet, grabbing my crutches, and hobbling to the door. "Ty?"

"I'm really sorry to bother you, but I saw your light on, and I thought we could talk."

"I was just going to hit the recliner, but come in. Can I get you anything?"

"No. I just stuffed myself at the Silver Bullet."

"I heard you helped decorate. Thanks." I motioned for him to take a seat across from me.

He nodded. "It was no trouble. They did a great job."

"I can't wait to see it."

There was a pause in the conversation, and I waited for Ty to tell me what was on his mind. I braced myself.

"I spoke with Roger Southwick. He seemed to think that you and Antoinette Chloe were upstairs snooping around in the private apartments. He said that you two might have been in his place. I guess a couple of things were disturbed."

There's going to be coal in my stocking on Christmas morning.

"Well, Ty, Antoinette Chloe and I ran into Roger by the back door as we were leaving. Remember, we spoke in the parking lot and you warned me about Margie

Grace. Oh, I have to tell you about Margie! Just listen to this!" I took a breath, but it was a big mistake.

He held up a hand as if he were directing traffic. "This isn't about Margie Grace. It's about whether or not you and Antoinette Chloe were in Roger's apartment." He let out a deep breath. "Just tell me the truth."

"I always do, more or less."

"Make it more of the truth, not less. I have to crack this case, and soon. I don't want a murderer walking around free."

"Will we go to jail?" I asked.

He looked at me with those sparkling blue eyes, and I knew he wouldn't lie, so why should I?

"No. You won't go to jail if you're honest with me," he said.

"Then, yes. Yes, we went to his apartment. And we also went to the Robinsons' apartment."

He sat back in his chair, hands folded.

"How did you get in?"

"Keys. I found keys in the office. We went up there when everyone was in church. Five more seconds and we wouldn't have run into Roger."

"What did you discover?" he asked.

"Do you really want to know?"

He nodded. "I interviewed the Robinsons and Roger in their respective apartments. Everything was clean. Then I got a search warrant, and went into both places, legally. Everything was clean."

"We found piles and piles of opened pull tabs in the Robinsons' place—three towers' worth of clear plastic garbage bags, stacked high, full of them. And there were more unopened pull tabs on their coffee table. I guess that one of them is addicted to pull tabs and opens them when they are watching TV."

Ty leaned forward. "Interesting. What else?"

"A pile of unpaid bills were on their kitchen table and there were even more on Darlene's desk."

"Uh-huh."

I moved the afghan over my feet. "What do you mean by that?"

"I mean that I already knew they were in financial trouble. So is the church."

"Maybe Liz knew that, too," I said. "And maybe she knew that one of them has a jones for pull tabs. She must receive everything that is ordered by the church."

"That's my guess." He leaned his arms on his thighs, intent on every word I said, or maybe he couldn't hear over the screaming Boca Babes.

He raised an eyebrow.

I smiled. "The Babes are busy playing pinochle and chugging highballs."

He chuckled. "Got it." He waited until the noise died down and then focused back on me. "Tell me about Roger's place."

"There was nothing exciting there—only a picture of Roger in a marine uniform standing with Darlene Robinson. Darlene was formerly known as Darlene Southwick, Roger's sister."

"I know." He smiled. "Internet search?"

"Yes."

"Did you know the stuff about the pull tabs?" I asked.

"No, but it's not illegal to have pull tabs."

"I know, Ty, but those heaping mountains of used pull tabs and unpaid bills seem to be an indication of a gambling habit. Don't you think?"

"Maybe."

There was silence between us for a while; then I said, "Did anyone find footprints or the like?"

"No. But like I said, Roger thought that some things were out of place."

"He's Mr. Clean. He would know. Now what?"

"I think I convinced him that you were exiting the building, and that you'd never do such a thing. I hope you put the keys back where you found them."

"Fudge!" My stomach did a flip. How could I be so forgetful? All Roger had to do was look for the keys and know that we were there.

"You two are not very good criminals. I think you both should give it up."

He seemed tired—tired of telling me the same thing over and over again.

"Ty, I shared information with you. Can you give me any information about the case?"

"You know I can't, and do you have any idea how tired I am of telling you to butt out?"

"Back atcha!" I said.

"I know it bothers you, but you know I'll figure out who did it."

"And you know I can't just sit back and not do anything about it."

It looked as if he was going to reach for my hand, but

he decided against it. My mouth suddenly went dry and I couldn't swallow.

This was one of those times where I enjoyed Ty's company. It almost felt as though he trusted me, as if we were working together.

"I don't think Margie Grace killed Liz," I said. "She's just lonely, Ty."

"I'd still be careful. Anything can set her off."

"I used to think that, but no more."

There was silence between us, and I thought he was going to leave, but he seemed to have more on his mind.

"Is there anything else you'd like to discuss?" I asked.

"What's your next move? I know you are keeping that job for some reason."

"I am going to help with whatever Liz was working on when she was killed. Maybe, just maybe, I'll get a clue or figure out who killed her."

"And you're going to put yourself in terrible jeopardy."

"I can handle myself, Ty."

"With a broken leg? You can't even run."

"Are you kidding? I can't run even with two good legs."

He laughed. "Will you keep me informed if you find out anything?" he asked.

"Sure, but only if you'll play Ebenezer Scrooge in the pageant."

He rolled his eyes. "Typecasting, huh?"

"Absolutely."

"I'll do it." He stood to leave. "Trixie, there's one more thing."

"Lay it on me, Sheriff."

He looked like he wanted to disappear. I've never seen him so uncomfortable. It must be horrendous news.

"My parents are coming from Houston for Christmas. They want to meet you, and they want to help out, too."

"That's wonderful! You haven't seen them in a long time, right?"

"In over three years."

He shifted from foot to foot, staring down. The part about his parents coming for Christmas wasn't all that was on his mind. Then finally he sighed deeply and looked at me.

"I'd like you to accompany me to the Tri-County Law Enforcement New Year's Ball. It's on a Saturday. January nineteenth. It's pretty fancy. But since I arrested you, I'll understand if you don't want to go with me."

Chapter 11

I could barely sleep the past night.

Ty asked me to the Law Enforcement Ball, and I accepted, cast and all.

I didn't have a clue that he was going to do that. I could tell he was nervous, and I'd never seen him like that. He was always so sure of himself, ready to take charge. He had the type of personality that everyone gravitated to, and the looks that had the women stacked up to date him like cordwood. When he turned on that good-ol'-boy Texas charm, the most hardened criminal confessed.

I was looking forward to the Law Enforcement Ball and being with Ty, but I was as anxious as Rudolph with a short circuit on a stormy Christmas Eve.

I was back at the Community Church's office and Darlene and Pastor Fritz were both thanking me profusely for the new laptops, but all I could think of was talking to Ty the previous night.

I knew I had to get back to the present.

"Darlene, I thought we could work on what you and Liz were working on."

I didn't miss the look Darlene gave her husband.

His expression telegraphed, *Don't do it.*

"Is something wrong?" I asked.

"Oh, no. Nothing in the least," Darlene said, waving her hand back and forth in dismissal.

"Then let's get to work," I said. "I am here all day. Then, after work, there are auditions. My friends will be bringing the food for tonight at about three o'clock and setting up. It's going to be a full day."

"Then I think you should rest and not do too much," Darlene said. "Maybe you'd like come with me to the Ladies' Yarn Circle this morning. We are making lap quilts for wheelchair citizens and baby blankets for the new babies. We'll have a delightful time."

"I can't even spell *crochet*, forget about doing it!"

"We knit, too," Darlene said.

"Does knit begin with an *n*?" I joked.

She chuckled nervously. What was it that she didn't want me to see of Liz's unfinished work?

I smiled. "You go right ahead to the Yarn Circle, Darlene. Just give me the disk or flash drive that you two were working off of and give me whatever you want me to enter. Okay? I'll figure it out."

Pastor Fritz tented his hands like a steeple. "Maybe Darlene's right, Trixie. Maybe you just relax and—"

"I insist that I pass the time doing something useful for the church," I said. "I want to help. Remember, it's my Christmas present to the church, and to you both. You've gone through so much lately. So let's rock and roll."

That ought to end this "relax" stuff once and for all.

"My dear," Pastor Fritz began, "why don't you show

Trixie the church bulletin template and give her all the announcements, and she can begin compiling something for next week."

"That's a good place to start, Fritz. I'll do that."

"What about entering all the church's records into a spreadsheet? Wasn't that what you and Liz were working on?" I asked, remembering all the empty folders that I'd found on my first day there. "That seems like something I could help with. Right, Darlene? Or do you have a bill-paying program? I could enter the information and cut some checks for you."

Darlene turned to her husband. "What do you think, Fritz?"

"Let Trixie work on the church bulletin first." He looked at the clock. "Oh, I'm late for an appointment. Please excuse me."

"And I'm late for the Yarn Circle," Darlene said, reaching under her desk for a tote bag.

"What about the church bulletin things?" I asked.

"Oh, that's right."

She reached into her desk, got a set of keys, and opened a two-drawer metal file cabinet to the right of her desk.

Pulling out a flash drive and a green folder, she handed both items to me, then made a point to relock everything, and check that she'd done so. Twice. She tossed the keys into the top left drawer of her desk, where all the other keys were kept.

Hmm . . . what else was in that little file cabinet?

I couldn't resist. When I heard her footsteps fade out down the hall, I headed for that drawer.

I hadn't seen the ring with all the little file cabinet

keys on them before, but I did now. They were way in the back.

There were about ten keys on the ring, but only one silver one. The others were brass-colored, probably for the tall, five-drawer file cabinets against the wall.

"Please let this work," I said, fumbling in my attempt to hurry. Finally the little button popped up, and I opened the drawer.

It was completely empty.

I opened the second drawer. Empty.

Huh. Where was everything?

I closed the drawers gently, pushed the silver button in, and placed the keys where I'd found them.

As I sat down at my desk, I realized that any kind of important folders had probably been moved because I might come across them.

I looked at the other file cabinets, wondering if I should try to open them, one at a time.

Nope. The important stuff wasn't in this room.

But where?

Oh, yes! Pastor Fritz's parlor!

I would've bet my nonexistent paycheck that Darlene had moved anything important into his parlor!

Getting into his office and snooping was going to take all my sneaky skills.

ACB and I could devise some kind of basic plan that would involve getting both the pastor and Roger out of the building, while Darlene was busy with her Yarn Circle.

Until I could talk to her and put our devious brains together, I'd play with the church bulletin.

I moved the laptop around to see where the little flash

drive should be plugged in, but as I did, I pushed the little thing off my desk, onto my skirt. Then it slid like a toboggan down my skirt and under my desk.

Ugh. I dreaded trying to get it.

I tried to move the little drive closer to me with the tip of my crutch, but I couldn't quite move it. Besides, it was too dark to see where it was under there.

I had no choice but to crawl under the desk and get it myself.

It was agony, but finally I managed to wiggle myself under the desk and grab the drive in my hand. But then my hair stuck to something.

Was that tape?

Ouch!

It *was* tape—masking tape—and there were several strips of it way back. And it was holding something in place.

I got up on my elbows and picked at the tape with a fingernail. Finally the tape released its treasure.

Another flash drive!

This was the one! I just knew it. It was the drive that Liz Fellows had been working on. It had to contain some kind of information that would point to whoever had killed her, and I held it in my hand!

I'd been under this desk before, but I hadn't seen it. Guess the second time was a charm.

"What on earth?" It was Darlene. She'd come back probably to catch me in the act of doing something strange . . . and she had. She was getting a nice view of me lying down on the rug with half of me under the desk.

I slid the flash drive, tape and all, into my cleavage like ACB always does. It worked.

"I dropped the flash drive that you gave me, and I was trying to get it," I said, and I'm sure it came out muffled. "And now I'm trying to get up."

"How can I help?" Darlene asked.

"You can't. I'll have to do it myself with this cast on."

I went into a backward crab crawl on my stomach. Finally I crawled into the light. Now to get up. I used my chair, the desk, the crutches, and it was all in vain. I was doomed to sit there like a slug.

I adjusted my skirt, fixed my blouse and my cleavage purse. That was about when Roger Southwick came into the room.

"What are you doing?" he snapped.

"Oh, I just thought I'd work from down here rather than my desk—just for something different."

He raised an eyebrow.

Darlene grunted as she bent over. "Let's help her get up, Roger, for heaven's sake. You take one arm, and I'll take the other."

It wasn't pretty, but finally I was out from under the desk, standing.

"Thank you both," I said, trying to catch my breath. "It's hard doing anything with this cast on."

"Even going up and down stairs?" Roger asked, eyebrow raised.

"I can't do that one bit. I sleep in my recliner in my front room because I can't go up and down the stairs," I said, looking right back at him. "I miss my comfortable bed."

He nodded, but it was the type of nod that meant *I don't believe you.*

"I don't particularly care if you believe me or not, Roger. So far you haven't done anything to make me feel welcome here."

His lips twitched as if he was going to smile . . . or sneer.

"Excuse me, both of you," I said sweetly. "I am going to get to work on the church's bulletin."

"I'm going back to the Yarn Circle," Darlene said.

"Oh, did you forget something?" I asked. "That's why you returned?

"My tote bag," she said.

"Oh, I distinctly remember you took it with you," I said.

She should have come up with a better excuse to spy on me, but she was a pastor's wife, so she was a definite amateur.

"I did, didn't I?" she said. "I'm just so scatterbrained today."

"Uh-huh." Then I turned to Roger. "I don't want to keep you from your work around here. I'm up, and I promise not to look for anything on the floor again."

He turned without a word and walked out.

"Don't mind him," Darlene said. "He's not very social."

"I noticed. Why did you hire him?"

"Well, uh . . . he needed a job." She paused and then continued, "Plus, he's my brother."

"Oh! I didn't know!" I lied. "You two don't look very much alike."

"We used to—when I was younger, thinner, and less blond." She laughed.

"I wish I could work with my brother, but he's in the Red Cross. Actually, both he and my sister work there."

"And I wish Roger would find a job elsewhere. He's a little too . . . uh . . . overprotective. And he doesn't really get along with Fritz."

I jumped on that. "Well, as we both know, your brother isn't the friendliest guy on the planet. But you say he's overprotective. Do you need protection from something or someone?"

She quickly looked at the door, to either make a fast exit or to find out if she was overheard.

"Is everything okay, Darlene?"

"I have to go," she said, on the verge of tears.

"Darlene . . . wait!"

But she didn't. I could hear her running down the hall.

Huh. What just happened?

She'd stated that her brother was overprotective, and I'd asked her if everything was okay. Then she'd burst into tears.

The masking tape was sticking to me and to my bra. I readjusted the flash drive that I'd found, but I didn't want to lose it, even though it was well cushioned.

I couldn't wait to get home and investigate Liz's flash drive and do some name searching.

Liz had hidden that little thing for a reason, which meant that there was good stuff on it. ACB and I were absolutely correct when we checked out Liz's laptop. She did have an external drive. And her house was trashed by someone looking for it. But by who?

And Ty and his deputies didn't find the flash drive

when they searched the church's office. Ty was thorough, but unless his hair got stuck on masking tape like mine, he would never have found it.

I called ACB on my cell phone.

"Hello. This is Antoinette Chloe Brown, formerly Brownelli, but that's a long story."

"It's Trixie. Are you alone?"

"I'm having such a good time with your parents, Aunt Stella, and the Boca Babes. We're decorating the Big House."

Translation: She couldn't talk, and she wasn't alone.

"Okay, then just listen, and don't make any funny expressions on your face. I found it, Antoinette Chloe. I found the flash drive. It was taped under Liz's desk."

She was silent for a while.

"Uh-huh. It's such a rewarding job doing work for the church."

Translation: She knew I'd find something sooner or later.

"And, get this, something's bothering Darlene. She seems pretty distraught over something, and her brother seems to be at the heart of it."

"I love the fact that you're getting closer to Darlene and her brother."

Translation: Keep talking to Darlene and find out what's going on with Roger.

"And Ty Brisco asked me to go to the Law Enforcement Ball with him."

"Wow. 'Tis the season to be jolly!"

Translation: She was very happy for me.

My stomach still flipped whenever I thought about going on a date with Ty. Or maybe I was just hungry.

"Antoinette Chloe, do you think you could drive here with my laptop and pick me up? I think that it's charged. I figure that if we drive to the parking lot of the library, we could pick up their network. Then we can look at the flash drive that I found and do some searches."

"Oh, you need to stop at the dentist and get your front tooth glued back in? I'd be thrilled to pick you up at noon. I'll meet you out back."

Translation: She couldn't wait. She'd meet me out back.

It was only ten o'clock, and for two hours, I wandered around the halls for no reason, and peeked through the window of Pastor Fritz's parlor twice. He was talking to someone on the phone both times and seemed . . . distraught.

I guessed it was a tough business saving souls.

On one of my trips down the hall, I knocked on the door while he was still on the phone. He held a finger up for me to wait, but I nodded, walked in anyway, and sat in one of the flowery Queen Anne chairs in front of him.

He raised both eyebrows at me, but I pretended not to notice. Getting up, I crutched around the room, looking at all the memorabilia that he had.

I toured the room. I was behind him, and he didn't like that, but on his desk was a pile of bills that looked very similar to the ones ACB and I found in his apartment.

Oh, he was calling about his bills! Maybe he was trying to resolve the high interest rate or the late fees that had been attached. Probably he was trying to fix the fallout from Darlene's pull tab addiction.

I was just about to sit down, when I noticed several dozen unopened boxes on a steel shelving unit off the main part of his office in a small side room. All of them were stenciled in dark blue ink: G.K. GAMING AND TOYS, BROOKLYN, NY. PULL TABS.

Fresh pull tabs.

This is where they were stored for the bingo games on bingo nights.

There was a paper clip on the floor, and I made like I was picking it up, when actually I was looking at the gray metal trash bin under his desk.

I didn't see any used pull tabs in his office.

I was convinced that the pull tab addict had to be Darlene.

And I'd just realized something.

By bingo night, the play would have been cast, and that would allow everyone to attend bingo in the community room. I decided to let practice out early to support the church and snoop at bingo.

And, even though I would've rather shot my eye out with a Red Ryder BB gun, I was going to play bingo.

Finally I sat down again, and Pastor Fritz hung up his phone. "Yes, Trixie? What can I do for you?"

"Nothing, really. I came to tell you that I was going out for lunch. Would you like me to pick up anything for you?"

"No. I'm fine. I'll make something for lunch in my apartment."

"Okay. I'll ask Darlene, too. Her circle is about to break up."

"Yes. Why don't you do that?"

"Pastor Fritz? May I ask you a personal question?" I asked.

"I doubt I could stop you."

He chuckled, and I put on my serious face. "Does . . . um . . . Roger have a problem with me?"

"You mean because he thought you and Antoinette Chloe were snooping around in his apartment?"

"Well, that and other things." I was going to glide over that one. "Maybe it's because I've replaced Liz in his eyes. Could that be it?"

Wow! That was quick thinking. I was impressing myself.

Pastor Fritz shrugged. "Roger did like Liz. Maybe you hit the nail on the head."

I got to my feet and adjusted my clothes. I could feel the flash drive in my blouse, and the tape was making me itchy.

Walking to the door, I turned and said, "It's always nice talking to you, Pastor Fritz."

"You, too, Trixie."

I crutched down the hall to the Ladies' Yarn Circle and opened the door. Much to my surprise, the ladies were intent on pulling piles of pull tabs.

My surprise must have shown. They all burst out laughing.

"This is our relaxation at the end of Yarn Circle," Darlene said.

Like it was so grueling sitting in a chair and knitting or crocheting . . .

The pull tabs were flying, and a couple of people won a couple of bucks. I'd hate to tally up all the amount of money they'd spent on them.

But what I noticed the most was that the biggest stack was right in front of Darlene.

"Darlene, I'm going to lunch. Would you like me to bring you back anything?" I asked.

"I usually join Fritz upstairs for lunch. But thanks for asking me, anyway. You're not coming back, are you?"

Gee, it was so nice to be wanted.

"Of course I'm coming back. I'm working on the church bulletin, and there are auditions tonight, remember? We're running behind. We have to start practicing for the pageant or else there won't be one."

"I hear that Margie Grace is out and about," Verna, one of the knitters, said, not looking up from her pull tabs.

"I think we should be very cautious of her," said Darlene, making like she was shuddering. "She could become violent at a moment's notice."

"Do you think that she stabbed Liz?" said Inez, a sweet, grandmotherly type.

"Margie is helping me with the pageant." I didn't know why, but I felt like I had to stick up for Margie somehow with these gossips.

"Now, *that's* going to be interesting," said Darlene. "I hope that the sheriff's department is going to be on hand."

"I know that I'm just not going to talk to her or go near her," said Verna.

"That's really too bad," I said. "Margie is obviously lonely and needs friends. And you know what they say: Peace on earth, goodwill to men—and women. I have to leave now and get a breath of fresh air."

And on that note, I turned and stomped out of the room on my crutches.

Steam was coming out of my ears by the time Antoinette Chloe pulled up to the back door.

"Gossiping hens!" I said. "The nerve of them! And Darlene should know better! She represents this church just as much as Pastor Fritz does."

"What are you babbling on about?" ACB asked as she pushed my butt up the step to the passenger seat in her van. Fingers, the chef of Brown's Four Corners, must have taken another kielbasa run to Utica, because it reeked of garlic.

"It's nothing. No vampires will come near us," I said, trying to lighten my mood.

But ACB was floating around the van to the driver's side in a poinsettia-covered muumuu and a red and green plaid cape. I was talking to myself.

Finally she pulled away from the church, and I could see the Yarn Circle watching out the window.

"You know," I said, "I don't really know if Margie killed Liz or not, but I think you should be innocent until proven guilty in this country."

"Beyond a reasonable doubt *and all that jazz,*" she said, singing and snapping her fingers like a Bob Fosse dancer.

"Antoinette Chloe, focus. Please. You're driving, and it's starting to snow," I pointed out.

"We're supposed to get a blizzard either tonight or tomorrow, according to Flip a Coin."

Heather "Flip a Coin" Flipelli, the local weather girl, was wrong more times than she was right, so the nickname given to her by the locals was rather apt.

"So we just might get a dusting, or it'll be cold and clear," I said, glad that the auditions wouldn't have to be canceled.

"I brought you some pizza from the Silver Bullet, by the way. It's one of the specials for today. Cindy called it everything-but-the-kitchen-sink pizza."

"Maybe that was the garlic I smelled."

Cindy was one of my cooks and was definitely skilled in pizza making, and her cinnamon buns were to die for.

ACB pulled into the library's parking lot. It was under construction due to the major damage it incurred during a previous blizzard when the roof collapsed. We joke that Sandy Harbor loses a roof a year due to the heavy snow.

"Pull up close to the building so we can get their network," I said, picking up the black case which contained my laptop. Unzipping it, I turned it on and got it ready to connect.

Then I fished Liz's little flash drive out of my bra, peeled off the masking tape with some of my hair strands still attached, and tossed it into the litter bag that was hanging from a magnetic hook in the van.

"I can't wait to see what's on this little thing," I said, hoping to get it to work. "Then we'll do searches on some folks and see if there's any information that could help us."

I found where the drive should be inserted, and as if by magic, I could follow what to do next.

Then a list of things on the H drive appeared.

"'Buff,'" I said. "There are a lot of *Buff*s. And we're pretty sure that it stands for *Buffalo*."

"Let's see one. Pick the oldest one," ACB said, getting a pizza box and setting it on the engine cover in the middle of the van.

"Oh my! We were right!" I said, skimming the article. "It's a newspaper clipping from the *Buffalo News* about someone named Darlene Osmond who was charged with a bunch of crimes because she had stolen over eight thousand dollars over the course of five years from—*are you sitting down?*—the church bingo games!"

"Who's Darlene Osmond?" ACB asked.

"Gee, I don't know. I was so excited . . . I don't know."

ACB handed me a slice of pizza on a paper plate with a napkin, but I put it on the dash for later.

"Is she our Darlene? Darlene Robinson? I mean, Darlene is not a common name, and there isn't any picture," I said.

"Open the next file. Buff2."

I did. This time it was another article from the *Buffalo News*. "It's another article. Apparently Darlene Osmond couldn't pay the restitution of eight thousand six hundred dollars. She only paid five hundred. So she was sentenced to Bedford Hills Correctional Facility, but this time there's a picture."

"Show me!"

I turned the laptop toward her so she could see the picture.

"That's our Darlene!" we both said together.

"If she stole from the church once, she might be tempted to do it again. Don't you think?" I asked.

ACB pulled the tab off an orange soda and handed it to me. "I mean, I wouldn't do it in the first place. But who knows what lengths people will go to for their addictions."

"Me neither," I said. "But let's think about this. Darlene seemed to be trying to throw suspicion on Margie Grace to the Yarn Circle gossipers. And she seems to be addicted to pull tabs—maybe she's hoping for a big score with them and is trying to make up money that she's already stolen from bingo before anyone notices." I took a gulp of the orange soda. Thinking always makes me thirsty. "But I think Liz Fellows had already noticed. Remember when we broke into Liz's house? Remember her answering machine messages? People the church owed money to, or whom the Robinsons owed personally, were calling Liz and asking her to intervene. Darlene is probably spending the church's money on pull tabs."

"For sure, Liz noticed, too. Open Buff3, Trixie."

Setting my soda down in the cup holder, I opened Buff3. "It's a dissolution of marriage, a divorce decree—Dirk Gregory Osmond vs. Darlene Southwick Osmond. It's dated before she was even arrested."

"How did she become Darlene Robinson? Open Buff4. Hurry!"

"Buff4 is another article, again from *Buffalo News*. It's called 'The Pastor and the Felon: A Love Story for Valentine's Day.'" I took another sip of orange soda as I read the screen. "Oh my, Antoinette Chloe, I have to read you the whole thing. This is so interesting. Are you ready?"

"Yes. Read it to me!" she said, taking a bite of pizza. It had peppers, onions, sausage, mushrooms, olives, pepperoni, and two kinds of cheese.

I was hungry, but something told me that the contents of this article were much more important.

Chapter 12

The Buffalo News
Buffalo, New York

THE PASTOR AND THE FELON:
A LOVE STORY FOR VALENTINE'S DAY

Pastor Fritz Robinson and Darlene Southwick Osmond met under unusual circumstances. She was one of the parishioners who volunteered to help with bingo at the Ontario Dunes Community Church in North Buffalo, and he was the pastor of the same church.

When it was discovered by the parish council that thousands of dollars were missing from the bingo proceeds, Darlene Osmond confessed to Pastor Fritz that she was the one who was responsible for the theft over the course of several years.

Pastor Fritz encouraged Ms. Osmond to contact sheriff's deputies and confess the theft. "Pastor Fritz was with me every step of the way, and gave me the courage to do what was right," she stated. "I have a gambling problem, and I needed help acknowledging that so I could turn my life around."

The defendant claimed that pull tabs, a facsimile of a slot machine on paper, were sold during bingo, and they were too hard to resist. She said that all the money she stole went to buying the pull tabs.

Her case was adjourned several times for her to pay restitution to the church. "Unfortunately, she couldn't come up with the eight thousand dollars," Pastor Fritz said, "and she had to go to jail."

But the story doesn't end there. Pastor Fritz was a frequent visitor to the Bedford Hills Correctional Facility, and the two eventually fell in love. After her release, they married on Valentine's Day.

"There's something special about Darlene," he said. "I owe everything to her."

And that, dear readers, is what love is all about.

"Isn't that a sweet story?" ACB wiped her eyes with a napkin.

"I guess." I had to think about that one. "But I wonder what Pastor Fritz meant when he said that he owed everything to her. That's kind of strange, isn't it?"

ACB chomped down on her slice of pizza. "People say all kinds of goofy things when they're in love."

"Very true." Then I looked at the rest of the files on the flash drive. "There's a lot of Bing files. Ten of them. Wonder what that means?"

"Bing Crosby." She laughed. "As in 'White Christmas'? Just as you said before."

"Speaking of which, it looks like it's shaping up to be a whiteout right now. Was Flip a Coin right and we are going to get a blizzard?"

"I'll turn up the heat. Now open one of those Bing files."

"I'll go with Bing1." I waited. "Oh, look, it's bingo receipts for the month of January of this year for the Sandy Harbor Community Church. Then expenditures. It looks like the church is in the red, even though a lot of money was taken in. Go figure."

"Keep going. Try Bing2."

"February receipts and expenses. Still in the red. It looks like Liz made a note that the number of bingo cards that were sold doesn't agree with the earnings that were recorded," I said.

"So the amount sold doesn't agree with the money that was taken in? Huh. Looks like someone was dipping into the bingo money . . . again. My bet is that Darlene is up to her old tricks," ACB said.

Finally I took a bite of pizza. *Yum.* "I have to agree with you, Antoinette Chloe. It doesn't look good for Darlene. And it might account for those stacks of used pull tabs in the Robinsons' apartment and the stack of unpaid bills on her desk. Bingo is supposed to pay for a lot of the church's expenses."

"Skip down to Bing10. That would be the most recent one—from October."

But before I could, there was a loud knock on my window, and I jumped a foot in the air. "What on earth?"

Through the heavy snow, I saw him standing there. Ty Brisco.

"It's Ty. Shoot!" I said to ACB. Then I rolled down the window. "Ty Brisco, are you stalking us?"

He didn't answer that, but I knew he was.

He gave a sideways grin and that dimple of his made an appearance. "Why are you sitting in Antoinette Chloe's van in the parking lot of the library in a blizzard? Has your car broken down? Do you need help?"

"No. We're just eating pizza," ACB said, leaning over me. "Want a slice? It's Cindy's everything-but-the-kitchen-sink pizza."

"Don't mind if I do." He opened the back door of the van and jumped in.

I thought that ACB was just going to hand him a slice and he'd disappear so we could go back to looking at the Bing files.

ACB handed him the pizza box. "It might be cold, although I had the heater on and the box on it."

He took the box. "Who didn't touch their pizza?" He pointed to mine on the dash. "Too busy with your laptop, Trixie?"

Geez, nothing gets by him.

"Yeah, I wanted to look something up. Caribbean cruises. I'm sick and tired of this snowy weather," I lied, pointing to the flakes falling outside. I didn't think I was fooling him, though.

"And you needed to do it here? Right now? You could have done it when you got home."

"Uh, it'd be too late, as I have to head the auditions at the church tonight."

"You could have looked it up on your laptop at work," he said.

He knew that this was my laptop because of the New York Giants stickers on it along with a couple of stickers that looked like bullet holes. Ray had given me those as a joke.

I glanced at ACB and raised an eyebrow. She nodded. "Might as well give it to him, Trixie."

I might as well. I think we'd found out most of what was on Liz's flash drive, anyway.

Pulling out the little thing, I handed it to Ty. "I found this under Liz's desk this morning. It was hidden under the desk with some masking tape. The tape stuck to my hair when I was under the desk picking up something."

He held out his hand, and I placed the drive on it.

"I knew you two were up to something, and I was hoping that this would be found. Good work, Trixie, although I wish you would have given it to me right away, instead of snooping first."

"Yeah, I know."

"What's on it?" he asked.

"Articles from the *Buffalo News*. There're about Darlene going to jail for stealing bingo money," I said.

ACB popped the top on another orange soda and handed it to Ty. "And there's an article about Pastor Fritz and Darlene falling in love at Bedford Hills Correctional Facility. It's so romantic!"

"She was married before," I added. "To someone named Dirk Osmond. But she was divorced before she was convicted of the crime."

"I know," he said.

"And there are some files called Bing."

He laughed. "As in Bing Crosby?"

"That's just what I said!" ACB snorted.

I took another bite of pizza. "As in bingo. It seems that Liz might have found some discrepancies between the bingo receipts and the church's overall earnings. She'd been tracking it all year. Up until the time she died. There's no November entry."

"I'll check it all out when I get back to headquarters," he said.

"Ty, do you think this flash drive is why Liz's house was tossed?"

"Yep. I think that's a good guess."

ACB sighed. "Darlene Robinson needs a good swift kick in the butt from the Ghost of Christmas Past and the Ghost of Christmas Presents. And, since I'm the Ghost of Christmas Presents, she won't be getting any presents from Santa or me."

"Ladies, you can't let on that she's a suspect. You need to carry on like nothing has happened. I can't prove that Darlene killed Liz. I can't prove that anyone killed Liz yet."

ACB shrugged. "But the money that's missing from bingo—"

"That's theft, not murder," he said. "It proves nothing."

"If you ask me, it all adds up," I said. "But then I'm the one who was convinced that Margie Grace killed Liz. Now I don't think so."

"Does Margie Grace work bingo here?" Ty asked.

"I don't know," I said, "but Antoinette Chloe and I plan on attending the next bingo. I'd rather drag a loaded sleigh up Mount Crumpit, but I will be playing bingo, as I observe."

"Maybe I'll do the same," Ty said. "And I'll bring the rest of the deputies."

"You mean you aren't going to tell us to stay away?" I asked, amazed.

"Would it do any good?" he asked.

"Nope," I said.

"Then I'm going to save my breath. But don't you let me catch you doing anything illegal or you know what I'll have to do."

"Coal in our stockings?" ACB asked.

"The electric chair," he deadpanned.

On that somber note, Ty took what was left of his pizza and his orange soda and went back to his car.

"We had to give it to him," I said out loud.

"Of course," ACB said. "But I still would have liked to look at the October files."

"It was probably more of the same as the rest of the Bings."

"Now what?" she asked.

I slapped my forehead. "I could have downloaded or uploaded the flash drive to my laptop."

ACB let out a breath. "We're lucky that you did as much as you did before Ty came."

That was my friend—always donning her gay apparel (or should I say donning her bright and shiny muu-muus?) and looking for the bright side.

I had to remember what Ty told me. Not to let on that anything was wrong, and I reminded myself of that when I crutched back to the office.

Darlene was in the office, at her desk, busily working on her laptop.

"Hi, Trixie. Did you have a good lunch?"

"I did. But we had to cut it short due to the weather."

"I hope the snow stops or we'll have to cancel auditions tonight."

"That'll put us even further behind," I said. "But I wouldn't want anyone getting hurt if this keeps up."

There was silence between us. I took off my one boot and coat and hung it up.

"Um . . . uh . . ."

"Yes, Darlene?"

"I . . . uh . . . just want to apologize for saying all of those uncharitable things about Margie Grace earlier. It wasn't nice of me at all," she said.

"You don't owe me an apology, Darlene, but maybe you can make it up to Margie by seeking her out and talking to her on occasion."

"That's a good idea. I'll talk to her tomorrow night at bingo," Darlene said.

"Is she a volunteer?" I asked.

"She is. She sells the bingo cards at the front desk."

Uh-oh . . . Margie touches money, but would she steal it? Maybe Liz had been watching Margie?

Interesting . . .

"Is there anything I can help you with, Darlene?"

"No. It would take too long to show you, and you'll be leaving us soon."

"So, you're not going to show me what you and Liz were working on? Getting all the handwritten ledgers on the computer?" I looked around. "Where are they all anyway?"

She looked very uncomfortable, but she answered me anyway. "I think they're in Fritz's office. He was doing something with them."

"I see. Well, then I'll just work on the church bulletin," I said. "It'll be pretty plain because I'm not able to do anything very fancy, but I do know how to insert pictures."

"That'll be fine, Trixie," she said. "Oh, here are some more announcements."

Darlene pushed away from her desk, but in her haste to get up, she dropped several papers, and they flew all over. Scrambling, she picked them up.

When she finally handed them to me, she looked like she was about to burst into tears.

I took her hand. "What on earth is wrong, Darlene? Can I help?"

She let out a stifled sob, and her shoulders started shaking. I stood and hugged her close. "It can't be all that bad, Darlene. It's Christmas. Miracles happen."

"I need a miracle, Trixie. I really do." She composed herself and pushed away from me gently. "I'm sorry to bother you."

"It's no bother. No bother at all. Please let me know if there's anything I can do to help you."

"No one can help me." She pulled out some tissues from a box on her desk. "I'm sorry, but I'm going upstairs. See you tonight, maybe."

"Sure. And if you need a shoulder . . ." I began.

But she was already gone.

* * *

The blizzard subsided and the auditions went on.

"Next up are Joey Faber and his twin brother, Joel Faber," I announced. "They both want to be twin Cats in the Hat, but we are not going to have Cats in the Hat in the pageant. Would Joey and Joel's parents like to choose another role for them from the list I've prepared?" I said loudly.

"Well, I never heard of such a thing. No Cat in the Hat twins at a Christmas pageant?" said a woman with an electronic cigarette in her mouth. She must be Mrs. Faber.

"They either pick something on the list, or they won't be eligible to participate," I said, using my no-nonsense voice. Then, I turned to the crowd of people sitting in the pews and milling about the aisles. "Everyone, please listen up . . . the parts that are available are on the list that I've prepared. Please see Antoinette Chloe for the list. Try out for one of those parts and you are in!"

"And no whining if a part's already been taken by someone else," ACB added. "It's Christmas."

"Nice touch," I said.

Margie Grace had gathered all the parents who wanted to be in the adult choir and took them in another room to practice their singing. ACB told me that she appointed Mr. Cam Pulaski to be the choir director. Cam was a music teacher at the high school.

"Brilliant," I said. "Now she can help with the children's choir, too."

"She's on it," ACB reported.

Then we got one adult to volunteer for each of the ten scenes that were in the pageant. That adult would oversee the players and make sure that the scene was polished and ready to be performed for dress rehearsal.

"Delegation," I said to ACB. "It's the key to my survival."

"Don't forget to enlist some help for putting up the scenery. You probably should ask Roger Southwick to chair that since he's in charge of church maintenance," ACB said. "And he's sitting all alone in the second pew. I triple dog dare you!"

There was a glaring breach of etiquette when ACB skipped over the double dog dare and went right to the triple.

"Oh, all right!"

So over I went to Roger. He watched me coming, and couldn't be bothered to meet me halfway or acknowledge me until I was standing right in front of him.

"Roger, would you mind accepting the chairperson job on the scenery committee? You are here and know where everything is. You're perfect for the job."

He shrugged. "Guess so."

"Thank you so much. If you'd like to gather some men or women from the pews here, you could go to a corner somewhere and meet with them."

"I'll do that," he said like a sullen teenager who was just asked to clean their room for the hundredth time.

"And, Roger?"

"Yeah?"

"Merry Christmas."

"Yeah. Whatever."

Margie, ACB, and I cast the Grinch scene—the one where he's stealing everything from the Whos. The 911 operator, Fanny Fowler, was going to be Cindy Lou Who. And the children's choir was going to sing the theme song.

We also cast the *A Christmas Story* scene—the Red Ryder BB gun scene.

And more of the same followed.

ACB, as the Ghost of Christmas Presents, and I, as Tiny Tim, were going to do the scene where the Ghost takes Scrooge to Bob Cratchit's house to watch them have a meal and toast him. Scrooge would be played by Ty. The Cratchits would be played by my mother and father.

The Boca Babes were going to be Santa's reindeer. Bob was a definite for Santa Claus. And Aunt Stella was a definite for Mrs. Claus.

My waitresses insisted on a choir of their own, which was fine with me.

"Is there anyone left who doesn't have a part in this play?" I asked loudly. "Speak now."

The two boys whose mothers were fighting because they always played the part of a camel—front and back— were left. I decided to get them into the light. One was going to play a Who from Whoville. The other was going to be one of the Cratchit kids.

At last count, I thought Bob Cratchit had a brood of twenty kids.

I had everyone covered! I was done.

"Dinner will be served in the community room," I announced. "Please adjourn there and help yourself to some food. Rehearsals will begin before bingo with each group rehearsing on their own for now."

* * *

By the time I got home, I was pooped. Information was whirling around in my brain like a tornado. All I wanted to do was sit in my recliner and not think about anything for a little while.

As we drove down Route 3, I let out a yell of awe when my house came into sight.

"Look at the Big House!"

It was beautiful. The eaves of the huge farmhouse were outlined with white icicle lights and lights of every color outlined the windows. The pines and shrubs also had lights, and lighting up both sides of the sidewalk up to the door were red-and-white candy canes.

"It's so pretty!"

The inside was exquisite, with more lights and decorations, but the tree was the most amazing. Colored lights twinkled, and a hand-painted manger set was under the tree. The tree had Polish glass ornaments sparkling from most every branch, courtesy of Aunt Stella, and glass candy canes were scattered on the tree.

I sat down and just stared at the tree, trying to take everything in.

I smiled, trying to offload all thoughts of Liz's murder and replace them with Christmas magic, like the scent of pine emanating from a beautifully decorated tree and the glow of lights.

"Antoinette Chloe, will you drive me to the Silver Bullet? I haven't seen the decorations there yet. Besides, I'm in the mood for a roast beef club sandwich."

"Sounds good to me!"

I hobbled down the stairs and the walkway and back

into her van for the short drive up to the diner. I loved how each window was decorated with multicolored twinkle lights and how the candy cane theme from the Big House was continued there as well. There was a sign that read, SANTA, PLEASE STOP HERE! and big plastic ornaments hung from various pine trees, which were bright with white lights.

It was just beautiful.

Everyone shouted my name as I entered, and I stopped at every booth and table to greet people. Then I went into the kitchen to see Cindy. She gave me a big hug, ever careful of my crutches.

Then Antoinette Chloe and I took a booth in the back. When Bettylou came over, we ordered two roast beef clubs and two cups of split pea soup, hot tea, and two cherry hand pies.

"I love the tree in here, too." The overhead lights were dimmer than usual, and diners ate under the glow of all the colored lights and the tree.

Brilliant.

But it was time to get back to business—the business of Liz's murder.

"Antoinette Chloe, got any idea how we can get Pastor Fritz out of his parlor, so I can see what files Darlene might have put in there?"

"Of course. I'll have a spiritual crisis, and ask him to meet me somewhere. Maybe here at the diner or in my restaurant," she said.

"What spiritual crisis?" I couldn't wait to hear this.

"Hmm . . . I think I'll tell him that I stole eight thousand bucks from . . . I don't know . . . a store's cash register when the cashier wasn't looking, and I don't know how to put it back."

"Brilliant," I said. "He can counsel you just like he did Darlene before he married her. Or he might tell you to go to St. Luke's—your church!"

She giggled. "When do you want to break in?"

"As soon as possible."

"I'm going to have my crisis tomorrow, then. Any particular time?"

"I think Darlene has her gossipy Yarn Circle tomorrow again. About nine-ish should work, but I'll call you for sure. The Yarn Circle is all morning long. She's in the front of the building, so she might not know if I'm in the pastor's parlor. I'll keep the lights off."

"What about Roger, our not-friendly maintenance man? He's all over the place, isn't he? I don't want him to see you. I think he's creepy with a side of dangerous."

"Yeah, I know, and he already caught us once." I shrugged. "It doesn't seem like he believed we were leaving at the time. He talked to Ty and blew us in. I'm just glad I slid down the stairs. I probably wiped away our tracks. But we'll have to get him out of the way, too, somehow, for this to work."

We made small talk, mostly discussing the beautiful decorations, talking about plans for the holidays, and we giggled like high schoolers about my going to the Law Enforcement Ball with Ty.

The pea soup was divine and the club sandwiches were loaded and nicely displayed with homemade potato chips and fancy-cut garnishes like radish roses, zigzags of carrots, spiral twists of cucumbers, and slices of tomatoes.

We lingered over tea and Sara Stolfus's cherry hand pies, and then we both started yawning.

"Let's hit the road, Trixie. We have a big day tomorrow," ACB said. "And we'll need all our energy if we're going to successfully pull this off and stay out of jail."

Back at the Big House, I heard a lot of noise coming from the dining room. "Sounds like the Boca Babes are having another pinochle and highball tournament. Boy, can they get loud."

"Do you want me to help you upstairs to your bedroom, Trixie?" ACB asked. "You'll never sleep down here with that racket."

"If you wouldn't mind. Oh, and my folks are having a late dinner at the Silver Bullet with some friends. They'll go right to their motor home, so we can lock up."

I had never locked my doors, but since Liz's death, I had every night.

I meandered to the stairs and hoisted my cast up every step. At the landing midpoint, I had to catch my breath. "My New Year's resolution is to lose weight and get in shape."

Antoinette Chloe rolled her eyes. "It's an annual thing, isn't it?"

"Yep."

"What are you going to wear to the Law Enforcement Ball?" she asked.

"No idea. I liked that brown sparkly dress of Aunt Stella's that I wore to the Miss Salmon Contest."

"He's seen it. Let's figure something else out. You need a sparkly red dress or maybe a royal blue. No, definitely red. You need red with your coloring. I'll see what

I can find," ACB said. "Oh, and by the way, I'll be going, too."

"What? Really?" I asked, thrilled that I'd know someone besides Ty. "Why didn't you tell me?"

"I didn't want to spoil your thunder, but Judge Glennie asked me to be his date."

We both did a high five, and I returned to climbing the stairs.

As I crutched to my room, I noticed that the upstairs smelled like perfume and powder. Lots of perfume and powder. I think it was time to crack the windows open a bit or maybe let the ceiling fans do their thing.

"Um . . . Little Red Riding Hood, looks like someone has been sleeping in my bed. And their stuff is in my room," I said.

"Oh, I forgot! it's Hattie McDougal. I didn't think you'd ever want to climb the stairs," ACB said. "So I said she could sleep in your room."

"But you kept asking me if I wanted to use *my* bedroom!"

Calm down, Trixie. It's not the end of the world. Let Hattie have the room.

I didn't know who was whispering in my ear. Maybe it was Clarence, the angel from *It's a Wonderful Life*, who was trying to get his wings. Either way, I was thankful for it.

"Hattie can have the room," I said. "I'll go back downstairs. It's not a problem. Just let me get some more clothes while I'm up here."

I found a tote bag and stuffed it full of the things I needed or wanted.

"I'm awful sorry, Trixie. With everything going on, I just plumb forgot all about it."

"It's no problem. Really. Plus, on the bright side, it'll be nice to sleep by the Christmas tree."

I went back downstairs, feeling like I was going to have a blue, blue, blue Christmas without my bed, bedroom, and my pillows.

I didn't know how long the Boca Babes were staying, but I'd heard they were spending Christmas there, and maybe even the first couple of weeks in January.

I was just cranky and tired of my cast and crutches. But I was grateful that everyone was there to help me. Letting Hattie use my bedroom was a small price to pay. The recliner *was* really comfortable, and now I could look at my Christmas tree as I drifted off to sleep.

Nice.

I tossed the tote bag downstairs, so I could concentrate on the stairs. When I got to where I'd tossed the bag, I picked it up and crutched to the laundry room. I noticed that the laundry had been done, and my things were piled neatly in a laundry basket.

Tears stung my eyes. I was mortified that I'd even thought about kicking Hattie out of my room.

I felt a hand on my back, and I jumped, having thought that I was alone.

"What's wrong, Trixie?" Aunt Stella said.

I shrugged, wiping my eyes on my blouse. "Just tired. It's been a long day. My brain is on overload. I'm tired of this cast and not being able to do much. Ty asked me to his Law Enforcement Ball, and I don't want to go in this cast. And I need something to wear."

I took a deep breath. Where had all this come from?

"But, Aunt Stella, I'm so very grateful for all the help, and the beautiful decorations, and it's great to see my parents again, and . . . and . . . I love you all."

She put her arm around me. "But you wanted to decorate yourself because you love Christmas and always have. I remember when you were young, Trixie. From after Thanksgiving dinner until midnight on Christmas, you embraced all the magic that Christmas has to offer. It's like that time recharged you for the whole year."

I sniffed. "Yes, and I haven't been able to do my own traditions and all of the Christmas rituals that I love."

"What's stopping you?" she asked. "Certainly not a broken leg."

"I've been kind of busy, Aunt Stella."

"So? Make the time to do what you like to do. Everyone's busy at Christmas."

How could I tell her that I had a murder to solve first?

She walked me to the front room, had me sit in the recliner, and tucked the afghan around me. "Get some rest, sweetie. I'll leave the tree on for you, and I'll tell the Babes to keep the noise down." She moved my bangs from my forehead and gave me a kiss. "See you tomorrow."

"Thanks, Aunt Stella."

The magic. I had to find the magic again, and I would. Right after I solved Liz's murder.

And I felt that I was close to doing so.

Very close.

Chapter 13

It was the day to search Pastor Robinson's office.

Gee, I hoped it worked.

If all the conditions were perfect, I'd be able to see what Darlene had hidden—like the contents to all of those empty files.

I'd found the key to Pastor Fritz's office earlier in Darlene's key drawer with the others. It wasn't hard because it was marked PARLOR, and I'd taken it home one night and ACB had made a duplicate at the hardware store, and I'd replaced the real key along with the keys to the upstairs.

The phone rang, and I answered it. It was Antoinette Chloe, right on time. Nine thirty.

My friend was never on time for anything, ever—with the exception of this cloak-and-dagger kind of stuff.

Or should I say parka-and-butcher-knife kind of stuff?

"Ready?" she asked.

"As I'll ever be."

"Are you at the Salmon River Bridge?" I asked.

"Yeah, and it's freezing out here."

"Remember how we rehearsed it?" I asked.

"Yes. I'm basically Jimmy Stewart, and everything in my life is going wrong. I lost my husband, Sal. My boyfriend, Nick. And now that it's Christmas, I'm depressed. I am alone in life and am very attracted to Roger, but he's not paying attention to me. I am going to jump, but I'd like to tell Roger that I love him before I do. Also, I'd like to speak with Pastor Robinson to confess my sins. I want them both to come before I end it all."

"Most excellent," I said. This was the best scenario yet.

"Is Clarence, the angel earning his wings, going to appear on the bridge and show me how life would have been in Sandy Harbor without me, like in *It's a Wonderful Life*?"

"No, girlfriend. That only happens in the movies."

"Darn it."

"Ready? I'm going to turn into Donna Reed now," I said.

"Hurry already. I'm freezing."

"Oh, no!" I screamed. "Antoinette Chloe, don't do it. Please, please don't do it. I'll get him. I'll get Pastor Fritz!"

I didn't have to go far down the hall because his head appeared out of his door, and he'd met me halfway.

"Pastor Fritz, please help my friend. Antoinette Chloe is going to jump off the bridge because she's despondent over Roger. She loves him, and he doesn't notice her."

"Roger? Roger Southwick?" he asked, brows furrowed.

Roger must have heard his name, as he appeared and hurried toward us.

"Oh, please go! Go now. There's no time. She's going to jump off the Salmon River Bridge." I made like I was going to faint.

They stood still, probably in shock.

"Go! Antoinette Chloe loves you, Roger. You can save her. You both can. Hurry!"

I could only hope that Pastor Fritz didn't have time to hide his things in his office.

"My coat is in my office," he said. "I'll be right back."

Luckily Roger had his coat on already. He looked puzzled. "Who are you talking about?"

"Antoinette Chloe Brown! Muumuus and flip-flops. Big hair. Fascinator on the side of her head."

"Fascinator?"

"Hat. She's partial to plastic peacocks."

"Oh, yes. I know her."

I passed the rest of the time with Roger with my hands over my face and my crutches under my arms, making like I was crying.

It didn't take Pastor Fritz long to get his coat, but he did lock the door behind him.

No problem.

Finally the two of them raced out of the building.

Yee-haw.

I went back to the office to make sure I saw them both leave toward the Salmon River Bridge. Then I called ACB, the frozen.

"The elves have left the workshop," I said.

"Gotcha. I am ready for my close-up, Mr. Capra."

Three minutes later, I was unlocking the door to Pastor Fritz's parlor, and I pulled the café curtains shut as he often did.

His desk had two of those huge ledger books on it,

both opened. I looked at what he'd been working on, compared the two books, then looked again.

He was "cooking the books," as they say on television. I didn't know much about things like that, but the book on the left was in the red, and the book on the right, had some of the same entries, but in different amounts. That book was in the black.

Interesting.

I opened up the drawers of his desk. Used pull tabs. More used pull tabs. I went over to the side storage room and lifted the lids on a couple of the boxes that I'd seen before. The boxes had been unopened. Now they were opened, and they were full of—wait for it—used pull tabs.

Darlene had confessed to pull tab gambling before, stealing money to feed her habit, and had gone to state prison. History was repeating itself.

He must be hiding the evidence of Darlene's addiction right there in his office, I thought. I assumed he was going to tape the boxes shut and dispose of them somehow.

If Pastor Fritz was cooking the books for the parish council's audit, it must mean that Darlene was up to her old tricks, and he was trying to protect her.

And he must be dumping the boxes of used pull tabs somewhere, so Roger wouldn't have to do it and get suspicious that his sister was committing the same crime as she had in the Buffalo parish when she ran bingo.

I couldn't wait to snoop at the next bingo night.

I crutched out of the parlor, pausing along the way to look through the window at the ladies of the Yarn Circle.

Their needles were working their magic and their tongues were wagging.

Darlene saw me watching and motioned for me to come in.

"Hello, ladies," I said. "How's everything going?"

There were nods and a chorus of *good* and *okay*, and I even got a couple of *Merry Christmas*es.

Maybe they weren't the gossips I thought they were.

"The Ladies' Yarn Circle would like to donate hats and mittens to some of our needier children," Darlene said. "I have a list from teachers at Sandy Harbor Grammar School. The teachers have noticed that some of the kids come to school without mittens and hats. We are going to wrap them, put names on them, and Santa will pass them out on Christmas Eve."

"That's a lovely gesture, ladies, but with all due respect, that'll probably hurt the 'needier children' instead of helping them."

Someone grunted. "How so?"

This was bringing back sad memories of fourth grade.

"The kids who get your gifts will be mortified and embarrassed because they'll be singled out."

"Oh, I hadn't thought of that," a knitter said. "Maybe you're right."

"This happened to one of my friends in fourth grade. She was singled out because she didn't have a good winter coat and boots. Sister Mary Mary generously presented them to her, from a mother whose daughter had outgrown them. My friend Debbie just about died of shame. We all knew that the coat came from Patty O'Brien because of the fake fur around the collar and cuffs. Patty was one of the more popular girls in school, and her parents had a lot of money. And when it got around that Debbie was given Patty's coat and boots, the kids in my school either kept bringing her things out of the goodness of their hearts, or they teased her for being poor and wearing other kids' clothes."

"I understand now," Darlene said. "I'm so glad we talked to you about this, Trixie. We want to help, not hurt."

"It's a great idea, but I think you'll have to give hats and mittens to *every* kid in that grammar school, or if you don't have enough inventory, pick a grade with the greatest need, and give to everyone in that grade."

"Excellent idea, Trixie," Darlene said. "We'll do that."

She looked so happy to be doing a good deed. It was hard to believe that she was my number one suspect.

"Trixie, can you talk right now?" It was Antoinette Chloe.

"I've been waiting for your call. How did the bridge drama go? Do you think they bought it?"

"Hook, line, and sinker. Roger even asked me to have lunch with him sometime, and Pastor Fritz wants me to leave St. Luke's and join him at the Community Church. But I told him I won't do that because my Italian Roman Catholic ancestors would haunt me."

"I'll tell you what I found out when you pick me up."

"Be there at four o'clock."

"Make it three. I want to have time to freshen up before bingo tonight. Oh, and I have tomorrow off. I have to go to the doctor's in Syracuse for my checkup. Can you drive me?"

"Sure can."

At three o'clock, ACB and I were headed back home. I filled her in on the double set of books and the boxes of used pull tabs that used to be new and unopened.

"Darlene must have callouses on her hands from pulling all those tabs. Maybe we can see what's going on at bingo tonight, and finally get to the bottom of Liz's murder," I said.

"I hope so, too, Trixie."

To me, bingo was like watching grass grow, but I passed the time watching Pastor Fritz, Darlene, and Roger flitting about. I also watched Margie Grace for a while, but she was very particular counting out cards, logging in what she'd sold, and making change for patrons.

Every so often, Roger would make a trip around the room. He'd pick up cash boxes from Margie, from the ladies selling pizza, donuts, and drinks, and from Darlene and her crew, who were circulating and selling pull tabs at the cost of a dollar each or six for five dollars, which I still thought was pretty steep.

He'd exchange a full box with another, which I was assuming was empty. Then he'd do it again and again. I wondered where he was taking all the money when he disappeared for a while—maybe his own apartment or another room in the complex. But he always looked over his shoulder and made sure no one was following him when he had the full cash boxes.

Were Darlene and Roger working together to steal the church's money?

Pastor Fritz was calling the numbers and making

jokes. Periodically he'd announce that the pull tabs were for sale and would ask that everyone, "Please support our church."

Antoinette Chloe nudged my arm. "Every time he says that, I keep thinking about all the bags of used pull tabs in their apartment. Do you think they could possibly be from bingo nights, and not Darlene?"

"No way. Roger keeps clearing piles of them off the tables and scooping them into a trash can along with used bingo cards and other paper trash. Then I see him tying up the plastic bags. The bags we saw were loaded with used pull tabs and only used pull tabs—there was no other paper. I wonder where Roger takes the plastic bags. Probably the Dumpster."

"I'll follow him and see what he does," she said, standing and smoothing down her magnolia-covered muumuu. She pushed up her fascinator, which displayed a snowman with a cardinal on its black top hat and white feathers. The snowman looked like it was doing a belly flop off her ear. "Remember, I'm supposed to be in love with him. I might as well keep the ruse going."

I listened to Pastor Fritz's corny jokes until I was ready to scream and listened to the bingo chatter around me. If I had convinced my mother, Aunt Stella, Juanita, and the Babes to come, it would have been more fun, but they all had things they were doing tonight.

The men were heading to Ty's apartment for Texas Hold'em poker along with Bob, Ray, Clyde, and Max.

And here I was, barely watching my bingo cards.

"You have bingo, Trixie. Yell it!" ACB said, returning.

"I do?"

"Yes! Bingo! Bingo!" ACB yelled. "Trixie has it."

Margie Grace came over and called back the numbers.

"We have a winner," said Pastor Fritz. "Pay Trixie twenty-five dollars, unless she'd like it in pull tabs."

"No. I'd like the cash, please." I knew just the people I'd like to give the money to, and much, much more. And I was going to stop there tomorrow on my way back from the doctor.

After we moved on to the next game, I whispered to ACB, "What did you find out?"

"Roger takes all the bingo trash out to the Dumpster. In fact, he said all trash goes out there."

"Must be that he never visits the Robinsons' apartment."

ACB shrugged. "And maybe Pastor Fritz takes the pull tab trash out to the Dumpster at night because he doesn't want Roger to know of Darlene's habit. Or he drives it to a paper recycling place."

"Poor Pastor Fritz is doing a lot of extra work to cover up for Darlene. I feel so bad for him," I said.

"Yeah, me, too," ACB said. "He must be exhausted."

"And Liz Fellows knew exactly what was going on, too. I'm starting to think Darlene had a very good reason for keeping her quiet."

I shuddered at the thought. Looked like Darlene just moved up to suspect number one on my list.

We drove to Syracuse bright and early the next morning.

"I think we can take this cast off after the first of the year," said Dr. Fanning. "You're healing very nicely. Are you keeping it elevated at night?"

"I've been sleeping in a recliner since Thanksgiving. Every night."

"It's done wonders."

"Really?" And here I was cranky at Hattie for being in my room. Actually she was doing me a favor. At this rate, I'd have the cast off before the Law Enforcement Ball!

"I still want you to sit as much as you possibly can, and keep it elevated."

"Will do." I would've done just about anything to have that cast off faster.

After the visit, I asked Antoinette Chloe to stop at a grocery store. "I'm shopping for the people under the highway bridge."

"Excellent idea! I will, too!" she said.

We filled her van with staples and a lot of canned goods, plus fruit, veggies, and Christmas cookies, bread, chocolate, and fruitcake. We added cereal and oatmeal and juice boxes for the kids. And we cleaned the store out of rotisserie chicken, baked ziti, ham salad, and chef salad.

We parked in front of the Ride 'Em Cowboy Saloon as we had before and waited. Soon our old friends Jud and Dan walked over.

"Ladies, you returned," said Jud.

"I said we would," I told him. "And we have a car full of wonderful things. Can we drive over to the bridge and drop it off?"

"Let me tell everyone that you are friends, not foes," said Dan. "When I give you the signal, come on over."

A short time later, Dan waved to us and we drove over. My heart broke for the people living under the bridge. As we unloaded, their gratitude was overwhelming, the hugs and handshakes were plentiful, and there were tears frozen on cold cheeks.

Both ACB and I passed out our business cards, and invited anyone who could use a free hot meal in Sandy Harbor to come on up.

Then we handed Dan and Jud a pile of cash so they could get what else the people needed for Christmas.

As we drove home, I felt the magic of Christmas glowing bright inside me.

Finally.

When we got home, the ladies were having tea and Christmas cookies at the kitchen table.

"She's here," I heard my mother say. "This is going to be great!"

"What's going on?" I asked, turning to ACB.

"You'll see."

Pretty packages wrapped in Christmas paper appeared on the table.

"It's a surprise party for you, Trixie," my mother said.

"Me? What on earth for?"

"Because you need a little Christmas spirit, right this very minute! Because you love Christmas so much and because we wanted to. So these are some pre-Christmas presents for you," Aunt Stella said. "Now sit down, put your foot up, and open the big one."

I enjoyed looking at the paper and the pretty silver bow, and then I tore the paper and tossed it on the ground as my father had us do every Christmas. It's a great tradition.

Our rug was always covered with colorful paper and bows on Christmas morning, like a big mosaic, until my mother made us clean it up.

I opened the box and parted the white paper with glitter on it.

"Oh my. It's beautiful!" It was a fabulous red-and-gold dress. The bodice was awash with gold and red sequins. But I wanted to see more! "Can someone hold this up for me?"

The rest of the dress draped into pretty folds and it was floor-length.

"Oh, Mom! I love it!"

"And, Trixie, I am an outstanding seamstress and used to work in the Garment District in New York City, so I can make any alterations you may need," said Frieda, one of the Boca Babes.

"Open the smaller ones," said Aunt Stella.

I opened a small green package that contained beautiful earrings that looked like diamond-encrusted snowflakes. "Oh, no! I couldn't!" I protested.

"You most certainly can," Aunt Stella said.

"If you insist . . ."

"This is for you, too, Trixie," Aunt Stella said, handing me a big box.

I tore open the beautiful paper. "A new Lenox crystal bowl. Thank you!"

"One more thing," ACB said. She pulled out a mug from behind her muumuu. "Look what I found online!"

It was the Santa Claus cocoa mug that my grandmother had given me years ago—the one that I broke when I fell.

"Oh, Antoinette Chloe!" That was the sweet white icing on the cupcake of my day. I was going to cry. "All of you are just wonderful. Thank you for helping me, and thank you for just being here."

"Don't cry, sweetie. Try on the dress," said my mother.

ACB got up with me, picked up the box, and we both went into the laundry room.

"I pray it fits," I said.

It did, and I loved it. I loved the way it draped from the bodice, the way it glittered, and the way it made me feel so special.

All I needed now was a pair of glass slippers!

Ty's parents arrived at Syracuse's Hancock International Airport in the late afternoon two days later.

Ty brought them immediately to pageant rehearsal so they could meet everyone and have something to eat.

I met them in the community room, where dining was under way. I had just walked into the room and deposited my notebook and a pen at a table, so I could make some notes on the pageant.

Ty's father, Justin Brisco, was an older version of Ty. His handshake was warm, friendly, and so enthusiastic that it rattled my teeth.

"When we used to rent a cottage here, I remember you running around in a purple bathing suit, playing in the sand for hours, and bobbing on the waves in a pink tube."

"I still do those things, pink tube and all."

He threw his head back and laughed. I wished that Ty would do that more, but he was always so serious.

His mother, Marylou, was tall, dark-haired, and looked like a model. Her smile lit up her face, especially when she looked at her son and husband, and her sense of humor had everyone laughing.

I remembered when Ty and I had shared a polka at my first summer Dancefest on the big deck by the Silver Bullet. He'd saved me from a world of embarrassment.

I was shocked that Ty could do the polka. He'd said that his mother taught him, and that her maiden name was Karpinski.

Ty was Polish on his mother's side, and I thought he'd said that his father's ancestors were from England.

That made Ty a Polish and British cowboy from Houston.

Hmm . . . fish and chips, pierogi, and chili.

Those would be my next specials at the diner in honor of Justin and Marylou Brisco.

I'd let Juanita, Cindy, and Bob know.

"Trixie, is there anything we can do for the pageant?" Marylou asked. "We've both done a little community theater."

"Professionals? Wow! I am sure there is." I raised my hands and crossed my fingers. "Can you sing or play the piano?"

"Justin is an outstanding pianist. I can sing a bit."

"She sings like an angel," Justin said, putting his arm around Marylou's slim waist.

With that tiny waist, she must have a black belt in Pilates!

"Then it's really fortunate for us that you're visiting. Our pianist, poor Mrs. Stump, has developed shingles.

I have sheet music somewhere. I'll find it and give it to you, Mr. Brisco."

"Justin. Please call me Justin." He had a smile just like Ty's, or vice versa, and he had the same little dimple on his right cheek.

Ty walked over. "Can I steal my parents away? I want them to meet Aunt Stella and Bob and your parents, too."

He nodded in the direction of where everyone was sitting. But it was Aunt Stella and Bob that I noticed first. They were sitting side by side at a back table not far from us. And, if I could believe my eyes, they were holding hands.

Holding hands?

When the Briscos approached, they dropped hands. My father and Bob stood, like the gentlemen they were, and three chairs were pulled out for them to sit.

Justin and Marylou sat down after Ty introduced them and the laughter and joking began as if the Briscos were long-lost friends.

That's what I liked about my family. No one was a stranger.

Ty said good-bye to them and walked toward me. He had a purposeful gait, combined with a bit of a swagger. His cowboy boots thumped on the floor and he wore a white Stetson hat (white, because he was a good guy). He sported a green and red long-sleeved shirt that had tiny gold threads woven into it. The Christmasy-looking shirt was tucked into a pair of dark blue jeans with a black belt, the buckle of which took up the same square footage as a toboggan.

Not that I noticed.

"Trixie, can I get you something to eat?" he asked.

"I'd love some chicken and biscuits. And a cola."

"You got it."

I caught his scent—pine and leather—over the chicken and biscuits that Bob and Juanita had made. The Boca Babes had made the salads with Aunt Stella, my mother, and ACB.

Darlene and Roger were eating together. It looked like they were having a serious, very secret discussion. I wondered what was up. It still tweaked me that they might be in cahoots together.

Ever since Darlene had had the mini-meltdown in the office, she'd made herself scarce. I'd often seen her eyes pink and puffy as if she'd been crying, but I'd stopped asking if I could help because whenever I did, it brought on a fresh batch of tears.

Ty came with the food and drinks on an orange plastic tray and sat down across from me.

I was surprised that he didn't want to eat with his parents, since they'd just arrived.

Something must be bothering him.

"What's on your mind, Ty?" I asked.

"Let's talk." He stabbed a piece of lettuce and swung his fork around in a tiny circle. "Tell me what you've been up to and why."

Okay, so I told him about how ACB had faked a jump on the Salmon River Bridge to get Pastor Fritz out of his office. I told him about how I'd found two sets of books and more boxes of used pull tabs. I even told him that we found out that Roger took all the bingo trash to the Dumpster, so the other pull tab trash was personal.

I asked Ty if he knew who had the pull tab habit.

Instead of answering, he asked me if *I* knew.

"Ty, do you suddenly have a policy of our working together on this?"

"I do not." He shook his head. "You're a civilian."

"So it'll be always a one-way conversation?"

"Yeah." He shrugged. "So, who?"

"I'd bet on Darlene. She has a past record of thievery. If anything, I think that Pastor Fritz is covering up her stealing by making up another set of books. Books that Liz was supposed to be computerizing. I think it's safe to assume that Liz probably confronted Darlene about it, and Darlene—who didn't want another scandal—killed Liz to shut her up."

He rubbed his forehead. I knew what he was thinking. How would he prove that Darlene had done it?

"Ty, put pressure on Darlene. She seems ready to snap anyway. Something's bothering her. She's been crying. Maybe she's just an emotional mess because she's overcome with the guilt of killing Liz." I took a sip of cola. "I also think you should check out if Roger has anything new to say. He's here for some reason, unless he really needs a job. And why is Roger the one collecting all the bingo money and all the church collection money? Doesn't he trust his sister? Or, more likely, they might be working together."

"All good questions. Thanks for the talk, Trixie. Gotta go."

He turned to walk away and gave me a smirk over his shoulder. "Oh, Trixie? It's standard operating procedure with suicide attempts to send the individual for a mental health evaluation. Ask Antoinette Chloe if she'd like me to make an appointment for her with a mental health professional, and let me know."

"I'll be sure to ask her."

Not!

Chapter 14

Time zoomed by in a frenzy of catering and mass consumption of Christmas cookies and cocoa.

I did a lot of catalog shopping since I couldn't get around, and spent a lot of days watching rehearsals at the community church.

Speaking of Christmas gifts, I couldn't wait to see the expressions on the Babes' faces when they saw the pink and white bowling type shirts that I had embroidered for them at the Sandy Harbor Stitchery. Their first names are on the pockets and "Busy Boca Babe" is across the back in black. I knew they'd love them, but I owed the Babes more than just fun shirts.

I also decided that Bob was finally a part of the Silver Bullet staff, so I ordered chef pants with air planes on them and his own white chef's coat. I hoped that he'd stick around, but I had a feeling that he would be headed for Boca with Aunt Stella.

The first dress rehearsal for the first half of the pageant was a major disaster with a couple of exceptions. The Busy Boca Babes did an excellent kick line as Santa's Reindeer.

Marylou did sing like an angel. Justin was an incredible pianist, and he developed a sound track for each "scene," if needed.

My part as Tiny Tim, with Ty as Scrooge, and my parents as the Cratchits, went well. I had the famous line, "God bless us, everyone," which always makes people happy and full of Christmas cheer.

The dress rehearsal for the second half of the pageant didn't fare much better.

Ralphie almost fell off the stage, and Randy just sat down and cried because he wanted to be either Captain America or the Hulk.

An angel decided that she couldn't be an angel without twinkling like a star, and wouldn't go on until her mother found some glitter and sprinkled it all over her.

The angels' halos wouldn't stay upright either, and someone had accidentally sewed their wings on upside down.

The Three Kings wanted to bring in three ostriches from their farm to act as camels. In fact, the ostriches were waiting in a trailer in the parking lot.

I asked ACB to handle that one.

The Grinch's costume was a furry, fuzzy, gray costume with orange, yellow, and purple feathers and shaped like a bird. The wardrobe department, Agatha Lutz, had thought I said we needed a *finch* costume. Oops.

Since it was too late to make another costume, we were going with *The Finch Who Stole Christmas*.

Other than that, we were ready to go!

All too soon, it was Christmas Eve, the night of the pageant and the Christmas Eve dinner. Santa would visit after dessert, which was a buffet of pies, cakes, and cookies.

Juanita, Cindy, and Bob were busy deboning cooked turkeys. The Babes, Marylou, and my mother had helped prepare big aluminum pans containing squash, gravy, mashed potatoes, and stuffing. There were cranberries, shaped like the can, which I loved, homemade applesauce donated by Harbor Orchard, and lots of pickles and olives and rolls for the tables.

The tables in the church's community room were already decorated and ready for hungry revelers. The Christmas tree was up, too, and had been decorated by Roger.

As many of us as could possibly fit piled into ACB's van. My father drove more people in my car, and Ty drove even more in his SUV.

When I got to the church, I sought out Roger Southwick. I wanted to tell him to lower the curtain after the pageant, then raise it again, because I had several people that I wanted to thank, him included, before the feast started.

I found him cleaning the men's room. "Roger, can we talk for a moment—outside?"

We took a seat on the bench in the hallway and I told him about raising the curtain. "And I want to thank you personally for everything you've done. I know you've done a lot of things behind the scenes, so thank you."

"You're welcome."

"And I'm sorry we got off on the wrong foot. I'll be quitting my job here after the pageant. I just wanted you to know that."

"I was pretty distraught after Liz's murder, so I was

rude. I liked Liz a lot, and we went out several times. Besides, she was going to help my sister," he said. "But no one can help Darlene now." He got up to leave, but I grabbed on to his arm.

No one can help Darlene now?

"Roger, please. It's a season of miracles. Darlene can be helped, but first, tell me how Liz was going to help Darlene."

He let out a big sigh. "Liz was looking into getting Darlene's conviction overturned because she wants to be a reverend."

Whoa!

"Darlene wasn't upset at Liz because she found out about Darlene's troubles in Buffalo?" I asked.

"Oh, so you know about her prison time? I thought that no one would know because she was Darlene Osmond back then. She didn't do it, you know."

I couldn't believe that this was Mr. Congeniality opening up to me. It *was* a Christmas miracle.

"Darlene is innocent?" I asked again. Of course he'd say that. "Who stole all that money, then? Was it you?"

He snorted and went back into the men's room.

"Wait . . . I have more questions!"

For heaven's sake!

That was all I was going to get from him?

I walked by Pastor Fritz's office and stopped when I heard a loud voice. "I want your brother out of here. Tomorrow. I saw him talking to that nosy Trixie Matkowski. I always knew she was up to something."

"It's Christmas and he's my only relative. You owe me, Fritz."

"How many times are you going to throw that in my face? I made you what you are."

"You made me a felon, Fritz! And I won't go back to prison. I will not. I can't. Don't even think it."

"When this stupid pageant is over, I want your brother gone! And I want Trixie Matkowski gone. And you're not to speak to Ty Brisco or anyone else without me there. Do you hear me?"

"I've already talked to a lawyer, Fritz. I want a divorce. You want my brother gone? Fine. I'm going with him."

"I'm not going to let you leave!"

"You can't stop me, Fritz. Don't even try."

"I must have been crazy when I married you!" he shouted.

"And you're still crazy," Darlene yelled.

This was Pastor Fritz? I never thought in a million years that he would speak to anyone like that. But maybe the stress of covering up for Darlene had finally gotten to him.

I didn't have time to think about it, though. It was almost time to get the pageant under way. I felt that I was close to finding out who killed Liz, but was still missing a crucial piece of evidence that would pin all of it on Darlene. There must have been something that I had overlooked, but I couldn't think of what it could be.

You made me a felon, Fritz.

I won't go back to prison.

From what I overheard, there was real trouble in Robinson land, and they were headed straight for divorce. Darlene had already seen a lawyer, but whether that was because she was filing for divorce or for something else, I couldn't say.

And what about Darlene's pull tab addiction? Why did her own brother keep the church collection and bingo money away from her? Or were they stealing together?

What was I missing?

I sat down at my desk in the office, exhausted, and suddenly remembered finding the cassette player on my first day in the office. I wondered whether Liz had made an incriminating tape and had hidden it underneath something, as she did with the flash drive. But where could it be?

What about Liz's car?

Without putting a coat on, I crutched to Liz's car, which was still parked out back and covered with snow. Ty hadn't taken it to be impounded yet.

I tried all the doors and they were locked—all except for the hatchback. I laughed, and then climbed in, closing the hatch behind me. I dove over the backseat, then did the same over the front seat, lifting my cast as I went.

I felt under the dash. "C'mon, Liz. You must have left something here . . . somewhere."

My fingers were numb from the cold. It seemed even colder inside Liz's car than outside.

Nothing was there, and it was getting dark.

On a whim, I opened the console in the middle. Nothing but some CDs and a few homemade cassette tapes, labeled ASSORTED SONGS FROM THE '50S, F'S GREATEST HITS, ELVIS BLUE HAWAII.

I put all three of the cassettes into my cleavage purse.

I checked for anyone watching, but it was impossible to tell with the windows all frosted over. Opening the driver's-side door, I hobbled back to the office to get both me and the tapes warm.

I opened Liz's middle drawer and got out the little cassette player/recorder. I was going to listen to F's Greatest Hits.

My heart started beating faster as I popped open the plastic door to the player, slid the cassette in place, and hit play. I put the buds into my ears and jumped as I heard a man's voice. I lowered the volume and slipped the player into my pocket.

"Did you tell anyone about this meeting, Liz?"

"No. I didn't tell anyone, Fritz."

"You don't call me 'pastor' anymore. Why not?"

"You don't seem like a pastor to me anymore. As a matter of fact, I think you should resign and turn yourself in. You'd save this parish and this community a lot of embarrassment. When I think of how the good people of Sandy Harbor donated their time and money to feed your gambling habit, it . . . well, let's just say it doesn't sit well with me. And you let Darlene take the rap and go to prison for you. How can you wear that collar? Where's your conscience?"

It hit me then. Liz wasn't using Darlene's criminal past against her. Liz was *helping* her.

"I didn't ask you to meet with me to talk about Darlene, or anything else for that matter," Fritz continued. *"I called you in to let you know that I've asked for a transfer, so all will be well."*

"You'll just commit the same crime again, won't you? First there was Buffalo, then Sandy Harbor. . . . You'll do it again

*wherever you go. It ends here, Fritz. I'm going to let your supe-
riors and Ty Brisco know."*

"You wouldn't dare!"

I heard Antoinette Chloe's voice as if from a distance.
"Trixie? Trixie, everyone is asking for you. What are you
doing in here?"

I pulled the earbuds out and noticed the time. Thirty
minutes before the curtain went up.

"I didn't think it was this late. Let's go!"

"What are you listening to?" ACB asked.

"Liz recorded her meeting with Pastor Fritz. I found
the cassette in Liz's car just now."

"Anything good on it?" she asked.

"Definitely! I have to finish listening to it, though.
But let me just tell you one thing: I think Fritz killed
Liz. He's the pull tab addict. And Liz was trying to help
Darlene, not hinder her. Darlene wants to be a priest."

"Wow!"

"Liz figured out that Darlene took the rap for Fritz
or else he framed her or something. And I think he's
about to do it again. I overheard them arguing. I'd love
to find Darlene and talk to her."

"You don't have to look very far, Trixie. She's coming
right down the hall."

"Antoinette Chloe, will you please go and handle
things for me for a while? I'll be right there."

"You got it."

Darlene crashed into me as I headed toward the
ladies' room.

"Have you seen my brother?" she asked, clearly
shaken.

"He was cleaning the men's room earlier. Maybe he's stocking it now. But are you okay, Darlene?"

"No." She stomped to the door of the men's room and stuck her head in. "Roger, get out here, please."

"What's wrong, Dar?"

"Just like we thought. It's happening again. We're leaving."

By this time, I'd caught up to them. "Darlene, I couldn't help overhearing. If you have a problem, talk to Ty. He'll help you."

"No way." She shook her head. "He'll help me right to jail. I'm leaving."

"If you leave, you'll look guilty, and I know that you didn't do anything. At first, I thought you murdered Liz because she found out about your crimes in Buffalo. I thought that you were stealing money from the church because you have a pull tab addiction and that maybe Roger was helping you—"

"No!" Darlene gasped. "My brother was helping Liz keep track of the receipts from bingo and the Sunday collections so Fritz wouldn't dip into it."

"Roger, you were helping Liz?" I said. "You and Liz were keeping track of receipts?"

"Yes. And finally Darlene had enough money to write checks," he said.

I smiled. "Liz saved the day on more than one occasion. I found a tape she made. She recorded a conversation between Fritz and herself. I haven't finished listening to it, but Fritz is clearly the culprit. Liz accused him of stealing money. She told him that she was going to turn him in to Ty Brisco, and therefore, he had a good reason to kill Liz."

Darlene slumped into the chair near the men's room, then looked up at me, sobbing.

"It's all over?" She was taking short, puffy breaths, and I thought she was going to pass out. "I loved Liz! She was my friend and confidant, and she was trying to help me. She was trying to help this church, too."

"I know she was. I know. But you have to talk to Ty, Darlene. And you can't let on that we know your husband is guilty of Liz's murder. Just do your part in the play. Do it for the kids."

"Fritz killed Liz," she whispered to herself. "I thought so, but I couldn't let myself believe it. I just couldn't."

"You can move in with me until things get . . . settled," Roger said, leaning against the door frame of the men's room. "We can move to one of the B&Bs in town."

Darlene was staring straight ahead and not blinking. It hadn't really sunk in yet that her husband had killed her friend.

"Darlene, do the pageant for the kids," I said, taking her hand. "You're a great Zuzu. Then we'll both talk to Ty."

She smiled sadly. "I'll do it."

"Good," I said, getting up. I wanted to hear the rest of the tape, but I had a pageant to put on.

"I just want to ask you one more thing, Darlene. It was Fritz who stole the money from the Buffalo church where you were a volunteer. Correct? And you went to jail . . . for him."

"He convinced me that I was guilty because I didn't do some things correctly as a volunteer. He said that if I pled guilty, he'd get me out of jail early, and he promised to marry me. To give me a good name, he said, and because he loved me. That was music to my ears after a hateful divorce from my husband. Here he was the great pastor of a church, and I was going to be like the First Lady. How stupid was I?"

"You were young, Dar. Don't beat yourself up. You've always had a good heart and that was your strength, but Fritz Robinson took advantage of you, and you paid the price."

"Thank you for that, Trixie."

"Don't go near Fritz until we can talk to Ty. His life is crumbling around him. He could get desperate."

I had to find Ty and keep an eye on Fritz.

But I couldn't find either of them. The place was packed and the adult choir was singing until the curtain went up in . . . ten minutes!

Where did the time go?

Two of my shepherds threw up backstage due to nerves and overindulging on Christmas candy. I found Margie Grace and asked her to find Roger for a cleanup. I guessed the nativity scene would be okay without shepherds tending their flock.

The Finch Who Stole Christmas was sucking on a candy cane through his beak.

ACB was ghostly in a white muumuu with white flip-flops, white makeup, and a white wig. A white fascinator with tiny, wrapped presents around a tiny Christmas tree jutted straight out from the side of her head. She was sitting down, holding hands with Judge Glennie.

Backstage, there was an excited buzz from the cast.

Margie walked around telling everyone to please be quiet, so the choir could be heard. Forget it! Everyone was just too excited.

I walked farther into the area behind the altar/stage, got out my cell phone, and called Ty. I got his voice mail.

"Ty, please find me. Hurry. I'm behind the stage. I have really important information for you about Fritz."

Just like Liz, I wasn't going to call him *pastor* anymore. He didn't deserve the respect of the title.

"You do, Trixie? What kind of really important information about me do you have for Ty?" Fritz asked through gritted teeth.

He was the Ghost of Christmas Future and wore a long black shapeless robe with a hood, and looked as pale as death. Which I guessed was the point.

"Trixie, my dear, why don't you come with me to my office, and we can discuss why you're upset. Shall we?"

"I'm not going anywhere with you, Fritz. You're a murderer, a gambler, and a thief. You aren't fit to be a pastor. In fact, you aren't fit to be in my pageant. You are hereby no longer the Ghost of Christmas Future."

I was stalling for time.

Question: Why wasn't anyone around back here?

Answer: Because the pageant was about to start.

They wouldn't start without me, would they?

Suddenly Fritz grabbed my arm, and I felt a prick in my side. A knife!

If he ruined my Tiny Tim costume—faux lederhosen made out of brown felt with red suspenders, a white peasant blouse, and red-and-green striped Christmas socks, our wardrobe department . . . um . . . Agatha Lutz would be mad.

"A knife, Fritz? Just like the butcher knife that you used to kill Liz Fellows?"

He was half dragging me to a room behind the stage.

He pushed me, and I crutched along slowly. Then there was another prick.

"Fritz, I'm telling you for the last time, leave the lederhosen alone!"

"*You* just couldn't leave things alone, could you?" he whispered in my ear as he kept pushing me. "I know that the whole thing with Antoinette Chloe, that fake suicide attempt on the bridge, was a ruse to get me out of here."

"You still went."

"I meant after. She overacted, and wasn't entirely convincing that she was going to jump because of Roger," he sniffed. "You saw my two sets of books, didn't you?"

"And a ton of used pull tabs in your apartment. Tell me, what do you do with them all when you are done?"

"I toss them into the Dumpster out back the night before the trash is picked up."

"So Roger won't see." I nodded. "And you trashed Liz's house, didn't you?"

"I must admit that was beneath me, but I had to find that stupid little . . ."

"Flash drive," I finished. "I found it the other day."

We stopped walking, and I decided to jump in with both feet and see if I could get a confession out of him.

"Why did you kill Liz, Fritz? Did she find out about

you? Did she figure out that Darlene took the hit for you in Buffalo? Did she find out that you were up to your old tricks and were going to lay the blame on Darlene again?"

His Adam's apple was bobbing in double time. "Who would believe that a pastor could do such a thing? It just wouldn't happen."

"Sure they'd believe it. I believe it! Liz believed it."

"And she's not here, is she?"

"Because you killed her!" I yelled, and got the satisfaction of seeing him flinch. "But Liz left the Sandy Harbor Community Church's parishioners and the Sandy Harbor Sheriff's Department a perfectly wonderful Christmas present." I held up Liz's tape recorder and hit the Play button. Fritz's voice was loud and clear.

"You wouldn't dare report me."

Liz laughed. *"I sure will. I have a record of all the money you've stolen on a little flash drive that you'll never find. I have records of the pull tabs that were ordered and paid for by the church, ones that you took and used for yourself. But above all, I am working to prove that you framed Darlene to take the rap for you back in Buffalo."*

"Is that enough, Fritz?" I knew I was taunting him, and I slipped the cassette back into my pocket. I'd guard it with my life because that little cassette was the best evidence of Fritz's crimes. "Is that why you killed Liz? Because she knew way too much about your illegal activity, huh?"

"Shut up!"

He was clutching his knife so hard that his knuckles were white, but I had a plan in case he came at me. But first, as they say on the television shows with all the initials, I needed backup.

There was a phone on the wall, and it had an intercom that went into the public address system. Moving in front of the phone, I managed to hide it from Fritz's view.

Then I looked around for something to hit him with. Some kind of wood thing would do, like a stick or a baseball bat. Maybe a golf club.

Or maybe crutches.

He made the mistake of turning away to see what I was looking at.

Whack! I hit him with a crutch on the back of the head.

Whack! I did it again.

He fell to the ground, and I hit the button on the intercom. "Attention, please. Your attention, please. Will Ebenezer Scrooge please report to Tiny Tim behind the stage, and hurry?"

Fritz started to move, so I plunked my casted leg on his back and shoved him back down.

"That's a major hurry, Ebenezer. STAT! Code Blue!" I said into the intercom.

Ty found me seconds later. The first thing he noticed was Fritz on the floor with his hands behind his back, and me with my foot on his butt like I was climbing Mount Crumpit. In the absence of handcuffs, I'd used one of my crutches and threaded his hands and arms through the middle of my crutch as far as they would go.

He looked like he was in the stocks.

"What have we here?" Ty asked me, picking up Fritz's knife, which I'd kicked away with my good leg.

"We have Liz Fellows's killer, the man who's been cooking the books and stealing from the church. The man who was wormy enough to talk a young girl into taking the blame for something he did many years ago. He dangled an early release and marriage in front of her."

"Is that right, Fritz?"

No answer. I pressed my foot into his back until he groaned. Then he said, "I want a lawyer."

"Good thinking." Ty replaced my crutch with his handcuffs and got Fritz up from the floor.

I was hot and flushed and pumped full of adrenaline.

"I'll take him out back and deliver him to Vern McCoy," Ty said. "Vern can start the paperwork. I'll be back."

"Good."

"Oh, and Trixie?"

"Yes?"

"Outstanding job," he said, giving me a snappy salute.

Wow!

Just like Ralphie on Christmas morning when his dad gave him the best Christmas present of his life—a Red Ryder BB gun—Ty had just given me the best Christmas present ever. I was sure that I'd get a lecture later about leaving the investigating to him, but until then, I was going to revel in his compliment and the fact that I caught Liz's killer.

I'd revel later. At that moment, I needed to get the show on the road.

I crutched to the stage, took a deep breath, and said to the audience, "Ladies and gentlemen and boys and girls, today's performance of our pageant is dedicated to the memory of our friend Liz Fellows." There was clapping by everyone. "And the part of the Ghost of Christmas Future will now be played by Roger Southwick." I hoped that Roger was okay with this. "And after the play, dinner will be served in the community room, and I hear that Santa and Mrs. Claus are going to visit."

There were *ooh*s and *aah*s from the audience. Then Ty's dad, Justin Brisco, broke into a rousing "Jingle Bells" on the piano, and everyone sang along as I hobbled off the stage.

The pageant wasn't perfect, but everyone loved it. There weren't any accidents, or at least nothing that required hospitalization.

Ty even made it for his part in the play. I had planned to play two parts—Scrooge and Tim—if need be. I would've bet it would have been the first time Scrooge was portrayed in lederhosen.

Onstage, Ty whispered to me that Darlene was going to testify against Fritz. More charges would be coming as soon as the church's records were audited.

When the play was over, I was given roses by the cast and crew. I called ACB and Margie Grace to the stage to share the honor with me. Then I said my thank-yous.

Bob then called us in rows to file into the community room. Darlene read a little Christmas prayer that she'd found. Later, when we talked privately about Fritz's arrest, her face glowed. "It's a Christmas miracle, Trixie."

If anyone wondered where Fritz was, no one asked.

The word would be out soon enough, anyway.

The food was delicious and everyone went up for seconds and thirds until there was nothing left.

I sat with my family, Ty's parents, and my extended family, the Boca Babes.

Santa and Mrs. Claus arrived to "Rudolph the Red-Nosed Reindeer," and the kids just about jumped out of their skin. They were so cute to watch.

The gloves-and-hat sets were a hit with the first, second, third, and fourth grades of Sandy Harbor Grammar School. Santa and Mrs. Claus passed out candy canes and other trinkets. And then it really hit me that Santa and Mrs. Claus, or should I say Bob and Aunt Stella, looked very much in love!

"Mom, have you noticed Bob and Aunt Stella?" I whispered.

"Stella told me all about it. Apparently Bob left when Porky died because he felt guilty. Bob had always loved Stella, and wanted to give her some time and space to heal before he came calling. They've reconnected, but Stella feels like she's betraying her beloved Porky by being with Bob. It's all a big mess, but there is always—"

"A Christmas miracle," I said.

I noticed Bob walk into the kitchen and return with a shiny black accordion. Clapping started as everyone noticed the person who Bob stopped and stood in front of.

Aunt Stella! Or should I say Mrs. Claus?

Aunt Stella grinned and held out her arms to take the accordion. Bob turned it around, gently handed it to her, and helped her with the straps. She unhooked it, let some air into the instrument, and ran her fingers up and down the keyboard and buttons.

The clapping increased and then a hush fell over the

room. Aunt Stella played several songs for the kids with everyone singing along. She ended with "Santa Claus Is Coming to Town."

Santa stood and called for everyone's attention, and the room became silent.

"Will Trixie Matkowski please join Santa and Mrs. Claus?"

My heart started beating wildly. What was this?

I settled down in a chair in front of the Christmas tree where Santa had pointed.

"Trixie, it has come to Santa's attention that you've been a little out of sorts this Christmas with your broken leg, but Santa and Mrs. Claus know that you've touched a lot of lives since you've come to Sandy Harbor. So several people have put together a little presentation for you, Trixie."

Aunt Stella stepped forward. "You've been like the daughter that I never had, Trixie, and I love you dearly." Then she whispered in my ear, "There's no one I'd rather see running the point than you."

Antoinette Chloe walked toward me. "You and I have had a lot of adventures, haven't we, Trixie? You've saved me from going insane on many occasions, you don't judge me, and we have a lot of laughs. BFFs forever!"

My parents talked about how I had encouraged them to buy a motor home and see the country, and how glad they were that they had listened to me.

Darlene had a very teary thank-you. "Trixie knows why I will always be so grateful to her. I can't express how my life is going to change for the better, and someday, if I can, someday, somehow, I will pay her back."

I was getting misty. This had better stop, and soon.

Ray Meyerson stepped up and told the crowd that I'd given him a job when no one would and saved him from going to jail.

Cindy, my cook, mentioned how I'd given her a job when she was fired from the Save-A-Lot. She even mentioned how I donate food to her large family from time to time. She shouldn't have said that.

Roger even stood up and thanked me. "You know why," he said. And I did. He was grateful that I'd found the cassette tape in Liz's car that proved his sister's innocence. I smiled when I remembered that Liz had labeled it F'S GREATEST HITS for Fritz!

Then echoes of "Speech! Speech!" echoed throughout the room, and I got to my feet.

"Thank you all so very much for this special honor. I am humbled and touched and . . . speechless. But before everyone leaves, I'd like to invite anyone who is alone for Christmas Day to come over to the Silver Bullet for a hot meal and some Christmas cheer. It's a tradition that was started by my uncle Porky back in 1952, when the diner was first opened, and I've continued it. That's where my family will be all day, and you are truly welcome to join our celebration."

Then a bell dropped from the Christmas tree, either accidentally or on purpose, and rolled toward me, tinkling.

I turned to see Darlene Robinson smiling. She took my hand and said, "Trixie, teacher says, every time a bell rings, an angel gets her wings. And you're our angel!"

Epilogue

I just had to write you both and tell you about the Law Enforcement Ball. First, it felt like I was going to the senior prom.

Ty looked gorgeous in a tux, and I even got a wolf whistle from him. Believe me, it was the dress.

He even gave me a corsage of white rosebuds that looked perfect.

We had to pose in front of the Christmas tree many times as everyone took pictures. (I didn't want to take the tree down until after the ball.)

We had a nice forty-five-minute ride to downtown Syracuse. The ball was held at the Onondaga Hotel, a historic hotel with big ballrooms.

The ballroom was awash in white twinkle lights. The mirrors around the room made it even more twinkly.

The tables were decorated with wreaths of white flowers and greens along with thin, gold tapers.

I was in heaven.

We found our table, and I was surprised to find that we were sitting with the mayor and sheriff of both Onondaga County and Oswego County, as well as a couple of other high-ranking officials from the State Police.

Puzzled at why we were seated at the head table, I looked at the program. Ty was getting an award for Law Enforcement Deputy of the Year. Nice! He'd never said a word.

I was thrilled for him.

He spent the night shaking hands with people who were congratulating him. They were queued up like a conga line.

And then finally it was time to eat.

Ty introduced me to our tablemates, and we all talked. They were very interested in my diner and housekeeping cottages, and Ty praised both to the limits. Plans were begun for a Silver Bullet / Law Enforcement fishing contest, and the sheriff of Oswego County promptly put Ty in charge of it.

He eagerly accepted!

Ty gave a short speech, and he thanked me! Me? He said that in a small town with a small force, he often sought out my opinion.

Huh? He fights me every step of the way. He even arrested Antoinette Chloe and me!

And then the dancing started. With my cast recently off and my magnificent dress glittering, I was dying to dance, but instead I spent the night watching the band and watching everyone dancing as Ty stood and received another conga line.

Finally he excused himself from the line, walked over to the bandleader, and whispered in his ear. Soon I heard the strains of "The Christmas Waltz." I don't know how Ty remembered that I love this song, but he hurried back to our table and held out his hand.

"This isn't a polka, but would you like to dance?" he asked.

I laughed and we went onto the dance floor, and he gave me a little twirl. My dress caught the lights and sparkled even more. I asked him how he'd gotten the band to play a Christmas song, and he said, "The Law Enforcement Deputy of the Year can do whatever he wants."

I closed my eyes, and enjoyed every second of the dance. Then I looked up at Ty, thinking about the many things that I liked about him.

You know, someday I might get over my divorce from Deputy Doug.

When I do, I hope Ty is still around and asks me to another ball.

The song ended, the evening ended, and I knew that I'd never forget that night.

It was magic. Just as magical as this past Christmas. It was wonderful having my family and friends here.

Miss you both.

Don't wait until I break my leg to visit again!

All my love,
Trixie

Recipes and Holiday Memories
from Trixie's Family and Friends

Ellen's Cranberry Relish

This recipe is from Ellen Connolly Breen, a friend of mine who lives on the sunny shores of Florida. She tells me that she's had this relish at Christmas since she was young, and it came to her by way of her dad's best friend, a police lieutenant in Yonkers, NY.

It goes great with any kind of meat!

4–5 cups water
4–5 cups sugar
3 bags (12 ounces each) fresh cranberries
1½ cups finely chopped walnuts
3 cups medium-chopped fresh pears
1½ cups raisins

Into a large pot, put 4–5 cups of water.

Add 4–5 cups of sugar.

Boil 5 minutes until the sugar dissolves.

Add cranberries, keeping heat high enough for the berries to start popping.

Turn down the heat and keep stirring.

Add nuts, pears, and raisins.

Let simmer for a few hours on the stove at a low heat, so that it thickens.

Put in jars and refrigerate.

Babci's Babka

From Babci Soja Kaczor (Grandma Sarah Kaczor)

Babci Sarah is no longer with us, but her memory lives on in her special cooking and baking, which she did with love. This is her babka bread recipe.

1 pound butter
1 tablespoon vanilla extract
1 tablespoon rum (optional)
1 teaspoon olive oil
1 whole orange peel
1 dozen eggs
2½ cups sugar
5 pounds bread flour
1 quart milk
¼ pound or a little more fresh yeast, or two strips
     (6 packages) dry
1 teaspoon salt
1 box golden raisins

TO START:

Melt butter and cool. Then add vanilla extract, rum, and oil into the butter. Set aside.

Grate orange peel on wax paper and set aside.

Separate egg yolks from whites and beat yolks until creamy and lemon-colored. Set aside. (Save egg whites for another time, may freeze.)

Measure 2 cups of sugar and from the sugar take 3

tablespoons out. Put into a cup, add 4 tablespoons of flour, and set aside.

Take 1 quart of milk and put it into a pot and scald; then let set until warm.

Add yeast to the warm milk and work it out until dissolved. Then add the sugar and flour mixture that's in the cup slowly to the yeast and milk, leaving a little flour to sprinkle on the top, and let bubble.

IN A LARGE BOWL OR 10-QUART PAN:

Put in 4 cups of flour and salt; then add sugar, orange peel, raisins, and butter mixture, and knead.

Keep adding flour and kneading dough until it doesn't stick to the bowl or your hands.

Pour dough out of the bowl and knead a bit more until smooth.

Oil the bowl lightly and place the dough back into it to rise.

Cover. Let the dough double in bulk in a warm place.

THEN:

On a floured surface, empty the dough from the pan and knead again.

Cut the dough into 6 equal pieces and put into 6 greased nonstick loaf pans or 8-inch round cake pans.

Cover and let rise again.

THEN:

Brush tops of loaves with beaten eggs.

Bake in a preheated 350-degree oven for 45 minutes.

Check the loaves after 20 minutes and change the top loaves to the bottom rack and vice versa.

When the baking time is up, remove one loaf and tap the bottom or sides. It is done if it sounds hollow.

THAT'S IT!

Good luck and love,
Babci Sarah

Mary Ann's Rum Cake

Mary Ann and I go way back to grammar school. We were library buddies and would walk together to the very old library, which was located in a very old house. We both loved the musty smell and loved finding a new "treasure" to read. As adults, we ended up working at the same place for a while, and Mary Ann would make this cake for all the Christmas parties. It was a big hit, and you'll see why!

CAKE

1 cup chopped pecans or walnuts
1 18-ounce package yellow cake mix
1 3.75-ounce package Jell-O instant vanilla pudding mix
4 eggs
½ cup cold water
½ cup vegetable oil
½ cup dark rum (80 proof)

GLAZE

> ¼ pound butter
> ¼ cup water
> 1 cup granulated sugar
> ½ cup dark rum (80 proof)

Preheat oven to 325 degrees.

Grease and flour 10-inch tube or 12-cup Bundt pan.

Sprinkle nuts over bottom of pan.

Mix all cake ingredients together.

Pour batter over nuts.

Bake 1 hour. Cool.

LATER:

Invert on serving plate. Prick top.

Drizzle and smooth glaze evenly over top and sides of cake.

Allow cake to absorb glaze. Repeat until all glaze is used.

FOR GLAZE

Melt butter in saucepan.

Stir in water and sugar.

Boil 5 minutes, stirring constantly.

Remove from heat.

Stir in rum.

Optional: Decorate with whole maraschino cherries and a border of sugar frosting or whipped cream. Serve with seedless green grapes dusted in powdered sugar.

Trutas
(Fried Portuguese Pastries)

Trutas are a Portuguese pastry made at Christmas. In fact, it can't be Christmas without trutas. Back in the day when my friend Doreen Kelly Alsen was growing up in Provincetown, MA, she said that Portuguese housewives would get together and make them and give them away. Doreen said that she was lucky that one of those generous women was a friend, named Ofelia Costa, who made sure that her family was supplied with trutas! This is Ofelia's recipe:

FILLING

> 4 pounds sweet potatoes cooked and peeled
> 1½ teaspoons fresh lemon juice
> 1 teaspoon grated lemon peel
> 1½ teaspoons cinnamon
> 1 pinch nutmeg
> 1 cup sugar

PASTRY

> 1 pound butter
> 1 pound lard (do not use vegetable shortening)
> 4 pounds flour, not self-rising
> 1 cup sugar
> 1½ cups warm orange juice
> 2 jiggers whiskey mixed in one cup warm water

MAKE THE FILLING

Mash the sweet potatoes and mix them with all the other ingredients in a pan.

Stir over a low fire until the sugar dissolves. Taste to see if you need more sugar.

Stir constantly so the potato won't stick or burn.

MAKE THE PASTRY

Melt the butter and lard together for frying later.

Put the flour in a deep pan and make a well in the flour with your hands and place all the other ingredients in the well.

Work the dough with your hands until it feels soft and leaves the sides of the pan.

Roll the dough on a pastry board until fairly thin. Cut out circles with a 3-inch pastry cutter and place a tablespoon of the filling in each dough circle.

Fold the dough over like it's a turnover and use a pastry wheel to close each one. Press down hard so the truta won't open when being deep-fried.

THEN:

Deep-fry the trutas in the melted butter and lard, drain, and let them cool.

Sprinkle the cool trutas with confectioner's sugar.

Makes 10 dozen trutas

Chocolate Whiskey Cookies

My friend Jen Gianetto Rowan gave me this recipe from her great-grandmother Mary Stella Azzarelli Savona. Nana Savona was born in Messina, Sicily, in 1901, and this recipe was one of her family recipes brought over when she immigrated. Unfortunately Jen doesn't know the year she came to America, but knows that she was young. For years, Nana Savona worked as the cook for one of the fraternities at SUNY Oswego. Nana was supposed to have been married through an arranged match, but had fallen in love with Jen's great-grandfather and asked her parents to let her marry him instead. They agreed!

8 cups flour
¼ teaspoon salt
2 teaspoons baking powder
1 teaspoon baking soda
2 cups sugar
¾ cup cocoa powder
1 teaspoon cinnamon
1 teaspoon ground cloves
⅛ teaspoon black pepper
1 cup shortening
4 to 5 jiggers of whiskey (any whiskey will do, but Jen highly recommends springing for Jack Daniel's)
2 cups milk
1 cup chopped nuts (optional)

Preheat oven to 350 degrees.

Sift flour, salt, powder, and soda together in a 6-quart bowl or soup pan.

Add sugar, cocoa, spices.

Add shortening and liquids.

Mix by hand (which means stick your hand in there and work it all together). The dough will be extremely sticky, especially if you've been "generous" with the whiskey. Add more milk a little at a time if the dough seems too dry.

Add nuts if desired, mix in.

Form into little balls, or, to make life easier, use a cookie scoop.

Place on parchment-lined cookie sheet.

Bake for 15 minutes. Remove to paper towels and frost while warm.

CHOCOLATE GLAZE FROSTING

1 box confectioner's sugar
cocoa powder
scant milk

GLAZE

Combine all ingredients in a bowl and mix until smooth.

It will need to be rather thick, but will still drizzle from a spoon, or the warm cookies will further thin the glaze and it will all run off the cookies.

Rosaline Matyjasik's Snowball Cookies

I've had this recipe forever! Christmas wouldn't be the same without these cookies. Good any time of the year, but especially at Christmas!

SIFT TOGETHER:

> 2 cups flour
> ½ teaspoon salt

BLEND TOGETHER:

> ¾ cup butter
> ½ cup sugar
> 2 teaspoons almond extract (or you could use vanilla or
>   peppermint)
> 1 egg

Mix dry ingredients into wet ingredients.

ADD:

> 1 cup chopped nuts
> 1 cup chocolate chips (chocolate mint chips are really
>   good, too, or even peanut butter chips)

Stir with wooden spoon or heavy spoon.
   Shape into 1-inch balls.
   Place on cookie sheet.
   Bake at 350 for 15–20 minutes.
   Cool slightly and roll in confectioner's sugar (or shake
in a plastic bag).

This recipe works well when doubled.

Snowballs can be frozen in plastic bags—just don't roll them in confectioner's sugar beforehand, and wait until they thaw to room temperature to do so.

From Andrea Hauge Kaczor

Andrea Hauge Kaczor's ancestors hail from Norway. She states, "Our favorite Christmas pastry is an almond-flavored coffee cake called Oslo Kringle. I make it every Christmas. . . . It's my kids' favorite (they call it Kris Kringle)."

CRUST:

1 cup flour
½ cup butter, softened
2 tablespoons cold water

Mix flour and softened butter; add cold water and mix as for pie crust. Roll out and transfer to cookie sheet in two long strips about 2 inches wide and a ¼-inch thick.

CREAM PUFF PASTE:

1 cup water
½ cup butter
1 cup flour

3 eggs
½ teaspoon almond flavoring

Bring water and butter to a boil. Remove from stove and immediately add all flour; stir until smooth. Add one egg at a time, beating well after each addition. Add flavoring.

Spread on the above strips and bake at 350 degrees for 45 minutes.

Frost when cool with the following icing:

1 cup confectioner's sugar
1 tablespoon butter
½ teaspoon almond flavoring
1 tablespoon cream

Combine all ingredients together and mix until blended.

Cappuccino Cookies

My friend Tracy Blair Funnel states that she first had these years and years ago, and now her relatives insist that she bring them to every holiday and event. She said, "Beware, they are addictive! They also have caffeine, so you have a good excuse to make these a grown-ups-only dessert."

1 cup butter, softened
1 cup firmly packed brown sugar

2 tablespoons milk
2 tablespoons instant coffee granules
2 large eggs
1 teaspoon rum extract
½ teaspoon vanilla extract
4 cups all-purpose flour
1 teaspoon baking powder
½ teaspoon ground nutmeg
¼ teaspoon salt
chocolate sprinkles or melted chocolate (optional)

Beat butter in large bowl with electric mixer at medium speed until smooth.

Add brown sugar and beat until well blended.

Heat milk in small saucepan over low heat. Add coffee granules, stirring to dissolve. Add milk mixture, eggs, rum extract, and vanilla extract to butter mixture. Beat at medium speed until well blended.

Combine flour, baking powder, nutmeg, and salt in large bowl. Gradually add flour mixture to butter mixture, beating at low speed after each addition until blended.

Shape dough into two logs, about 8 inches long and 2 inches in diameter. Dough will be soft. Sprinkle lightly with flour if too sticky to handle.

Roll logs in chocolate sprinkles, if desired, coating evenly (⅓ cup sprinkles per roll). Or leave rolls plain and dip cookies in melted chocolate after baking.

Wrap each log in plastic wrap and refrigerate overnight.

Tracy says: I prefer the dip option. I use a nice dark chocolate and only dip the cookie a little bit. Makes a nice presentation and you can pick how much to use. Add colored sprinkles to the soft chocolate if you want a real holiday look. Might be good with white chocolate, too (although I haven't tried that).

Preheat oven to 350. Grease cookie sheets. Cut rolls into ¼-inch-thick slices. Place 1 inch apart on cookie sheets (keep unbaked cookie rolls or slices chilled until ready to bake). Bake 10–12 minutes or until golden brown. Transfer to wire racks to cool. Dip in chocolate if desired. Store in airtight container.

For dipping chocolate: Melt one cup chocolate chips in small saucepan over very low heat until smooth.

Makes about 60 cookies

Molasses Cookies

I wanted to include this very old recipe, also from Tracy Blair Funnel, who reports that it's a family recipe on her husband, Doug's, side. The name of the person who it came from is lost, but another relative remembers that the baker baked them on a woodstove and gave them as gifts for Christmas.

1 cup shortening
1 cup molasses
2 eggs
1 cup sugar
½ cup hot water
2 teaspoons baking soda
1 teaspoon ginger
1 teaspoon cinnamon
½ teaspoon salt
4½ cups flour

Mix together shortening, molasses, eggs, and sugar until creamed.

Mix separately hot water and baking soda, and add to molasses mixture.

Sift together remaining ingredients and add slowly. Let stand in refrigerator overnight.

Roll chilled dough mixture onto a floured surface, and use a cookie cutter or cup to cut out cookies.

As an optional step, pat down lightly with sugar before baking (can also be done after baking).

Place on cookie sheet and bake at 350 for about 10 minutes.

Grandma's Mandelbrodt
(Mandel Bread)

My friend Jenn Kettell's grandmother used to send each of her grandchildren a cookie tin full of her Mandelbrodt when they were in college. If you returned the tin when you came home for breaks, she'd refill it and send you more. Jenn said that she and her aunt still bake it for family occasions.

> 6 eggs
> 2 cups sugar
> 2 cups canola oil or Crisco
> 2 teaspoons vanilla extract
> 6 cups flour
> 3 teaspoons baking powder

OPTIONAL

> 8–12 ounces chocolate chips
> 1–2 cups chopped nuts (pecan, walnut, or almonds)

Preheat oven to 375.

Beat eggs and sugar.

Add oil and mix.

Mix in vanilla extract, flour, and baking powder until fully incorporated.

Fold in optional ingredients.

Spoon dough onto greased pan and shape into strips, approximately 1½ inches wide.

(Hint: square off each end to avoid burning.)

Bake for approximately 25 minutes, until golden brown.

Let cool slightly; then slice strips into even pieces, approximately ¾ inch wide.

Lay pieces on their sides and return to the oven.

Toast in oven for 10–15 minutes.

Pack in a cookie tin or other sealed container. Allow the pieces to cool completely before packing. Mandelbrodt freezes well for an extended period of time.

Grandma Theobald's Sugar Cutout Cookies

My friend Gayle Kloecker Callen tells me that her grandmother Mary Vargo Theobald came from Czechoslovakia as a little girl. She said she remembers Grandma Theobald for the tuna fish and egg salad sandwiches she packed whenever she accompanied Gayle's family on road trips. Gayle loves to bake, and the recipe she uses most is Grandma Theobald's recipe for cutout cookies at Christmas. She told me, "I grew up baking them, and I made sure my kids did the same. Even now, my grown kids make me wait to bake them until they can travel home to help. So, in honor of my grandma Theobald, here's the recipe, and of course I included the frosting recipe, for what are cutouts without frosting?"

1 cup butter
1½ cups sugar

3½ cups flour
3 eggs
1 teaspoon vanilla extract
2 teaspoons cream of tartar
1 teaspoon baking soda
½ teaspoon salt

Cream butter and add sugar, gradually creaming until light and fluffy. Add eggs one at a time, beating after each egg. Stir in vanilla extract. Stir dry ingredients together; then add gradually to mixture.

Chill 3–4 hours or overnight.

Roll on floured surface; cut shapes.

Bake on ungreased sheets at 375 for 6–8 minutes.

BUTTERCREAM FROSTING

1 stick butter
3 tablespoons milk
1 teaspoon vanilla extract
4 cups powdered sugar

Slightly soften butter. Mix liquids together. Alternate adding liquid with a cup of powdered sugar until the consistency is right. (Powdered sugar is only a rough estimate.)

Makes 8 dozen cookies

Christmas Eve French-Canadian Poutine

This recipe came to me via my very funny French-Canadian friend Kris Fletcher.

She said that it's been a family favorite from the first bite.

NOTE: All quantities are to taste. There's no hard-and-fast rule when it comes to poutine. Just play around, sample, and tweak to your heart's delight.

> French fries—a bag of frozen, or homemade if you have nothing else to do on Christmas Eve
> cheese curds
> cooked turkey or chicken, cut into smallish cubes
> cranberry sauce
> cooked peas
> gravy, preferably turkey or chicken (Homemade is best, but if you have to use frozen or canned, do what you must. It's Christmas Eve. No one is going to judge.)

Cook the fries by whichever method you prefer. (I myself prefer to toss the frozen ones in the oven, the way it says on the bag.)

While they are cooking, break the cheese curds into small pieces, cook the peas if necessary, dice anything that needs dicing, and heat the gravy.

When the fries are piping hot, scoop half of them into a big bowl. Add half of all the other ingredients. Repeat the layers.

Ring the dinner bell and tell Santa to come to the table. Enjoy with a cold beer or hard cider.

Grandma Flossie's Fabulous Chocolate Fudge

My friend MJ Compton remembers her grandmother making this fudge every year between Thanksgiving and Christmas. Somehow, between working long hours at an industrial laundry, bowling leagues, and holiday banquets, she was able to give each of her twenty-six grandchildren (yikes!) a batch as part of their Christmas gift. MJ remembers Grandma Flossie sewing Barbie-doll clothes for all the granddaughters as Christmas gifts, too.

   3 cups sugar
   ¾ cup margarine
   ⅔ cup evaporated milk
   1 12-ounce package semisweet chocolate chips
   1 7-ounce jar marshmallow cream
   1 teaspoon vanilla extract

Combine sugar, margarine, and milk in heavy 2½-quart saucepan.

Bring to full rolling boil, stirring constantly.

Continue boiling 5 minutes over medium heat, stirring.

Remove from heat and stir in chocolate until melted.
Add marshmallow cream and vanilla extract.
Beat until blended.
Pour into greased 13-x-9-inch baking pan.
Let cool and cut into 1-inch squares.

Chapter 1

*W*hat on earth did I do?

A thrill of excitement shot through me as I stood in front of the Silver Bullet Diner. It was still hard to think of it as *my* diner, but the wad of keys in my pocket assured me that it was.

It was mid-March in upstate New York, Sandy Harbor to be exact, and the snow was falling in big fat flakes, adding to the six-foot banks around the parking lot. Still, the bright red neon of the diner's name and the blue neon proclaiming AIR-CONDITIONED and OPEN 24 HOURS shone through the snow and lit the way for patrons arriving for lunch.

It was my diner now.

Maybe it wasn't excitement that I felt, but more like anxiety. In diner lingo, maybe I had bitten off more than I could chew. Or maybe I was having buyer's remorse.

Probably all of the above!

As I surveyed my new kingdom on the frozen shore of Lake Ontario, I mentally listed all the things with which I needed to familiarize myself.

A huge gingerbread Victorian house located to the

left of the diner and closer to the water had been recently vacated by my aunt Stella. It was also now mine. It had almost disappeared in the heavy snow, with its pristine white paint and dark green shutters. It had a major wrap-around porch that I planned to use in the summer. I'd sit in a forest green Adirondack chair and watch the waves of Lake Ontario lap at the shore.

I looked over at the twelve little white cottages that dotted the lakefront. It looked like the big Victorian had a litter.

They were called—*care to guess?*—the Sandy Harbor Guest Cottages.

My mind flashed back to the two weeks every summer that my family rented here. We always rented Cottage Number Six, on the front row of the first chain of cottages. My sister, my brother, and I would stay in the water from sunrise until sunset. Mom and Dad had to drag us out of the water, slather us with sunscreen, feed us, and listen to our pleas to go back in.

Now all twelve cottages belonged to me, and I'd be renting them out to the next generation of fishermen and families who'd enjoy them.

The Silver Bullet was the centerpiece of my little kingdom. Smiling, I saw that the parking lot was filled with cars that were frosted with a couple inches of snow. Customers entered the diner in groups, laughing and talking and looking forward to a good meal. They left the same way they came, but now sated by delicious comfort food and finishing their conversations before brushing the snow off their cars.

The scent of baking bread drifted on the crisp winter

air and mixed with other cooking scents. My mouth was watering just thinking of what I was going to order later.

Slogging through the snow to the side of the diner, I savored every aspect of its outside appearance: the curved lines, the metallic diamond-shaped edging around the windows, and the porchlike entranceway. The Silver Bullet looked like it had just been towed into place, not like it had been there since 1950.

I looked for the cement cornerstone, which I'd always thought was so romantic, but it was buried under several feet of snow. I knew what it said by heart: STELLA AND MORRIS "PORKY" MATKOWSKI, MARRIED 1950, TOGETHER FOREVER IN OUR LOVE.

They were together until Uncle Porky died a month ago.

I sighed, thinking about the two of them. Porky and Stella always finished each other's sentences and walked hand in hand. But now Stella was alone, just like I was alone, but I hoped to change that as soon as I met more people in the community. I remembered Sandy Harbor as being a friendly place, and that was just what I needed—friends.

Actually, Aunt Stella wasn't alone right now. A gaggle of her friends came for Porky's funeral and stayed at the house. They helped her through the first month of losing her husband, and now she was en route to a senior community in Boca with them. They planned on living like the *Golden Girls* characters, but first they were going on a cruise around the world.

Because she was busy entertaining her friends, packing to leave, and searching for her missing passport,

Aunt Stella didn't have much time to show me the entire operation.

"The same people have been working here forever. They know what to do," she'd told me several times.

I pointed my boots toward a slushy path that led to my new house. Maybe I should unpack and get settled, but I was eager to get more acquainted with everyone and everything.

I took a deep breath and let it out. All this was so overwhelming. Mostly because I, Beatrix Matkowski (formerly known as Beatrix Burnham), was starting over at age thirtysomething.

I was freshly divorced from Deputy Doug Burnham after ten years of marital nonbliss. And, after ten years of trying to start a family and failing at it, Deputy Doug proved that it wasn't his fault by getting Wendy, his twenty-one-year-old girlfriend, pregnant with twins.

The day after I found out about Doug and Wendy, I was downsized from my job as a City of Philadelphia tourist information specialist, a position that meant I sat at a walk-in tourist information site and dispensed heaps of tourist information.

How things had changed in a few months!

They say that bad things always come in threes: Uncle Porky died before my divorce and the downsizing.

After the cemetery, where we left Uncle Porky's ashes in the Matkowski family crypt, everyone came back to the diner for food and remembering. My mother, who had rolled into town with my father in their motor home, cried and laughed with relatives and friends who she hadn't seen in years. My father told humorous tales of Uncle Porky, his older brother.

My mom, Aunt Stella, and Aunt Beatrix all got a little tipsy and giggly, and they fell asleep in one of the back booths of the diner.

When my mom sobered up, she decided that since Stella was going around the world, she and my dad should go to Key West and take Aunt Beatrix with them. I didn't get the parallel, but early the next morning they all took off, except for Aunt Beatrix, who was taking Amtrak back to NYC because she'd been to Key West "fifty years ago, and it's probably the same."

It was over the Wednesday special at the diner, ironically a Philly steak sandwich and a small chef salad, that Aunt Stella discussed selling me "the point." "The point" is local talk for the Silver Bullet, the cottages, and her Victorian house—everything that Stella and Porky owned.

"I'll make you an offer that you can't refuse," she'd said. "And we'll figure out a payment plan." She wrote down some dates and dollar amounts in columns on the back of a paper place mat that advertised local businesses.

Aunt Stella was far too generous. She was practically just handing me the whole pierogi. Almost.

So I went back home to think about it, and then my life fell apart with Doug.

Then the pieces fell together again.

Doug, acting very civilly, offered to buy out my share of the house, furniture, and whatever. Apparently Wendy liked my faux–Williamsburg colonial and the school district, and she had just come into a trust fund. She wanted Deputy Doug, my house, and its entire contents enough to buy me off handsomely, on the condition that I leave town.

I shook hands with my husband of ten years and took a last look at my beautiful house just outside Philadelphia. I had a pang of regret at leaving all the lovely antiques that we'd accumulated throughout our marriage.

But I wasn't going to be an antique! I was going to start over—clean slate, fresh, new, reborn.

I stuffed my personal belongings into my boring gray Ford Focus and drove from Philly to Sandy Harbor in one day.

Suddenly, I had a nice chunk of money for a down payment—Wendy's "kiss-off" check—that was burning a hole in my Walmart purse.

Aunt Stella told me that the mayor of Sandy Harbor had made a purchase offer on "the point" but she'd turned him down. He wasn't family, she'd said, and besides, "He owns half of Sandy Harbor already."

She'd also turned down another restaurateur who wanted to add another restaurant to his empire, because he wasn't family either.

Aunt Stella emphatically stated that the figures on the place mat were only a guideline . . . that I was her niece, and she knew that I'd take good care of what she and Uncle Porky had built.

I'd told her that I absolutely would take care of everything and keep our family memories safe, from the smallest black-and-white picture of Porky hanging on the wall to the huge collection of recipes from family and friends.

But the diner had me worried. As the flickering red neon sign on the top of the diner said, it was open twenty-four hours and had been since 1950. The Silver Bullet was an icon in these parts.

Aunt Stella shook off my concern with a wave of her hand, telling me not to worry.

Yeah, right, I had thought as I'd pushed a check for partial payment over to her and she'd dropped the keys into my hand.

Aunt Stella had patted my cheek and said that Uncle Porky would've been very happy. They hadn't had children of their own, and they had often wondered what they'd do with their property.

Owning my own diner was heaven-sent. I just loved to cook. It had been my salvation on those lonely nights when Deputy Doug wasn't home. I made comfort food, and heaven knew that I needed comfort. As a matter of fact, I comforted the whole neighborhood with stews, pierogi, mac and cheese, pot roasts, chili, and hip-enlarging desserts.

Perfect diner food.

I decided to savor my first trip to the Silver Bullet as its owner and save it for last on my list of places to visit and observe.

Or maybe I was procrastinating. I could cook; I knew that. I grew up in the Silver Bullet kitchen and waitressed there when I was in college, but I didn't know if I could handle the business aspect of it all. I'd learn, however. My first step would probably be ordering food and supplies and how to do payroll.

I headed to the bait shop on the other side of the boat launch. It didn't belong to me, but there was someone there who I needed to visit. It'd been a long time since I'd seen Mr. Farnsworth.

Opening the front door of the bait shop, I walked in. Smiling down at me from a high ladder was Mr. Farnsworth. He hadn't changed a bit since I was a kid . . . well, maybe a bit. His hair was as white as the snow falling outside, and I noticed a few more lines on his face, but he was as slim and as friendly as ever.

"If it isn't little Trixie Matkowski!" He slowly climbed down the ladder and pulled me into a bear hug against his red flannel shirt. "Stella told me that she sold to you. Wanted to keep it in the family, she said."

"Well, Mr. Farnsworth, I'm not so little anymore, but, yes, I'm the new owner."

He dropped his hands and stepped away. "You're the spitting image of your aunt Beatrix. She's a looker, that gal."

Aunt Beatrix is my dad's older sister and like my fairy godmother. I could never predict when she'd surface from her penthouse on Fifth Avenue in New York City and appear, but she always seemed to know when I needed her the most.

So, Aunt Beatrix (and don't call her Trixie!) should be arriving any time now.

I walked over to look at the cement tubs that usually

contained minnows and the like. They were empty, and the familiar gurgling of the water pumps was absent.

Way back when, my sister, brother, and I, along with a bunch of friends, would hit the bait shop at least once a day to watch the bait swim around.

It was almost better than TV.

"Mr. Farnsworth, are you getting ready for trout season? Getting worms?" I expected a big fishing season when the lake defrosted. The more fishermen, the more business I'd have.

"Sure. I've ordered worms for those who use natural bait, but I've also ordered poppers, spoons, plugs, and jigs. And for the fancy fishermen types, I've ordered buzzes, blades, cranks, tubes, and vibrators."

Vibrators?

"Is there anything I can do to help?"

"Not a thing, Trixie. I'll be fully loaded and ready for trout season."

"Good. Thanks, Mr. Farnsworth. I'll help you stock the shelves if you'd like."

He shook his head and grinned. "No way. It's my favorite part of my job."

I half expected him to hand me a lollipop and send me on my way, as he'd done when I was a kid. Mr. Farnsworth always had an ample supply of them. Then I noticed a fishbowl on the counter by the register. It was full of colorful lollipops.

As if he'd read my mind, he walked to the bowl, pulled out a grape one—my favorite—and handed it to me with a slight bow.

It had been years since I'd had a grape lollipop. I tore open the plastic wrapper and popped it into my mouth.

I pulled out the lollipop. "You remembered?" I asked, stunned.

He shrugged his thin shoulders. "Of course."

I heard a thumping noise from the side of the shop. From what I could recall, the stairs led to a storage area above. The noise got closer, then stopped.

Then at the bottom of the steps, by a display of army green waders, was a . . . cowboy?

He tweaked the brim of his hat to me. "Howdy, ma'am."

This guy seemed like a bona fide, real cowboy. Museum quality. Now, he was something you didn't see every day in little old Sandy Harbor.

His black cowboy hat and boots made him seem about six foot four. He had on a pair of dark jeans that he was born to wear. A crisp-looking white shirt was tucked in, and a brown leather belt with silver conchos surrounded his waist. A belt buckle the size of one of the Silver Bullet's platters sat on his flat stomach. His boots were spit shined—maybe snakeskin—and he wore a brown suede bomber jacket.

I managed to pull the grape sucker from my mouth. "Hi."

I noticed that his sky blue eyes traveled down the length of my body, taking in my red, puffy knee-length parka, my shin-high hiking boots, and the purple scarf draped around my head and neck like a mummy. I wondered if he noticed how my purple mittens and purple scarf matched my grape sucker.

Mr. Farnsworth walked to the cowboy's side. "Trixie, this is Mr. Tyler Brisco. He's all the way from Houston, Texas, and he's renting the apartment above my shop. Ty, Trixie is the new owner of the Silver Bullet."

The cowboy held out his hand. "I guess that makes you my neighbor, Mrs. Matkowski."

His voice was low and gravelly and incredibly sexy with a hint of a drawl, not that I'd noticed. I moved my grape sucker to my left hand and held out my right.

We shook hands, my purple-mittened hand in his. I hoped that it wasn't sticky.

"Just call me Trixie. And I'm not a Mrs. anymore. Just Trixie. Trixie Matkowski. I took my maiden name back after my divorce." Why on earth did I find it necessary to tell everyone about my divorce? I changed the subject. "I didn't know that there was an apartment up there."

Mr. Farnsworth nodded enthusiastically. "Yeah, your uncle Porky helped me renovate it a while back."

I couldn't take my eyes off the Texas cowboy. "How long have you lived in Sandy Harbor, Mr. Brisco?"

"Call me Ty." With his drawl, those three simple words lasted forever. His smile was warm and infectious. "I moved in just after the first of the year."

His voice was so mesmerizing, I'd listen to him read the Silver Bullet's dinner menu. I jerked back to reality, and my reality was to concentrate on my new business ventures, not a Texas cowboy.

"So we're both new to Sandy Harbor. What brings you here, Ty?"

I told myself that I was just making conversation, that I really didn't care what he was doing here.

"I'd had enough of big-city crime," he said. "You know, I'm just going over for lunch at the Silver Bullet. Join me and we'll talk?"

His eyes twinkled, and I wondered if he knew how sexy he actually was. Of course he did. A guy as good-looking as Ty had women stacked up like cordwood.

I wasn't going to be one of them. No, thanks.

But I was headed over to the diner anyway, wasn't I?

"Uh . . . I'd love to join you, but I'm a bit busy right now," I finally answered.

Mr. Farnsworth butted in. "Trixie, go and keep Ty company. There's nothing that can't wait. We take things a little slow here in Sandy Harbor."

Oh great. I was trapped into having lunch with the cowboy.

I pulled out my notebook and a pen from the recesses of my coat. I'd take the opportunity to jot down some ideas I had for making the diner my own.

"What do you say, Trixie?" the cowboy drawled again, and my knees turned to mashed potatoes. My two-syllable name took on a life of its own.

Reluctantly I nodded. At another point in my life, maybe fifty years from now, I wouldn't mind spending time with the cowboy. He might be interesting to get to know, but right now, all I could think of was that he was a man, and I was in a world of hurt, courtesy of Deputy Doug.

"I eat all my meals at the Silver Bullet." Ty patted his flat stomach. "I think I've gained sixty pounds since I moved here."

Yeah, right, cowboy.

I pulled out a crumpled tissue from the pocket of my coat and wrapped it around what was left of my sucker. I probably had purple teeth and tongue, but I didn't care.

We went outside, walked around the boat launch between the diner and the bait shop, and cut through the launch's empty parking lot to the back door of my diner.

"Let's cut through the kitchen this time, Ty. I want to check on the cook."

"Juanita?"

The man even knew the name of the morning cook. "You do come here often, don't you?"

I smiled and waved to Juanita, whom I'd met briefly when she came to the Victorian to say good-bye to Aunt Stella.

"Everything okay?" I asked.

Juanita gave me a quick nod, and we hurried to the front of the diner to get out of her way.

I just loved the kitchen. Everything was aluminum or chrome and just shone. The smell of bacon frying permeated the air as did bread taking a ride on the toaster. Aunt Stella always called the revolving toaster a Ferris wheel for bread. I could just picture Uncle Porky at the cast-iron stove, working several orders at a time.

A good crowd was already gathered at the diner, but there were at least two booths available.

"Over there?" I pointed to the booth toward the back.

"Lead the way, darlin'."

"I'm not your darlin'," I mumbled. Doug used to call me darling. It rang hollow even then.

"Pardon me?"

"I said, 'I love this diner.'"

A hush fell over the patrons, forks stopped moving, and it seemed like every pair of eyes looked in my direction. Several customers—mostly women—smiled and waved.

Happy to be recognized after all these years, I did the same back.

Then I realized they weren't greeting me. It was all for Ty Brisco.

Glancing back at him, I saw that he was waving and tweaking his hat. The women were swooning.

Good grief.